The Four Corners of the Earth

(Matt Drake #16)

By

David Leadbeater

Copyright 2017 by David Leadbeater
ISBN: 978-1544178967

All rights reserved. No part of this publication may be reproduced, distributed, or transmitted in any form or by any means, including photocopying, recording, or other electronic or mechanical methods, without the prior written permission of the publisher/author except in the case of brief quotations embodied in critical reviews and certain other non-commercial uses permitted by copyright law.

All characters in this book are fictitious, and any resemblance to actual persons living or dead is purely coincidental.

This ebook is for your personal enjoyment only. This ebook may not be re-sold or given away to other people. If you would like to share this ebook with another person, please purchase any additional copy for each reader. If you're reading this book and did not purchase it, or it was not purchased for your use only, then please return it and purchase your own copy. Thank you for respecting the hard work of this author.

Thriller, adventure, action, mystery, suspense, archaeological, military, historical

Other Books by David Leadbeater:

The Matt Drake Series
The Bones of Odin (Matt Drake #1)
The Blood King Conspiracy (Matt Drake #2)
The Gates of Hell (Matt Drake 3)
The Tomb of the Gods (Matt Drake #4)
Brothers in Arms (Matt Drake #5)
The Swords of Babylon (Matt Drake #6)
Blood Vengeance (Matt Drake #7)
Last Man Standing (Matt Drake #8)
The Plagues of Pandora (Matt Drake #9)
The Lost Kingdom (Matt Drake #10)
The Ghost Ships of Arizona (Matt Drake #11)
The Last Bazaar (Matt Drake #12)
The Edge of Armageddon (Matt Drake #13)
The Treasures of Saint Germain (Matt Drake #14)
Inca Kings (Matt Drake #15)

The Alicia Myles Series
Aztec Gold (Alicia Myles #1)
Crusader's Gold (Alicia Myles #2)
Caribbean Gold (Alicia Myles #3)

The Torsten Dahl Thriller Series
Stand Your Ground (Dahl Thriller #1)

The Disavowed Series:
The Razor's Edge (Disavowed #1)
In Harm's Way (Disavowed #2)
Threat Level: Red (Disavowed #3)

The Chosen Few Series
Chosen (The Chosen Trilogy #1)
Guardians (The Chosen Tribology #2)

Short Stories
Walking with Ghosts (A short story)
A Whispering of Ghosts (A short story)

Connect with the author on Twitter: @dleadbeater2011
Visit the author's website: www.davidleadbeater.com

All helpful, genuine comments are welcome. I would love to hear from you.
davidleadbeater2011@hotmail.co.uk

The Four Corners of the Earth

CHAPTER ONE

Secretary of Defense, Kimberly Crowe, sat down with a growing sense of trepidation in her already pounding heart. Admittedly she hadn't been in the job for long, but she guessed it wasn't every day that a four-star army general and a CIA high-flyer all but demanded an audience with someone of her stature.

It was a small, dim, but lavishly adorned room inside a hotel at the heart of DC; a place she had grown used to using when matters required a tad more tact than was usual. Low lighting glistened faintly off a hundred golden and solid oak objects, lending the room a more relaxed air and complimenting the features and ever-changing expressions of those that met there. Crowe waited for the first of them to speak.

Mark Digby, the CIA man, got straight down to business. "Your team is off the rails, Kimberly," he said, his tone cutting through the ambience like acid through metal. "Writing its own ticket."

Crowe, expecting this acidic barb, hated going on the defensive but really had no choice. Even as she spoke she knew this was exactly what Digby wanted. "They made a judgment call. In the field. I might not like it, Mark, but I do stand by it."

"And now we're behind," General George Gleeson rumbled unhappily. The new engagement was all he cared about.

"In the race for the so-called 'resting places'? The Horsemen? Please. Our best minds haven't cracked the code yet."

"Stand by it, huh?" Digby went on as if Gleeson hadn't

interrupted. "And what of their *decision* to murder a civilian?"

Crowe opened her mouth, but didn't speak. Best not to. Digby clearly knew more than her and was going to use every last fragment of it.

He glared straight at her. "What about that, Kimberly?"

She stared back at him, saying nothing, the air now crackling between them. It was clear that Digby was going to break first. The man was practically wriggling with his need to share and vent and mold her to his way of thinking.

"Man named Joshua Vidal was helping them with their enquiries. My team on the ground didn't know why they sought him out, or why they killed all the cameras in the surveillance room—" he paused "—until they checked later and found . . ." He shook his head, feigning distress worse than most soap stars.

Crowe read between the lines, sensing many layers of bullshit. "You have a full report?"

"I do." Digby nodded decisively. "It'll be on your desk by tonight."

Crowe kept silent about all she knew regarding the last mission. The SPEAR team had kept in touch—barely—but she knew a little of what went down. That said—the murder of this Joshua Vidal, if in any way accurate, would have deep and far-ranging repercussions for the team. Add to that Mark Digby, who was the kind of individual happy to chase down any mistake that furthered his own particular agenda, and Hayden's team could easily be marked down as an embarrassment to the United States. They could be disbanded, classed as fugitives marked for arrest, or . . . even worse.

It all depended on Digby's agenda.

Crowe needed to tread very carefully, keeping in mind her own rather rocky career. Coming this far, climbing so high, hadn't been without its dangers—and some still lurked at her back.

General Gleeson grunted. "This ain't moving anything forward. In particular those guys out in the field."

Crowe nodded at the general. "I agree, George. But SPEAR have and are one of our most effective teams, along with SEAL Teams 6 and 7. They're . . . unique in so many ways. I mean, quite literally, there is no other team in the world quite like them."

Digby's eyes were hard. "I see that more as a highly volatile position, not a superior one. These Special Forces teams need shorter leashes, not more loose chains."

Crowe sensed the atmosphere deteriorating and knew there was worse to come. "Your team are off the rails. They have internal problems. External secrets that may yet come to bite us all in the ass . . ." He paused.

General Gleeson offered another grunt. "Last thing we need is a team of rogue multinationals employed by the United States going crazy abroad, creating yet one more shitstorm. Best to cut ties while we can."

Crowe couldn't hide her surprise. "What are you saying?"

"We're not saying anything." Digby glanced at the walls as if expecting to see Dumbo ears.

"You're saying they should be arrested?" she pressed.

Digby gave the slightest shake of his head; barely noticeable, but a movement that rang warning bells deep in Crowe's soul. She didn't like it, not the smallest sliver of it, but the only way to break the terrible tension in the room and move away was to move on.

"Put a pin in it," she said in as light a voice as she could muster. "And let's discuss the other reason we're here. The four corners of the earth."

"Let's speak plainly," the general said. "And look at the facts, not the fables. The facts state some bunch of crackpots stumbled across thirty-year-old manuscripts that were written by war criminals whilst hiding in Cuba. The facts state that this bunch of crackpots went right ahead and fucking *leaked* them onto the goddamn Web, par for the course for this bunch. Those are the facts."

Crowe knew of the general's distaste for archaeological folklore and his complete lack of imagination. "I think they are, George."

"Would you like some more?"

"Well, I'm quite sure we're about to hear them."

"Every mad scientist, every wannabe Indiana fucking Jones and enterprising criminal in the world now has access to the same information we do. Every government, every Special Forces team, every branch of black ops, has seen it. Even the ones that don't exist. And right now . . . they've all got their dirtiest attentions fixed on one place."

Crowe wasn't sure she liked his analogy, but said, "Which is?"

"The blueprint of the Order of the Last Judgment. The blueprint to end the world."

"Now that sounds a little dramatic coming from you, General."

"I was reading verbatim, that's all."

"We've all read it. All of it," Digby interjected. "Of course, it has to be taken seriously until it can be discounted. The main document, the one they're calling the Order of the Last Judgment, refers to the Horsemen and, we believe, an order in which to look for them."

"But—" Gleeson clearly couldn't help himself. "Four *corners*. It's completely illogical."

Crowe eased him along. "I'm guessing it's coded purposely, George. To make it harder to solve. Or to make it discoverable only by those the Order chose."

"I don't like it." Gleeson looked like his mind had been blown.

"I'm sure." Crowe tapped the table before her. "But look—the manuscript throws up many questions, all of which are so far unanswered. Chiefly, where are they now . . . the Order?"

"That is by no means the biggest riddle we face," Digby disagreed. "This blueprint—that is what we must address with all haste."

Crowe enjoyed winning that particular manipulation. "SPEAR are already in Egypt," she affirmed. "Taking the manuscript at face value and assuming our early interpretations are correct—that is where we should be."

Digby chewed at his lower lip. "That's all good," he said, "but brings us full circle also to where we want to be. A decision must now be made, Kimberly."

"Now?" She was genuinely surprised. "They're not going anywhere, and it would be a mistake to take them out of the field. You've understood the manuscript, I'm assuming? The Four Horsemen? The final four weapons? War, Conquest, Famine, Death. If this is a valid claim, we need them doing what they do best."

"Kimberly." Digby rubbed at his eyes. "You and I have a wildly different view of what that is."

"Surely you can't dispute their previous successes?"

"How do you define success?" Digby spread his hands in an infuriatingly smug manner. "Yes, they neutralized a few threats but so could the SEALs, the Rangers, the CIA's Special Activities Division, SOG, Marine Raiders . . ." He paused. "See where I'm going?"

"You're saying we don't need SPEAR."

Digby rolled his eyes on purpose. "Never have."

Crowe took more than a moment to consider the intended slight. She looked between Digby and Gleeson, but the general only offered an emotionless, stoic glare, the exterior expression of his creative streak no doubt. It was clear to her where SPEAR excelled. Gleeson genuinely didn't see it, and Digby was seeking a different goal.

"So far," she said, "we only have words and reports, basically hearsay. This team have put their lives on the line, lost their own people, and sacrificed again and again for this country. They have a right to speak."

Digby screwed his face up, but said nothing. Crowe sat back, drinking in the calm ambience that still existed around the four corners of the room in an effort to stay focused. One required focus and calm when dealing with poisonous snakes.

"I propose we send people to TerraLeaks in an effort to staunch this flow of information," she said. "Until the authenticity of this Order can be determined. Which will be soon," she added. "We investigate the Cuban bunker where it was found. And we let Team SPEAR do their job. Nobody will get it done faster."

General Gleeson nodded in agreement. "They are on site," he rumbled.

Digby then gave her a wide smile, intimating the cat that got the cream. "I accept all your proposals," he said. "I want to go on record as not agreeing with them, but I will go along. And in return, I want you to accept a small proposal of mine."

Dear God, no. "Which is?"

"We send a second team. To cover for and possibly assist them."

Crowe knew what he was saying. "Cover for" meant *watch,* and assist quite possibly meant *execute.*

"Which team?"

"SEAL Team 7. They're already close by."

"Incredible." Crowe shook her head. "We have two of our best teams in the same area at the same time. How did that happen?"

Digby managed to stay impassive. "Pure chance. But you gotta agree, two is better than one."

"All right." Crowe knew she had no recourse but to agree. "But under no circumstances do the two teams meet. Not for *any* reason. Are we clear?"

"Only if the world depends on it." Digby smiled, dodging the question and drawing forth a groan from Gleeson.

"Staying professional," Gleeson said. "I can have Seven in the right area in a few hours. Providing we wrap this up pretty soon."

"Consider it wrapped." Crowe refrained from telling the pair not to let the door hit them in the ass on the way out. For SPEAR this could hardly get more serious. For the man that killed Joshua Vidal it was severe. For her, it could be any of those things and worse. *But first, let's save the world,* she thought.

Again.

CHAPTER TWO

Alexandria sprawled in all its modern glory beyond the plate-glass window; a thriving, concrete metropolis, bordered by a glittering sea, marked by palm trees and hotels, a curving coastline and the enormously impressive Bibliotheca Alexandrina.

The CIA safe house looked out over six jam-packed lanes that carried traffic slowly around the bow of the coast. All access to the feeble balcony outside was restricted by the heavy glass and bars. Only the main living room offered any signs of comfort; the kitchen was small and makeshift, the two bedrooms long since converted into steel cages. Only one person manned the safe house on a permanent basis, and he was clearly way out of his comfort zone.

Alicia ordered a round of coffees. "Hey, dude, that's four black, two with milk, three with creamer and one with a sniff of cinnamon. Got it?"

"I don't . . ." The thirty-something man with thin-rimmed glasses and bushy eyebrows blinked furiously. "I don't . . . make coffee. Do *you* get it?"

"You don't? Well, what the hell are you here for?"

"Liaison. Local contact. Housekeeper. I—"

Alicia squinted hard. "Housekeeper?"

"Yeah. But not like *that*. I—"

Alicia turned away. "Fuck, dude. You don't make beds. You don't make coffee. What the hell are we paying you for?"

Drake was trying hard to tune the Englishwoman out, concentrating instead on the meeting between Smyth and Lauren. The New Yorker had been prepped and flown out to Egypt the moment the new threat went from somewhat concerning to red hot priority. Standing at the center of the room, hair down and game-face on, she was ready to update the team, but as Smyth now approached Lauren a whole range of emotions struck her head-on.

"Not now," she said immediately.

"I'm alive," Smyth growled. "Thought you might be interested."

Instead of snapping back, Lauren took a deep breath. "I worry about you every day, every minute. I do. Is that pleasing to you, Smyth?"

The soldier opened his mouth to retort, but Alicia stepped smartly in. "Shit, didn't you hear? His name's Lancelot. He prefers it to Smyth. We all call him it now."

Lauren was taken aback for the second time in a minute. "Lance-a-*what?* Isn't that the name of an old knight?"

"Sure is," Alicia said happily. "Same guy that committed infidelity with the king's wife."

"Are you saying I should be worried? Or care?"

Alicia stared at Smyth. "Nah. If he loses you the best he's gonna get is a baboon and there are no red-arsed monkeys in Egypt." She swept the room with a questing air. "At least, not outside this room."

Mai was now standing beside Lauren, having drifted over after double-checking the safe house's security. "Shall we catch up with the op? I'm assuming that's why Lauren is here?"

"Yeah, yeah." The New Yorker quickly recaptured her composure. "You all wanna sit down? This might take a while."

Yorgi found a seat. Drake perched on the arm of a chair, watching the room closely. It was clear to him, seeing from the outside, how Dahl and Kenzie drifted closer, how Hayden glided away from Kinimaka and, thankfully, how Alicia and Mai now seemed more accepting of each other's presence. Drake felt hugely relieved over that outcome, but the next big thing was about to erupt. Yorgi had been almost completely silent since his revelation of only three days ago.

I am the one who killed my parents in cold blood.

Yeah, it had put a dampener on the celebrations but nobody pressed the Russian. He had come far indeed to confess the act; he needed time now to decipher the memory into real words.

Lauren looked a little uncomfortable standing at the head of the room, but when Smyth backed away she started to speak. "Firstly, we may have a lead as to the whereabouts of Tyler Webb's secret stash. Remember—he promised more secrets would be unearthed?"

Drake remembered it well. They'd been worrying about the potential fallout ever since. *Or at least, two or three have.*

"But we have no time for that now. Later, I hope we can all take a trip. But this . . . this new threat began when the organization TerraLeaks dropped a whole slew of documents onto the Internet." She grimaced. "More like a physical bomb dropped onto a digital foundation. The documents were all handwritten, clearly fanatical, and entirely self-aggrandizing. The usual old dross. Employees of TerraLeaks discovered them inside an old bunker in Cuba, something left over from decades ago. It seems the bunker used to be the headquarters of a group of madmen that called themselves the Order of the Last Judgment."

"Sounds like a bunch of laughs," Drake said.

"Sure it was. But in truth, it gets much worse. These men were all war criminals, escaped from Nazi Germany and hiding in Cuba. Now, as you all know, it's easier to make a list of weird shit the Nazis *weren't* interested in than a list of the things they were. This Order was created to pass things on to future generations. If they were caught or killed, they wanted some glorious repercussion somewhere down the line."

"And you're saying they've got it?" Hayden asked.

"Well, not yet. Nothing is proven. The Order were made up of two generals, two powerful government figures and two wealthy businessmen. Together, they would have wielded considerable power and resources."

"How do we know this?" Mai asked.

"Oh, they've kept nothing hidden. Names, events, places. It's all there in the documents. And TerraLeaks have followed suit," Lauren shook her head, "as they do."

"You're saying everyone knows?" Drake said softly. "Every bloody organization in the world? Shit." He swung his head toward the window as if beholding the whole world out there, converging.

"The document in question isn't fully finished—" Lauren began.

Alicia snorted. "If course it isn't."

"So we don't have all of the information. We can only assume these war criminals that vanished from the face of the earth around twenty seven years ago didn't get chance to finish their work."

"Vanished?" Dahl murmured, shuffling a little. "That usually means secret police. Or Special Forces. Makes sense since they were war criminals."

Lauren nodded. "That's the consensus. But whoever 'vanished' them didn't think to look for a secret bunker."

"Probably the SAS then." Dahl glanced over at Drake. "Thick bastards."

"At least our Special Forces aren't called ABBA."

Kinimaka wandered over to the window to take a look. "Sounds like the mother of all mistakes," he rumbled at the glass. "Letting this info go free. How many governments are going to be hunting it down at the same time?"

"At least six," Lauren said. "That we know of. Could be more than that by now. The race began whilst you guys were finishing off in Peru."

"Finishing off?" Smyth repeated. "We were saving lives."

Lauren shrugged. "Nobody blames you for it."

Drake distinctly remembered Smyth's repeated requests to hurry the hell up during the last mission. But this was no time to bring it up. Instead, he quietly caught the New Yorker's attention.

"So," he said. "Why don't you tell us exactly what this Order of the Last Judgment planned and how it's going to destroy the world?"

Lauren took a deep breath. "All right then. I hope you're ready for this."

CHAPTER THREE

"Through spy satellites, hidden agents and cameras, drones, the NSA . . . you name it, we know that at least six other countries are rushing to find the four corners of the earth first. The Americans—" she paused, thinking "—well . . . being the Americans . . . want to get there ahead of the others. Not only for the prestige, but because we simply can't tell what anyone else will do with what they find. The feeling is . . . what if Israel finds a covert country killer? What if China find all four?"

"So these are the confirmed countries involved?" Kenzie asked quietly. "Israel?"

"Yeah. Plus China, France, Sweden, Russia and Britain."

Drake wondered if he might know some of the people involved. It didn't sit right that he should be working against them.

"Tricky," he said. "What are the *exact* orders?"

Lauren consulted her laptop to be sure. "They contain an awful lot of 'without fails' and 'at all costs.'"

"They're seeing it as a global threat," Hayden said. "And why wouldn't they? The next apocalypse is always just a few days away."

"Still," Drake said, "essentially we're all on the same side."

Hayden blinked at him. "Whoa. Get off the drugs, dude."

"No, I meant—"

"Too many knocks have finally addled his head." Dahl laughed.

Drake stared. "Shut yer gob." He paused. "Have you been brushing up on yer Yorkshire? Anyway, what I *meant* was we're all Special Forces. Cut from the same cloth. We bloody well shouldn't be racing and fighting each other across the world."

"Agreed," Hayden said without emotion. "So who ya gonna take it up with?"

Drake spread his hands. "President Coburn?"

"You'd have to get past the Secretary of Defense first. And others. Cole has more than physical walls surrounding him and some of them aren't without their battlements."

"Not all of the teams will be friendlies," Kenzie added with surety.

"Of course." Drake gave in and took a seat. "Sorry, Lauren. Go on."

"Right. So everyone has read the leaked documents. Most are Nazi bullshit, to be honest. And I'm reading that verbatim. A page named after this wretched group, called the Order of the Last Judgment, points firmly to the so-called 'resting places' of the Four Horsemen: War, Conquest, Famine and Death."

"From the Book of Revelation?" Hayden asked. "Those Four Horsemen?"

"Yep." Lauren nodded, still consulting an abundance of notes proved by some of America's top geeks. "The Lamb of God opens the first four of seven seals, which summons four creatures that ride out on white, red, black and pale horses. Of course, through the years they have been tied to everything, and reimagined time and again in popular culture. They were even described as a symbol of the Roman Empire, and its subsequent history. But, hey, the Nazis could twist it however they want, right? Now, it might be better if I hand these out." She dug a sheaf of papers from her briefcase, looking more efficient than Drake had ever seen her. An interesting change for Lauren, and one she looked to be taking to heart. He glanced quickly at the paper.

"This is the thing that's got everyone fired up? The Order?"

"Yeah, read it."

Dahl read it aloud as the others took it in.

"At the Four Corners of the Earth we found the Four Horsemen and laid with them the blueprint of the Order of the Last Judgment. Those who survive the Judgment quest and its aftermath will rightly reign supreme. If you are reading this, we are lost, so read and follow with cautious eyes. Our last years were spent assembling the four final weapons, the world revolutions: War, Conquest, Famine and Death. Unleashed together, they will destroy all governments and unveil a new future. Be prepared. Find them. Go to the Four Corners of the Earth. Find the resting places of the Father of Strategy and then the Khagan; the Worst Indian Who Ever Lived and then the Scourge of God. But all is not as it seems. We visited the Khagan in 1960, five years after completion, placing Conquest in his coffin. We found the Scourge who guards the true last judgment. And the only kill code is when the Horsemen arose. The Father's bones are unmarked. The Indian is surrounded by guns. The Order of the Last Judgment now live through you, and will forever reign supreme."

Drake took it all in. Many clues, many truths. Much labor. Dahl beat him to the first comment though. "Arose? Not arise?"

"Yeah, seems off." Lauren agreed. "But it ain't a typo."

Mai commented, "It does appear to show the *order* in which to look, albeit subtly."

Lauren nodded in agreement. "It does. But do you also see why they're terming it as 'resting places?' Not tombs, or graves or whatever?"

"All is not as it seems," Dahl read aloud.

"Yeah. Obviously there's a ton more research required."

"The Indian is surrounded by guns," Alicia read aloud. "What the hell does that mean?"

"Let's not get too far ahead," Hayden said.

"It's believed the knowledge of all these final resting places died with the Nazi Order." Lauren said. "Maybe they were planning on writing something down. Maybe coding it. Or passing the knowledge on to other generations. We don't know for sure, but we do know this is all we have to go on," she shrugged, "and everyone's in the same boat." She stared at Drake. "Dinghy. Survival raft. You get the idea."

The Yorkshireman nodded proudly. "Sure do. The SAS could make a rock float."

"Well, whoever we're up against, they have the same clues we do," Hayden said. "How about we make a start?"

Kinimaka turned away from the window. "The four corners of the earth?" he asked. "Where are they?"

The room looked blank. "Hard to say," Dahl said. "When the world's round."

"Okay, how about the first Horseman that they referenced. This Father of Strategy." Kinimaka moved into the room, blocking all light from the window at his back. "What references do we have to him?"

"As you would expect—" Lauren tapped at the screen "—the think tank back home has that covered too . . ." She took a moment to read.

Drake took the same moment to reflect. Lauren's mention of "the think tank back home" only clarified that which was absent.

Karin Blake.

Granted time flew when you were part of the SPEAR team, but they were long past the day and even the week when Karin should have been in touch. Every time he resolved to contact her something stopped him—whether it be a raft of enemies, a world crisis, or his own prerequisite for not being irritating. Karin needed her space, but—

Where the hell is she?

Lauren started to speak and again thoughts of Karin had to be shelved.

"It seems a historical figure was known as the Father of Strategy. Hannibal."

Smyth looked unsure. "Which one?"

Alicia pursed her lips. "If it's the Anthony Hopkins dude I ain't leaving this room."

"Hannibal Barca was the legendary military commander from Carthage. Born in 247 BC, he was the man that marched a whole army, including war elephants, over the Pyrenees and the Alps into Italy. He had an ability to determine his strengths and the enemies' weaknesses, and defeated a whole slew of Rome's allies. The only way he was eventually beaten was when some guy studied his own brilliant tactics and devised a way to use them against him. This was at Carthage."

"So this guy is the Father of Strategy?" Smyth asked. "This Hannibal?"

"Considered one of the greatest military strategists in history and one of the paramount generals of antiquity along with Alexander the Great and Caesar. He was named the Father of Strategy because his worst enemy, Rome, eventually adopted his military tactics into their own schemes."

"Now that's a win," Dahl said, "if ever there was one."

Lauren nodded. "Even better. Hannibal was considered such a nightmare to Rome that they adopted a saying whenever any kind of disaster struck. Translated it is, *Hannibal is at the gates!* The Latin phrase became common and is still used today."

"Getting back to the Order," Hayden prompted them. "How does it fit?"

"Well, we can safely say Hannibal is one of the Four Horsemen. Beyond the physical fact that he obviously rode a horse, he's named throughout history as the Father of Strategy. He then, is War, the first Horseman. He certainly brought war to the Roman empire."

Drake scanned the text. "So it says the blueprint of the Order of the Last Judgment was laid with the Horsemen. Are we to assume that the Order buried a devastating weapon inside Hannibal's grave? Leaving it for a future generation?"

Lauren nodded. "That's the general feeling. A weapon in every grave. A grave at every corner of the earth."

Kinimaka raised a brow. "Which again makes as much sense as a grass skirt."

Hayden waved him down. "Forget that," she said. "For now. Surely a man such as Hannibal will have a tomb or mausoleum?"

Lauren sat back. "Yeah, that's where it gets tricky. Poor old Hannibal was exiled and died a poor death, probably from poison. He was buried in an unmarked grave."

Drake stared. "Bollocks."

"Kinda makes you wonder, doesn't it?"

"Do we have a location?" Mai asked.

"Oh yeah." Lauren smiled. "Africa."

CHAPTER FOUR

Alicia walked over to a side cabinet and pulled out a bottle of water from the mini-fridge on top. The start of a new op was always a fraught affair. Her forte was out in the field; this time though they clearly needed a plan. Hayden had already joined Lauren at the laptop and Smyth was attempting to look interested, no doubt because the New Yorker was embracing a different role. *Oh yeah, and because she isn't in prison visiting a mad terrorist.*

Alicia kept her own council, but found it hard to see the logic of Lauren's thinking. Still, it wasn't her place to judge, not after the life she'd already led. Lauren Fox was worldly wise and shrewd enough to see what was coming.

Hope so. Alicia drank half the bottle, then turned to Drake. The Yorkshireman was currently standing beside Dahl and Kenzie. She was about to move in when there was a movement at her side.

"Oh, hey Yogi. How's it hanging?"

"Okay." The Russian thief had been downcast ever since his abrupt revelation. "Do you think they hate me now?"

"Who? Them? Are you kidding? Nobody judges you, especially not me." She grunted and looked around. "Or Mai. Or Drake. And especially not Kenzie. Bitch probably has a dungeon full of nasty little secrets."

"Oh."

"Not that yours is a nasty little secret." *Shit!* "Hey I'm still trying to change here. I'm no friggin' good with the pep talks."

"I see that."

She reached out, "C'mere!" and lunged for his head as he

slipped away, trying to drag him into a headlock. Yorgi skipped toward the end of the room, light on his feet. Alicia saw the futility of pursuit.

"Next time, boy."

Drake watched her approach. "Y'know he's scared of you."

"Didn't think the kid was afraid of anything. Not after spending time in that Russian prison and running up walls. Then, you find out he's afraid of this." She tapped her head.

"Most powerful weapon of all," Dahl said. "Just ask Hannibal."

"Ooh, Torsty cracks a witticism. Let's all mark the calendar. Seriously though," Alicia added. "Kid needs to talk. I'm not best qualified."

Kenzie barked. "Really? I am astounded."

"Were you mentioned in Webb's statement? Oh yeah, I think so."

The Israeli shrugged. "I find it hard to sleep at night. So what?"

"It's *why*," Alicia said. "Not *what*."

"For the same reason as you, I expect."

A deep silence fell. Dahl met Drake's eyes over the top of the women's heads and made a slight roll. Drake looked away fast, not belittling the women but not wanting to get dragged down a well of misery either. Alicia looked up when Hayden started to speak.

"Okay," their boss said. "It's better than what Lauren initially thought. Who's up for a trip to the Hellespont?"

Alicia sighed. "Sounds perfect for this bloody team. Sign me up."

First in helicopters and then speedboats, the SPEAR team approached the Dardanelles. The sun was already sinking toward the horizon, the light transforming from a bright orb to a panoramic backcloth to a horizontal slash. Drake found the bumpy ride barely changed between modes of transport and found time to wonder how the pilots made it safely through the day. Alicia, at his side aboard the chopper, made her feelings a little clearer.

"Hey, people, do ya think this dude's trying to kill us?"

Kinimaka, buckled in tight and grasping as many spare straps as he could hold, spoke through gritted teeth. "I'm pretty sure he thinks they bounce."

Comms were fully operational and open. Silence filled the air as they team checked their CIA-supplied weapons. The usual suspects, Drake found, which included Glocks, HKs, combat knives, and a various assortment of grenades. Night vision tools had also been provided. In just a few minutes Hayden began to speak over the comms.

"Okay people, time to face another, more personal aspect of this mission. The competing teams. CIA still says it's six, so let's be thankful it ain't a lot more. The Alexandria cell are being fed information constantly, a drip-feed from CIA cells all around the world, from the NSA and undercovers. They're passing on any pertinent facts to me—"

"If it suits their interests," Kenzie put in.

Hayden coughed. "I realize you've had bad experiences with government agencies and the CIA do get a bad press, but I did use to work for them. And I, at least, did my job right. They have an entire nation to protect. Rest assured I'll pass the facts on to you."

"I wonder what's blowing *her* skirt up," Alicia whispered over the comms. "Sure as hell ain't anything good."

Kenzie stared over at her. "What could be *good* that blows your skirt up?"

"I dunno." Alicia blinked quickly. "Johnny Depp's mouth?"

Hayden cleared her throat and continued. "Six Special Forces teams. Hard to say who's sympathetic and who's downright hostile. Do not assume. We must treat everyone as an enemy. Not one of the countries we know to be involved are acknowledging it. I realize you may know some of these guys, but the song remains the same."

As Hayden paused, Drake wondered about the British contingent. The SAS had quite a few regiments and he'd been gone many years but still, the world of ultra-elite soldiery was not exactly a large one. Hayden was right to bring up potential confrontations and reservations now rather than be surprised by them in the field. Dahl might wonder about the Swedish contingent and Kenzie the Israeli one. Good job there wasn't a conventional American presence.

"I can't see China being friendly," he said. "Nor Russia."

"At this rate," Mai said, staring out of the window. "They'll be shapes in the dark."

"Do we have an idea of each country's current position?" Dahl asked.

"Yeah, I was coming to that. As far as we can tell the Swedes are hours away. The French are still at home. Mossad are the closest, very close."

"Of course," Dahl said. "Nobody really knows where they're going."

Drake coughed lightly. "Trying to make excuses for Sweden's shoddy attempt?"

"Now you sound like Eurovision. And nobody mentioned Britain. Where are they? Still brewing a pot of tea?" Dahl lifted a pretend cup, little finger sticking out at an angle.

It was a fair point. "Well, Sweden probably started back to front."

"At least they started."

"Guys," Hayden cut in. "Don't forget *we're* a part of this too. And Washington expect us to win."

Drake grunted. Dahl grinned. Smyth looked up when Lauren started speaking.

"An interesting aside to all this, is that some of these countries are vehemently protesting any involvement. Of course, there's always a high bullshit level, but we could be dealing with some rogue elements too."

"Off the books? Splinter groups?" Kinimaka asked.

"That's a possibility."

"Just brings us back to the main brief," Hayden said. "Everyone's a hostile."

Drake wondered what Smyth might be thinking about her statement. Back in Cusco, Joshua had been a hostile, but because his death hadn't been sanctioned by the government and their stay had been in flux, contested, nobody knew what would happen. The man's death had been an accident, but fueled by inattention and over-eagerness. Yes, he was a parasite and a murderer, but the circumstances were different.

After the chopper they filled the boats. Wearing black and with faces camouflaged, bouncing smoothly across the waters of the Hellespont, darkness finally filled the night. The route they chose was empty, the lights twinkling beyond the far shore. The Hellespont was an important channel that forms part of the boundary between Europe and Asia. A narrow strait, its northern shores harbored Gallipoli whilst most of its other boundaries were relatively sparsely settled. As they skimmed across the waters, Hayden and Lauren used the comms.

"Hannibal never had a tomb, not even a grave marker. After an illustrious career this legendary general died almost alone, poisoned in old age. So, how do you find an unmarked grave?"

Drake looked up as Lauren paused. Was she asking them?

Smyth went gamely for a solution. "Sonar?"

"It's possible, but you would have to have a pretty good idea of where to look," Dahl answered.

"They found an obscure document, a matter of record yes, but lost in time," Hayden said. "The fate of Hannibal has always galled those that loved the hero who stood against Roman imperialism. One such man was the President of Tunisia, who visited Istanbul in the sixties. During this visit the only thing he wanted was to be able to take the remains of Hannibal back to Tunisia with him. Nothing else mattered. The Turks eventually relented somewhat and took him on a little trip."

"The sixties?" Dahl said. "Wasn't this when the war criminals started devising their nasty little plan?"

"Most likely." Hayden said. "After they settled in Cuba and established new lives. Their new Order then continued for almost twenty years."

"Plenty of time to get devious," Alicia said.

"And to choose their Four Horsemen," Mai added. "Hannibal—the Horseman of War? Makes sense. But who the hell are Conquest, Famine and Death? And why is the Dardanelles in Africa one of the four corners of the earth?"

"Good point," Alicia backed Mai, causing Drake to double-take. "You need to get that little thinking cap back on, Foxy."

Lauren smiled. Drake could tell by the tone of her voice. "So the Turks, particularly embarrassed by their own lack of respect for Hannibal, took the Tunisian president to a spot on the Hellespont. It reads 'on a hill where there is a dilapidated building.' This is the reputed resting place of Hannibal Barca."

Drake waited, but no more information was forthcoming. "Still," he said, "that was thirty years ago."

"It stood that long," Lauren said, "and the Turks no doubt post some kind of honor guard."

Drake looked dubious. "Could just be an honor grave, truth be told."

"They took the President of Tunisia there, Matt. He even took away vials of sand, attested by his bodyguards, vouchsafing them as 'sand from Hannibal's gravesite' on his return home. In that situation, in that year, would the Turks really have hoodwinked the Tunisian President?"

Drake nodded ahead to the approaching dark curve of the coastline. "We're about to find out."

CHAPTER FIVE

Drake helped pull the sable-colored speedboat out of the water, mooring it to a nearby cluster of old roots and stowing the outboard. Mai, Alicia and Smyth rushed off to establish an outpost. Kinimaka hefted the heavy rucksacks with Dahl's help. Drake felt sand under his boots. The air smelled earthy. Waves lapped hard at the shore to his left, given momentum by the boats. No other sound broke the stillness as the SPEAR team took stock.

Hayden held a portable GPS unit. "All right. I have the coordinates programmed in. We good to go?"

"Ready," several voices breathed back.

Hayden moved out and Drake fell in behind, working against the shifting sands beneath his feet. They scanned the area constantly, but no other lights were in evidence. Maybe they'd gotten here first after all. Maybe the other teams were holding off, letting somebody else do all the hard work. Maybe, even now, they were being watched.

The possibilities were infinite. Drake nodded at Alicia as they passed and the Englishwoman fell into line. "Mai's ranging from side to side."

"And Smyth?"

"I'm out here. Coast is clear."

Oh aye, but we're heading inland, Drake thought but said nothing. The soft sand gave way to hard-packed earth and then they were climbing an embankment. Just a few feet high and with a rolling top, they soon crossed over to find the edge of the desert and a stretch of flat ground. Hayden pointed the way and they traversed the barren wasteland. No need to post sentries now. They could see for miles, but

Mai and Smyth stayed further afield, adding range to their sight.

The GPS screen blinked silently, guiding them ever closer to their goal, and the dark arch of the night stretched imposingly above. With this much space the sky was vast; stars barely visible and the moon but a tiny sliver. Ten minutes became twenty and then thirty, and still they walked alone. Hayden kept in touch through the comms, both with the team and Alexandria. Drake let the environment sink inside him, drawing breath with the unsteady beat of nature. Animal sounds, breezes, rustling earth—it was all there but nothing untoward. He realized the teams they were up against may be every bit as good as them but trusted his own abilities and those of his friends.

"Up ahead," Hayden whispered. "The GPS shows the topography rising about forty feet. That could be the hill we're looking for. Eyes up."

The hill appeared slowly out of the gloom, a steadily rising mound of earth with tangled roots and boulders dotting the dry ground, and they made a steady path through the obstacles. Drake and Alicia took a moment to pause and look back, noting the smooth blackness stretching all the way to the undulating sea. And way beyond that, twinkling harbor lights, a whole different existence.

"One day?" Alicia asked wonderingly.

Drake hoped so. "We'll get there," he said.

"It should be easy."

"Aye love. Like riding a bike. But you fall and you get cuts and bruises and scrapes long before you find your balance."

"Half way there then." She touched him briefly and then continued up the hill.

Drake followed her in silence. The future really did hold a new wealth of possibilities now that Alicia Myles had broken away from a cycle of self-annihilation. All they had to do was overcome the next set of madmen and megalomaniacs hellbent on making the people of the world suffer.

And that right there was why soldiers like himself put everything on the line. For Adrian next door and Graeme across the road. For Chloe who struggled to get her two kids to school on time every single day. For the couples that bitched and moaned their way around the supermarket. For the good of those that sat good-naturedly in ring-road traffic jams and those that jumped the queues. Not for the gutter-trash that stole into your van or garage after dark, making off with whatever they could. Not for the bullies, the power-hungry and the back-stabbers. Let those that struggled hard to respect and love and care, be cared for. Let those that fought for their children's future be assured a safe one. Let those that helped others, be helped.

Hayden caught his attention with a low grunt. "This could be the place. GPS says it is and I see a derelict structure ahead."

He saw the overlapping colored dots. This was ground zero then. This was now no longer a time for subtlety. They may as well set off fireworks in their quest to locate Hannibal's grave if, now that they were here, they could find it faster. Because Drake was certain—if they could find it, all the other teams could.

Hayden marked the approximate area. Kinimaka and Dahl swung their heavy packs down. Mai and Smyth took up the best surveillance positions. Drake and Alicia moved close to Hayden to help. Only Yorgi hung back, lack of confidence showing as he waited to be told what to do.

Kinimaka and Dahl broke out the good flashlights, setting a trio up on carbon-fiber cradles and handing more out. These were not simply bright bulbs, they were manufactured to imitate sunlight as close as possible.

Admittedly, even the CIA's vast reach was limited in Egypt but Drake thought the apparatus didn't look half bad. Kinimaka used the cradle-mounted light to illuminate a general large area and then Hayden and Dahl roamed to check the earth.

"Now be aware," Hayden told them. "The Order of the Last Judgment states a weapon was buried here long after Hannibal's death. This is an unmarked grave, not a tomb. So we're looking for disturbed earth, not bones or blocks or pillars. We're looking for items more recently interred, not ancient relics. It shouldn't be too hard to—"

"Don't say it!" Dahl barked. "You'll jinx bloody everything."

"I'm just saying we don't have to find Hannibal. Just the weapon."

"Good point." Kinimaka adjusted the perimeter lights a little.

Hayden marked three places in the earth. All looked as if they'd been tampered with and none recently. Yorgi walked up carefully, shovel in hand. Drake and Alicia joined him and then Kinimaka.

"Just dig," Hayden said. "Hurry."

"What if it's booby-trapped?" Alicia asked.

Drake looked over at the dilapidated building. Walls hung sadly, drooping as if holding the weight of the world. One side had been chopped in half as if by a giant cleaver, blocks now exposed to both sides like ragged teeth. The roof had long since collapsed, doors and windows gone. "Well, it's not like we can take shelter in there."

"Thanks."

"No worries, love. Chin up."

Drake ignored the vehement glare and got to work. "So what's the significance of the Four Horsemen anyway?" he asked Hayden through the comms.

"Think tank's best guess? They fit the historical figures we're searching for and the weapons we hope to find. So Hannibal, raised to hate Romans, brought an almost endless war to Rome, yes? This is where we'll find a weapon of war."

"Could also be that they're horsemen," Kinimaka put in. "I mean, Hannibal was."

"Yeah, bit too vague, Mano."

"So nothing to do with the Bible?" Drake dug out another mound of earth. " 'Cause we don't want none of those silly codes."

"Well, they appeared in Revelation and—"

"Whoa!" Alicia suddenly cried out. "I think I hit something!"

"And heads up," Mai's voice rustled over the comms. "There are new lights on the water, coming fast."

CHAPTER SIX

Drake threw his shovel to the floor and strode over to watch Alicia. Yorgi was already there, helping her dig. Kinimaka also moved in fast.

"How long do we have?" Hayden asked urgently.

"Judging their speed, thirty minutes tops," Smyth responded.

Dahl stared hard. "Any clue?"

"Probably Mossad," Kenzie replied. "They were closest."

Drake cursed. "The only time I ever wished for the bloody Swedes to come first."

Alicia was knee deep in the hole, slamming the edge of her spade into soft earth, trying to ease the object free. She struggled, pulling at the obscure edges with no joy. Kinimaka cleared soil from above as Yorgi joined Alicia in the ever-widening gash in the earth.

"What is it?" Drake asked.

Hayden crouched, resting her hands on her knees. "Can't quite tell yet."

"Put yer friggin' back into it, Alicia." Drake grinned.

A glare and a raised finger was his only reply. The object in question was covered in dirt and clad all around in earth but it did have a shape. Oblong, measuring approximately two meters by one meter, it had a definite box shape and shifted easily, showing that it wasn't at all heavy. The problem was, it was surrounded and packed by hard earth and roots. Drake stared from the box to the sea, watching the lights move ever closer and wondering how the hell such a small, light container could hold a devastating weapon of war.

"Fifteen minutes," Smyth reported. "No other signs of approach."

Alicia wrestled with the earth, cursing and getting nowhere at first but finally exposing the object and letting Yorgi pull it free. Even then, buried vines and tangled roots clung to it, gleefully it seemed, presenting a hard, twisted cluster that refused to let go. They were up to their waists now, brushing at muddy clothes and resting on their shovels. Drake refrained from making the obvious men at work crack, and stooped down to help lift. Dahl reached down too and between them they managed to find purchase along the side of the object and tug it free. Roots protested, snapping and unravelling. Some held on for dear life. Drake heaved, and felt it scoot up the hole and over the rim. Rivers of displaced soil ran from the top. Together, he and Dahl then rose and stared down at Alicia and Yorgi. Both were red-faced and panting.

"What?" Drake asked. "You two planning a tea break? Get the hell up here."

Both Alicia and Yorgi double-checked the bottom of the hole, searching for more boxes or, perhaps, old bones. Nothing turned up. A moment later the young Russian ran at the side of the hole, finding purchase where there seemed to be none to bounce up the slope and over the edge of the hole. Alicia watched with chagrin and then leapt a little ungainly for the rim. Drake caught her hand, pulled her up.

He clucked. "You forgot the shovel."

"You wanna go fetch? I propose head first."

"Temper, temper."

Hayden remained staring down into the hole. "I thought a moment for poor old Hannibal Barca is in order. We mean no disrespect to a fellow soldier."

Drake nodded in agreement. "Legend."

"If he's even down there."

"The Nazis did their research," Hayden said. "And, grudgingly I admit they did it well. Hannibal achieved enduring fame simply because he was good at his job. His journey across the Alps is still one of the most prodigious military accomplishments of early warfare. He introduced military strategies that are still lauded today."

After a moment they looked up. Dahl was with them. Kinimaka brushed off the object to reveal a sturdy box, made of dark wood. A small crest had been emblazoned in the top, and the Hawaiian sought to expose it.

Hayden leaned in. "That's it. Their self-made emblem. The Order of the Last Judgment."

Drake studied it, committing the symbol to memory. It resembled a small center circle with four swirling scythes positioned around it at odd compass points. The circle was the infinity symbol.

"Scythes are weapons," Hayden said. "Protecting their world within?" She shrugged. "We'll figure it out later if we have to. C'mon."

The lights were no longer offshore, which meant Mossad, if that's who were closest, had reached solid ground and were less than fifteen minutes away at full pace. Drake wondered once more how the confrontation would go down. SPEAR had been ordered to secure all four weapons at all costs, but orders rarely translated perfectly to the field of action. He saw twitchy expressions on other faces and knew they felt the same, even Hayden who was closest to the command structure.

They readied to move out.

"Try to avoid a confrontation," Hayden said. "Obviously."

"And if we can't?" Dahl asked.

"Well, if it's Mossad maybe we can talk."

"I doubt they'll have ID vests," Alicia muttered. "This ain't a cop show."

Hayden momentarily flicked her comms to the off position. "If we're fired upon, we fight," she said. "What else can we do?"

Drake saw it as the best compromise. In a perfect world they would sneak past the approaching soldiers and make it back to their transport, unscathed and undetected. Of course, SPEAR wouldn't exist in a perfect world. He checked his weapons again as the team made ready to move out.

"Take the long route," Hayden suggested. "They won't."

Every precaution. Every trick to avoid conflict.

Lauren's voice was a splinter in his ear. "Just got word, people. The Swedes are inbound too."

CHAPTER SEVEN

Drake led the way, first moving behind the dilapidated building and then heading downhill. Darkness still pooled across the land but sunrise was not far away. Drake wound his way in a ragged loop until he was traveling back toward the sea.

Senses alert, heads up, the team followed.

Dahl took possession of the box, careful to keep the lid tight under his arm. To his side ran Kenzie, helping him navigate. The team wore their night-vision gear, all except for Smyth who preferred to fully sense his environment. It was a good mix. Side by side and in file they ran until they reached the bottom of the hill and the flat plain where there was no cover. Drake kept to his loop, bringing them around in the general direction of the boats. No words were passed—all used their senses to test the environment.

They knew how deadly their enemies were. No half-interested mercenaries this time. Today, and the next and the next, they were up against soldiers as good as them.

Almost.

Drake slowed, sensing they were moving just a little too fast. The terrain was not in their favor. A pale glow crept toward the eastern horizon. Soon, there would be no cover. Smyth ranged to his right and Mai to his left. The team kept low. The hill with the dilapidated building on top shrank to their rear. A row of brush dotted by a few trees appeared up ahead and Drake felt a little relief. They were a good way to the northeast of where they needed to be, but the end result would be worth it.

Best case scenario? No fighting.

He moved on, watching for dangers and keeping his body language neutral. The comms remained quiet. As they approached the cover they slowed, just in case somebody was already there, waiting. Being Special Forces they might expect a warning, but nothing could be taken for granted on this mission.

Drake saw a large area bordered by several trees and straggly brush, and stopped, signaling the others to take a break. A check of the landscape revealed nothing. The hilltop was deserted as far as he could see. To their left, sparse cover led all the way to the flat plain and then the shores of the sea. He guessed their boats might be a fifteen minute hike away. Quietly, he keyed the comms.

"Lauren, any news on the Swedes?"

"Nope. But they must be close."

"Other teams?"

"Russia's in the air." She sounded embarrassed. "Can't give you a position."

"Place is about to become a hot zone," Smyth said. "We gotta move."

Drake agreed. "Let's move out."

He rose, and a shout blasted at him as shocking as any bullet.

"Stop there! We want the box. Do not move."

Drake didn't hesitate, but dropped fast, both grateful for the warning and shaken that they hadn't spotted the enemy. Dahl glared at him and Alicia looked confused. Even Mai exhibited surprise.

Kenzie clicked her tongue. "That has to be Mossad."

"Did you get a bead on 'em?" Hayden asked.

"Yeah," Drake said. "Speaker's dead ahead and probably has mates to the sides. Right where we wanna be."

"We can't go forward," Mai said. "We go back. That way." She pointed to the east. "There's cover and a road, some farms. A city not too far away. We can call an evac."

Drake glanced at Hayden. Their boss seemed to be weighing up the choices between heading north along the coast, east toward civilization, or facing the battle.

"Nothing good happens if we stay here," Dahl said. "Facing one elite enemy would be tough but we know more are on their way."

Drake already knew Mai was right. North offered no means of escape. They would be running alongside the Hellespont with bare cover and trusting everything to sheer luck that they might stumble across a mode of transport. Traveling east guaranteed an opportunity.

Plus, the other teams were unlikely to be coming from a city.

Hayden called it and then turned toward the east, gauging the ground and the chance of a quick getaway. Right then, the voice rang out again.

"Stay right there!"

"Crap," Alicia breathed. "The dude's psychic."

"Just got good eyes," Smyth said, meaning visual tech. "Get behind something solid. We're about to take fire."

The team moved, heading east. The Israelis opened fire, bullets slamming above the SPEAR team's heads into tree trunks and between branches. Leaves rained down. Drake scrambled fast, knowing the shots were aimed deliberately high and wondering what the hell kind of new warfare they had ventured into here.

"Just like a friggin' army exercise," Alicia said.

"I really hope they're using rubber bullets," Dahl replied.

They scrambled and improvised movement toward the east, reaching more sturdy trees and grabbing a look. Drake fired back, deliberately high. He saw no signs of movement.

"Tricky bastards."

"Small team," Kenzie said. "Cautious. Automatons. They will be awaiting a decision."

Drake sought to take full advantage. The team wound a cautious path to the east, right into the pale dawn that still threatened the far horizon. As he reached another clearing, Drake heard and practically felt the whizz of a bullet.

"Shit." He dived for cover. "That one was close."

More gunfire, more lead slamming among the cover. Hayden stared Drake in the eyes. "Their orders have changed."

Drake breathed deeply, scarcely believing it. The Israelis were firing hard, and no doubt advancing at a careful but advantageous rate. Another bullet took a chunk of bark from a tree just behind Yorgi's head, making the Russian flinch hard.

"Not good," Kenzie grunted furiously. "Not good at all."

Drake's eyes were like flint. "Hayden, get on to Lauren. Ask her to confirm with Crowe that we fire back!"

"We *have* to fire back," Kenzie cried out. "You guys never checked before."

"*No!* They're paid soldiers, elite forces, trained and following orders. They're fucking allies, potential friends. Check, Hayden. *Check now!*"

More bullets rifled the undergrowth. The enemy remained unseen, unheard, their advance known only through SPEAR's own experience. Drake watched Hayden click the comms and speak to Lauren, then prayed for a fast response.

The Mossad soldiers came closer.

"Reconfirm our status." Even Dahl sounded stressed. "Lauren! Get the decision? *Do we engage?*"

Already driven away from their boats, the SPEAR team were forced to move further east. Under fire, they were driven hard. Reluctant to fight known allies, they were neck deep in danger.

Scrambling, scraped and bloody, they employed every trick in their arsenal, every ploy, to put distance between themselves and Mossad. It only took minutes for Lauren to come back, but those minutes dragged on longer than a Justin Bieber CD.

"Crowe ain't happy. Says you got your orders. Secure the weapons at all costs. All four of them."

"That's it?" Drake asked. "You told her who we're up against?"

"Of course. She sounded pissed. I think we pissed her off."

Drake shook his head. *Doesn't make sense. We should be working together on this.*

Dahl leant an opinion. "We did go against her orders in Peru. Maybe this is payback."

Drake didn't believe it. "Nah. That'd be petty. She's not that kind of politician. We're up against allies. *Shit.*"

"We have our orders," Hayden said. "Let's survive today and argue tomorrow."

Drake knew she was right, but couldn't help thinking that the Israelis had probably said the exact same thing. This was how age-old grievances began. As a team now they blazed a trail to the east, staying within their shield of forestation, and organized a rearguard, nothing too aggressive but enough to slow down the Israelis. Smyth, Kinimaka and Mai were outstanding at showing that they now meant business, hobbling their adversaries at every turn.

It came from behind them as Drake flitted between trees. A chopper thundered overhead, then banked and dropped to a landing in some discreet clearing. Hayden didn't have to say a word.

"Swedes? Russians? Jesus, this is bad shit, guys!"

Drake immediately heard gunfire from that direction. Whoever had just exited that chopper had been fired upon, and not by Mossad.

That meant four Special Forces teams were now in the fray.

Ahead, the forest ended and a wide field bordered by stone walls revealed an old farmhouse.

"Make some time up," he cried. "Go hard and fast. We can regroup there."

The team ran like the hounds of Hell were racing at their heels.

Running at a full but controlled pace, the team randomly broke cover and pelted toward the farmhouse. The walls and window openings were almost as beat-up as the hillhouse had been, signifying the lack of human presence. Three Special Forces teams lay at their backs but how close?

Drake didn't know. He jogged hard across the rutted ground, taking his night-vision apparatus off and using the lightening skies to mark the way. Half the team scanned the way ahead, half the way behind. Mai whispered that she'd seen the Mossad team reach the edge of the forest, but then Drake reached the first low wall and Mai and Smyth put down a little suppressing fire.

Together, they huddled behind the stone wall.

The farmhouse stood another twenty paces ahead. Drake knew it would do them no good to allow the Israelis and others to get settled and establish perfect lines of sight. Also the other teams would be wary now of each other. He spoke into the comms.

"Best haul ass, folks."

Alicia shifted to stare at him. "That your best American accent?"

Drake looked worried. "Crap. I've finally turned." Then he saw Dahl. "But, hey, could be worse, I guess."

As one they broke cover. Mai and Smyth again provided containing fire and received only two rounds in return. No other sounds were heard. Drake found a sturdy wall and stopped. Hayden immediately put Mai and Smyth and Kinimaka on perimeter watch and then scurried over to join the others.

"We're good for a few minutes. What do we have?"

Dahl was already breaking out the map as Lauren's voice filled their ears.

"Plan B is still possible. Head inland. If you're fast you won't need transport."

"Plan fucking B." Drake shook his head. "Always plan B."

The perimeter watch reported all was clear.

Hayden indicated the box Dahl carried. "We gotta take responsibility here. If you lose that we have no idea what's inside. And if you lose it to an enemy . . ." She didn't need to go on. The Swede placed the box on the ground and knelt beside it.

Hayden brushed at the symbol engraved into the top. The swirling blades cast an ominous warning. Dahl urged the lid open gently.

Drake held his breath. Nothing happened. It was always a risk, but they had been unable to see any hidden locks or mechanisms. Now, Dahl pulled the lid up fully and peered into the space within.

Kenzie grunted. "This is what? A weapon of war? Tied to Hannibal and hidden by the order? All I see is a bunch of paper."

Dahl sat back on his haunches. "War can be waged through words too."

Hayden carefully lifted a handful of sheets out and scanned the text. "I don't know," she admitted. "Looks like a research file and . . . a record of . . ." She paused. "Tests? Testing?" She flicked through more pages. "Build specs."

Drake frowned. "Now that sounds bad. They're calling it Project Babylon, Lauren. See what you can dig up on that."

"Got it," the New Yorker said. "Anything else?"

"I'm just getting a feel for these specs," Dahl began. "It's a gigantic—"

"Down!" Smyth yelled. "Incoming."

The team dropped and prepared. A volley of gunfire ripped across the stone walls, harsh and deafening. Smyth returned fire from the right, sighting from a niche in the wall. Hayden shook her head.

"We're gonna have to pack this up. Get out of here."

"Haul ass?" Drake asked.

"Haul ass."

"Plan B," Alicia said.

Staying safe, they moved from wall to wall toward the rear of the farmhouse. Debris littered the floor and chunks of masonry and timber marked where the roof had given way. Mai, Smyth and Kinimaka watched the rear. Drake paused as they reached the back windows and glanced at the route ahead.

"This can only get harder," he said.

The rising sun slipped over the horizon in a rush of color.

CHAPTER EIGHT

The race continued, but now the odds were drawing in. As Drake and Alicia, in front, broke cover and headed inland, careful to keep the farmhouse between them and their pursuers, the Mossad team finally emerged from the forest. Clad all in black and with face masks, they came low and cautious, guns up and firing. Mai and Smyth quickly fell behind the cover of the farmhouse. Hayden sprinted forward.

"Move!"

Drake fought the instinct to stand and fight; Dahl to his left clearly fought it too. Normally they battled and outwitted their opponents—sometimes it was down to brute force and numbers. But often it was down to the numb-headedness of their opponents. Most paid mercenaries were slow and dull-witted, relying on their size, ferocity and lack of morals to get the job done.

Not today.

Drake was acutely aware of the need to protect the prize. Dahl carried the box and kept it as protected as it was ever going to be. Yorgi now ranged ahead, sampling the ground and trying to find the paths with the most cover. They traversed a hilly field and then dropped through a small, sparse stand of trees. The Israelis stopped their fire for a period, perhaps sensing other teams and not wanting to broadcast their position.

Many tactics were now on display.

But, for Drake, Alicia summed it up best. "For fuck's sake, Yogi. Get your Russkie head down and run!"

Lauren was tracking their progress by GPS and

announced the plan B rendezvous was just over the next horizon.

Drake breathed a little easier. The stand of trees ended and Yorgi led the way up a slight hill, Kinimaka hot on his heels. The Hawaiian's trousers were caked in mud where he'd fallen—three times. Alicia glanced across at Mai, moving nimbly between folds in the ground.

"Friggin' Sprite. Looks like a spring lamb gamboling along."

"Everything she does, she does it well," Drake agreed.

Alicia skidded in shale, but managed to keep her stride. "We all do it well."

"Yeah, but some of us look more like goats."

Alicia raised her weapon. "Hope you don't mean me, Drakey." Her voice held a note of warning.

"Oh, of course not, dear. Obviously, I meant the Swede."

"*Dear?*"

Shots rang out from behind, cutting Dahl's retort off before it even began. Experience told Drake the shots were not meant for them, and consisted of two different notes. Mossad were engaging with either the Russians or the Swedes.

The Swedes probably, he thought, *ran headlong into Mossad.*

He couldn't help the private chuckle.

Dahl glanced over as if sensing the outrage. Drake offered innocent eyes. They crested the minor hill and slipped down the other side.

"Transport incoming," Lauren said.

"There!" Hayden pointed to the skies, far away, where a black speck moved. Drake viewed the area and dragged Yorgi down just as a bullet skimmed its way over the top of the hill. Someone had suddenly become more interested in them.

"Into the valley," Kinimaka said. "If we can reach that set of trees..."

The team readied for the final sprint. Drake glanced again at the oncoming speck. For a second he thought he might be seeing a shadow, but then saw the truth.

"Um, people, that's another chopper."

Kinimaka stared hard. "Crap."

"And there." Mai pointed to the left, high toward a bank of clouds. "A third."

"Lauren," Hayden said urgently. "Lauren, talk to us!"

"Just getting confirmation." The calm voice came back. "You have the Chinese and the Brits in the air. Russia, Swedes and Israelis on the ground. Look, I'm gonna patch you into the chatter now so you can get first time information. Some of it's crap, but anything could be valuable."

"The French?" Kinimaka wondered for some reason.

"Nothing," Lauren said.

"Good job they're not all like Beau," Alicia said with a twist of bitterness and melancholy. "The French, I mean. The guy was a traitor, but damn good at his job."

Dahl screwed his face up. "If they're like Beau," he said quietly. "They could already be here."

Alicia blinked at that, studying the nearby mounds of dirt. Nothing moved.

"We're surrounded," Hayden said.

"Special Forces teams to all sides," Drake agreed. "Rats in a trap."

"Speak for yourself." Mai evaluated everything quickly. "Take two minutes. Memorize what's inside that box as best you can." She raised her hands. "Do it."

Drake caught the gist of it. The box, at the end of the day, wasn't worth their lives. If things got really tight and the friendlier team overcame them, giving up the box might just save their lives. Dahl flipped the lid open as the team walked straight toward the oncoming choppers.

He handed sheaves of paper all around.

"Whoa, this is weird," Alicia said.

Kenzie shuffled several sheets. "Walking into a fight whilst reading a thirty to fifty-year-old document written by Nazis and hidden in Hannibal Barca's grave? What's weird about that?"

Drake tried to commit the passages to memory. "She has a point. Par for the course for SPEAR."

High altitude research project, he read. *Initially created with the goal of studying the ballistics of re-entry at lesser cost. Instead of expensive rockets . . .*

"I don't know what the hell this is."

Non-rocket space launch. The project suggests a very large gun could be used to fire objects at high speed to high altitudes . . .

"Oh, shit."

Dahl and Alicia were similarly ashen faced. "This can't be good."

Hayden pointed out the oncoming choppers, now in plain sight. They could see individual weapons hanging out of the helos.

"And neither is that!"

Drake handed over the papers and readied his weapons. Time for something he was used to and good at. Chatter flew at him from Hayden, Mai and Smyth, and also from the comms system that Lauren had patched in.

"Israelis engaged with Swedes. Russia unknown . . ." Then came bursts of static and quick translations from live feed communications that the NSA and other organizations had managed to listen in on.

The French: "We are approaching the area . . ."

The British: "Yes sir, targets seen. We have multiple enemies in the field . . ."

The Chinese: "Are you certain they have the box?"

Hayden led the way. They ran from the field. They ran without a plan. Careful gunfire made the choppers shy away and forced their ground pursuit to move with extreme caution.

And then, as Drake had almost tuned out and concentrated on their new escape route, another voice cut through the static.

Only briefly.

Partially hidden under the noise, hard to properly make out, a deep drawl jabbed at his ears.

American: "SEAL Team 7 here. We're real close now . . ."

Shock jolted him to the core. But there was no time. No chance to talk. Not even a second to absorb it.

His eyes though met Torsten Dahl's.

What the . . . ?

CHAPTER NINE

"Tell the helo to back off!" Hayden snapped through the comms. "We're gonna find a different way."

"You want it to hang around?" Lauren asked, making Alicia laugh even as she ran for her life.

"Of course. Duck and cover. Don't call us, we'll call you!"

Drake wondered if the day would ever end, then saw the full disc of sun hanging over the horizon and saw the irony. The ground ran in a series of hills, each one steeper than the next. SPEAR covered their asses as they reached the top of the hill, stepping carefully, then ran full-pelt down the other side.

Gunfire erupted spasmodically from the rear, but it wasn't aimed at them, probably the Israelis and Swedes trading blows. Appearing to the left and right were several more decrepit buildings, most built in shallow valleys, all deserted. Drake wasn't sure what had made the people leave, but it had happened a long time ago.

More hills and then a stand of trees to the left. Offering cover, the greenery and boughs clustered thickly. Hayden steered the team in that direction, and Drake breathed a little easier. Any kind of concealment was better than none at all. First Hayden and then Alicia flitted through the trees, now followed by Dahl, Kenzie and Kinimaka. Drake entered the wood, which left Mai, Yorgi and Smyth at the rear. Shots rang out, closer now, sending a bolt of apprehension for his friends through Drake.

Turning, he saw Mai stumble.

Watched her face bounce off the ground.

"Noooo!"

Hayden skidded to an instant stop and turned. Mai lay collapsed on the ground in that instant, Drake stepping up to her, Smyth already bending down. Bullets thudded into the outer trees. Someone was close.

Then the undergrowth erupted. Figures leapt out, one striking Hayden in the lower body. She staggered, but kept her feet. A tree trunk struck her spine. She ignored the jolt of pain, raised her gun. Then the black figure was at her again, striking with an elbow, a knee, a knife . . .

Hayden twisted with the lunge, and felt the edge of the blade pass her stomach by a hair's-breadth. She fought back, an elbow to the face and a knee to the stomach to force a little space between them. She was aware of Kinimaka and Alicia struggling to the right, of Dahl kicking out at a figure he'd felled.

Of Drake lifting up a limp Mai.

Bullets flew between the trees, shredding the leaves and vegetation. One felled an adversary, but not for long. The man soon rose, clearly wearing some form of Kevlar. Hayden's vision was then full of her own opponent—a man from the Mossad, features engrained with raw and vicious purpose.

"Stop," she said. "We're on the same—"

The punch in the mouth stopped her. Hayden tasted blood.

"Orders," came the thick reply.

She blocked more blows, forcing the man away, trying not to bring up her gun even as he wielded his knife. The blade tasted bark, then dirt. Hayden kicked the man's legs out as Drake pelted past, racing along the trail and further into the trees. Smyth watched his back, striking an Israeli in the face and sending him back into the underbrush. Kenzie came next, face for once hesitant and eyes wide as if searching for someone familiar.

Hayden pushed her way toward Drake.

"Mai?"

"She's fine. Just a bullet to the spine is all. Nothing spectacular."

Hayden blanched. "What?"

"Jacket stopped it. She fell, hit her skull. No biggie."

"Oh."

Alicia ducked under a vicious elbow attack and used a judo throw to send her opponent crashing beyond the trees. Kinimaka bulldozed his way through another Mossad soldier. For a few moments the way was clear, and the SPEAR team took full advantage.

Every ounce of experience came into play as they ran at full pace, without thought of slowing down, through the twisting, dipping, hazardous cluster of trees. A gap was introduced between them and the Mossad team, and the thick foliage was the perfect cover.

"How the hell did they get around us?" Drake yelled.

"Must have been when we stopped to check the box," Hayden said.

Smyth clucked loudly. "We were watching."

"Don't beat yourself up—" Hayden began.

"No, my friend," Kenzie said. "They are the best at what they do."

Smyth grunted as if to say *so are we,* but otherwise held his silence. Hayden saw Kinimaka stumble, huge feet landing in a pile of springy loam, and moved to help but Dahl had already steadied the big man. The Swede swopped the box to the other arm, pushing the Hawaiian with his right.

And now another danger added to the mix—the unmistakable sound of a chopper sweeping overhead.

Would they open fire?

Would they sweep the forest with bullets?

Hayden didn't think so. A thousand things could go wrong with such irresponsible action. Of course, these guys were under orders from their governments and some of the clowns sat back home in their warm or air-conditioned offices cared naught for what happened outside their ivory towers.

The clapping of rotors passed above. Hayden kept running. Already, she knew Mossad would be hot on their team, and perhaps the Swedes and Russians behind them. Noises came from the left and she thought she saw more figures—it had to be the Russians, she thought.

Or maybe the Brits?

Fuck!

They were too exposed. Too unprepared. In real effect, so were all the teams out there. Nobody had expected everyone to arrive at once—and that had been a mistake. *But tell me a plan that would cater for this?*

Drake trail-blazed ahead, slowed down not at all by Mai's weight. Alicia pounded at his heels, watching to left and right. The path meandered aimlessly, but generally in the right direction, and Hayden sent out a thanks for that. She heard Smyth spray bullets to their rear, discouraging the pursuers. She heard several cries to the left, as if two forces had met.

Crap, this is some crazy shit.

Drake hurdled a fallen tree. Kinimaka smashed through it with barely a grunt. Splinters exploded in all directions. The terrain began to slope down and then they saw the edge of the forest. Hayden snapped into the comms that they should slow—nobody knew what on earth could be waiting beyond that tree line.

Drake slackened the pace only a little. Alicia flanked him to the right and Dahl pounded up to the left; together the three of them breached the cover and entered a narrow valley protected on both sides by steep brown slopes. Kinimaka and Kenzie were hammering their heels in an effort to provide support and then Hayden broke cover too, now trying to ignore the growing burn in her chest.

They'd been running for longer than she wanted to think about.

And the nearest town was miles away.

CHAPTER TEN

Drake felt Mai start to struggle a little. He gave her a minute, knowing she'd come around fast. In that fleeting moment he spotted something flat, gray and winding that made his pounding heart skip a beat.

"Left!"

The whole group broke to the left, guarding their flanks carefully but unnecessarily as their competitors were still unseen. Drake allowed Mai to struggle a bit but held on. Pretty soon she drove a fist into his ribs.

"Let me down."

"One sec, love . . ."

Alicia glared over. "You enjoying it that much?"

Drake hesitated, then grinned. "There's no safe answer to that one, love."

"Really?"

"Well, think about it from my point of view."

Mai solved his dilemma by using his spine to push off and flip to the floor. She landed well but swayed in place, holding her head.

"See," Drake said. "In my defense, she does seem shaky."

"Your *head* will be shaky if we don't get a move on." Alicia pushed past and Drake followed, watching Mai a little longer until she straightened and fell into the pace. The group raced up an embankment toward the blacktop.

"First tangle with Mossad." Dahl stretched. "Nothing spectacular."

"They were holding back," Kenzie said. "As you were."

"Second tangle," Drake said. "Remember that village in England? Yonks ago."

"Yonks?"

"Ages."

"Oh." Dahl paused for a second then delivered: "BC or AD?"

"I think they're calling it BCE now."

"Bollocks to that."

The road stretched in both directions, deserted, potholed and in need of repair. Drake heard the flak-flak of the chopper coming around and then more gunfire. He turned to see it being fired upon from the forest, wondered if it would simply carpet the area with bullets, and then saw it veer away sharply.

"Can't take the chance," Dahl said. "Guess that must be the Chinese and they can't hear chatter as we can."

Drake nodded silently. The chatter hadn't revealed anything new recently. Not since . . .

Hayden gave out a quiet cheer. "I see a vehicle."

Drake dropped low and scanned the area. "So what do we have behind us? Mossad and the Russians in the trees, hindering each other. The Swedes somewhere near the Russians? SAS?" He shook his head. "Who knows? Best guess—skirting the forest. They all know if they expose themselves they're dead. Which is why were still alive."

"Chinese in the helo," Smyth said. "Landing there." He pointed to a series of shallow dips.

"French?" Yorgi asked.

Drake shook his head. Joking aside, the French may even have held back to test the water and allow their opponents to thin themselves out. Shrewdly winning the day at the last minute. He stared at the approaching van.

"Guns up."

Smyth and Kenzie took point, standing at the side of the road and pointing their weapons at the approaching van. Dahl and Drake had placed a couple of heavy boulders in the road. As the van slowed, the rest of the team came from the rear, carefully covering the vehicle and ordering its occupants out.

Alicia threw open the rear door.

"Whoa, it stinks!"

But it was empty. And Drake heard Kenzie asking a question in Turkish. He shook his head as Dahl smiled triumphantly. Full of surprises that girl. "Is there any language she can't speak?"

The Swede guffawed. "C'mon man. Don't leave yourself so wide open."

"Ah," Drake nodded. "Yeah. The language of the gods."

"Ey up, love. Fancy a shag? Yeah, I can just hear your sweet accent rolling off Odin's tongue."

Drake ignored it, concentrating on the two Turkish people, who appeared genuinely terrified.

And genuinely Turkish.

Hayden bundled them back into the truck, following close at their heels. Dahl grinned once more and then followed her, gesturing at the rest to jump in the back. Drake saw his reason for mirth an instant later, then stared back at Alicia.

"How bad is it back there?"

The truck bounced and jounced and tried to destroy itself on the decrepit road.

Alicia held on for dear life. "Is he *trying* to hit the bloody bad bits?"

"Probably," Smyth said miserably, holding his nose and a filthy strap tied to a strut inside the van. "I smell goats."

Alicia narrowed her eyes. "Oh yeah? Friend of yours?"

Kinimaka sat at the rear of the truck, desperately gulping lungfuls of fresh air through gaps where the rear doors met. "Must . . . be . . . farmers, I guess."

"Or goat smugglers," Alicia said. "Never can tell."

Smyth grunted in anger. "When I said goats, I meant *generally*."

"Yeah, yeah, yeah."

Drake kept out of it, taking shallow breaths and trying to focus on other things. They had to trust Hayden and Dahl up front to keep them safe and find the best place to go. The comms remained silent except for the occasional blast of static. Even Lauren stayed quiet, which also helped in its own way. It told them they were relatively safe.

The team complained loudly around him—their way of coping and taking their minds off the animal stench. Comparisons to Swedish bathhouses, American restaurants and London hotels were proffered in good sport.

Drake let his mind wander from Yorgi's recent outburst and need to share a terrible secret, to the new understanding between Alicia and Mai, to the other troubles that beset the SPEAR team. Hayden and Kinimaka remained at odds, as did Lauren and Smyth—though the latter were dissected by a little more than disagreement. Dahl was working his socks off with Johanna, but there again the job stood in the way.

Something more urgent and implacable prodded his brain. Secretary Crowe's irritation that they hadn't followed orders in Peru and the sure knowledge that a clandestine, top-secret second American team was here. Somewhere.

SEAL Team 7.

The questions were countless and inexplicable. What was the answer? Did Crowe no longer trust the SPEAR team? Were they backup?

He hadn't forgotten about the large question mark still hanging over Smyth's head, but couldn't imagine any other scenario. Crowe had sent Seven to watch over them.

Drake quelled the anger. She had her own job to do. Black and white was a life vision shared only by fools and crazy people. His deep musings were interrupted by Hayden.

"All clear behind and up front. Looks like we're approaching a place called Çanakkale, on the coast. I'll wait until we've found a place before contacting the helo. Oh, and Dahl's had chance to pick this box apart."

The Swede took their minds off their situation for a while as he explained what the sheaves of paper appeared to represent. More than war, it was its very *declaration*. Hannibal, it seemed, had been chosen merely as a symbol.

"No clue as to how Africa became one of the four corners of the earth?" Mai asked.

"Not a bloody thing. So we can't anticipate where the next Horseman will be."

"Look into the past," Kenzie spoke up. "In my job, my *old* job, the answers were always buried back in time. You just have to know where to look."

Lauren chipped in then. "I'll try that."

Drake fought the plunge and sway of the truck. "How far to Çanakkale?"

"Entering the outskirts now. Doesn't look too big. I can see the sea."

"Oh, you win." Drake remembered a game from when he was a kid.

"I saw it first," Dahl said with a smile in his voice.

"Yeah, we used to play that too."

The truck pulled over, and pretty soon the rear doors were opening outward. The team jumped out and took in amazing lungfuls of fresh air. Alicia complained she felt ill and Kenzie pretended to faint in the English manner. This perked Alicia right up. Drake found himself staring hard and staring in amazement.

"By 'eck," he muttered on purpose. "Well I'll be a monkey's uncle."

Dahl was too gobstruck to comment.

An enormous wooden horse stood before them, somehow familiar, brooding over a small square surrounded by buildings. Rope seemed to bind its legs and was strung around its head. Drake thought it appeared armored and majestic, a proud manmade animal.

"What the hell?"

Crowds flocked around it, staring and posing and taking pictures.

Lauren spoke via the comms. "I guess you just found the Troy horse."

Smyth guffawed. "It's far from a toy."

"No *Troy*. You know? Brad Pitt?"

Alicia almost broke her neck, glancing in all directions. "What? Where?"

"Whoa." Kenzie laughed. "I've seen vipers strike slower."

Alicia was still scrutinizing the area. "Where, Lauren? Is he *in* the horse?"

The New Yorker let out a chuckle. "Well, he was once. Remember the modern movie—*Troy*? Well, after filming they left the horse right where you stand, in Çanakkale."

"Bollocks." Alicia vented. "I thought all my Christmases had come at once." She shook her head.

Drake cleared his throat. "I'm still here, love."

"Oh yeah. Great."

"And don't worry, if Brad Pitt jumps out of the arse-end of that horse and tries to kidnap you, I'll save you."

"Don't you fucking dare."

Lauren's voice cut across their chatter like the hard descent of a samurai sword. "Incoming, guys! Multiple enemies. Approaching Çanakkale right now. They must be linked into the comms as we are. *Move!*"

"See that?" Drake pointed at the fortress. "Call the chopper. If we can climb the castle and defend ourselves, it can take us from there."

Hayden cast a glance back toward the outskirts of Çanakkale. "*If* we can defend a castle, in a tourist city, against six Special Forces teams."

Dahl hefted the box. "Only one way to find out."

CHAPTER ELEVEN

Instinctively, they moved toward the coastal path, knowing it would wind around toward the town's impressive fort. Lauren elicited very little information from the blasts of comms chatter and Drake heard even less from the various team overseers, but the general consensus was that they were all closing in fast.

The path led past many white-fronted buildings: houses, shops and restaurants facing the Hellespont's rippling blue waters. Cars stood parked to the left and beyond them, several small boats, with the high, sand-colored fort walls towering above all. Tourist coaches passed by, grumbling slowly through the narrow streets. Horns honked. Locals gathered outside a popular coffee shop, smoking and talking. The team hurried as fast as they could without attracting suspicion.

Not easy when wearing combat gear, but purposely for this mission they wore all black and could remove and conceal those items that might attract attention. Still, a group moving as they were turned heads and Drake saw more than one phone flipped open.

"Call the damn chopper in fast," he said. "We've run out of land and bloody time here."

"On its way. Ten-fifteen minutes out."

An age in combat, he knew. Some of the other Special Forces teams would have no qualms about raising hell in the city, confident of their orders and ability to escape, knowing the authorities would usually put a terrorist spin on any intensely threatening situation.

Sand-colored walls rose sharply right in front of them.

The fort of Çanakkale had two rounded, sea-facing castle walls and a central keep and, beyond that, a sweeping arm of battlements that ran downhill back toward the sea. Drake followed the line of the first curving wall, wondering what lay at the conjunction of this and its sister. Hayden paused ahead and glanced back.

"We go up."

A brave decision but one Drake agreed with. To go up meant they'd be stuck in the fort, defending from a high position but exposed, trapped. To continue meant they had other options besides running into the sea: they could hide in the city, find a car, potentially go to ground or split up for a while.

But Hayden's option kept them at the head of the game. There were other Horsemen out there. The chopper would find them easier. Their skills were better employed in a tactical battle.

Rough walls gave way to an arched entrance and then a set of winding stairs. Hayden went first, followed by Dahl and Kenzie, then the others. Smyth brought up the rear. Darkness made a mantle for their eyes, hanging thick and impenetrable until they became used to it. Still, up they went, climbing the stairs and heading back to the light. Drake tried to filter all the relevant information to his brain and make sense of it.

Hannibal. The Horseman of War. The Order of the Last Judgment and their blueprint to make a better world for those that survived. The governments of the world should be working together on this, but ruthless, greedy individuals wanted the spoils and the knowledge for themselves.

The four corners of the earth? How did that work? And what the hell was coming next?

"Interestingly . . ." Lauren's voice crackled through the

comms at that moment. "Çanakkale is situated on two continents and was one of the launching points for Gallipoli. Now, the Russians have entered the town and so have the Israelis. Don't know where. Local police chatter is rife, though. Some of the citizens must have reported you and are now calling in the new arrivals. It won't be long before the Turks call in their own elite forces."

Drake shook his head. *Bollocks.*

"We'll be long gone by then." Hayden moved cautiously into the light above. "Ten minutes guys. C'mon."

The mid-morning sunshine beat down on the wide-open, sparse area of land almost at the top of the tower. The tower's circular top lip jutted up another eight feet above their heads, but this was as high as they went without getting inside. Broken battlements lay all about, projecting like ragged fingers, and a dusty path bordered a series of low mounds off to the right. Drake saw a plethora of defensible positions and breathed a little easier.

"We're here," Hayden said to Lauren. "Tell the helo to prepare for a hot pick up."

"Hotter than you think," Smyth said.

The entire team stared downward.

"Not down," Smyth said. "Up. *Up.*"

Above the castle, the town still littered the hills. Houses stood overlooking the battlements and walls stretched high and thick toward them. It was across these walls that a team of four men ran, faces covered, guns fully exposed.

Drake recognized the style. "Fuck, that's trouble. SAS."

Dahl was first into action, but instead of loosing his weapon he tucked it away, gripped the box, and jumped up onto the battlements themselves. "British have the right idea for a change. Look . . ."

Drake followed his eye. The battlements swept in a wide arc all the way back down to the beach and the undulating sea. If they timed it right the chopper would be able to pluck them right off the top or at the very end. Drake took the responsibility of firing a couple of shots into the craggy concrete under the British feet, slowing them and allowing the team time to climb onto the top of the slightly roll-topped fortifications.

Alicia wobbled. "Not keen on heights!"

"Do you ever stop whining?" Kenzie intentionally squeezed past her, giving her a tiny nudge on the way.

"Ooh bitch, you'll pay for that." Alicia sounded unsure.

"Will I? Just make sure you stay behind me. That way when they shoot you and I hear you scream I'll know to pick up the pace."

Alicia fumed. Drake steadied her. "Just Mossad banter." He spread his arms.

"Right. Well when we get down from here I'm gonna properly Mossad her ass."

Drake guided her the first few steps. "Is that *supposed* to sound arousing?"

"Fuck off, Drake."

He thought it best not to mention that the battlements, far below, turned into spaced crenellations where they would have to jump from one to the other. Dahl jogged down the three-foot-wide wall first, leading the team. Kinimaka relieved Smyth at the back for once, observing the British. Drake and the rest kept eyes open for any other signs of enemies.

The race down the battlements began. The SAS soldiers kept formation and came in pursuit, weapons raised but silent. Of course, professional leniency might be only one of the reasons; in addition to tourists, locals, the preference toward secrecy, and highly secure orders.

Drake found he needed full concentration for his feet. The drop to each side and the gradual descent to the sea didn't matter, only the safe zone beneath his feet. It wound gradually, gracefully even, in a steady curve. Nobody slowed, nobody slipped. They were halfway to their goal when the sound of thudding rotors filled their ears.

Drake slowed, looked to the skies. "Not ours," he shouted. "Bloody French!"

It wasn't a definitive deduction but would explain their absence until now. Swooping in at the last minute. Team SPEAR were forced to slow their pace. Drake saw the faces of two soldiers leering out the windows, whilst two more dangled from the half-open doors, weapons coming around to get a proper lock.

"Truth be told," Dahl panted. "This might not have been the best idea. Bloody British bell-ends."

As one, Drake, Smyth, Hayden and Mai elevated their guns and opened fire. Bullets ricocheted off the approaching chopper. Glass smashed and one man fell from his rope, smashing hard to the ground below. The chopper veered away, chased by Hayden's bullets.

"The French are not fans," she said grimly.

"Tell us something we don't know," Alicia muttered.

Yorgi sprinted nimbly ahead of Dahl, passing him on the outside lip of the wall, and reached back for the box. "Here, give it to me," he said. "I am better on the wall, no?"

Dahl looked like he wanted to argue, but handed the box over mid-run. The Swede wasn't a stranger to a bit of Parkour, but Yorgi was a pro. The Russian sped off at top speed, racing down the wall and already approaching the crenellations.

Alicia spotted them. "Oh hell, shoot me now."

"That may yet happen." Drake saw the French helicopter banking and coming around. Trouble was, if they stopped to aim, the British would catch them. If they ran firing, they could possibly fall or be easily picked off.

Dahl swung his weapon around. Both he and Hayden fired upon the chopper as it came back into play. This time the soldiers aboard fired back. Rounds stitched the castle walls in a deadly pattern, striking below the rim. Hayden's own fire struck the helo's cockpit, clanging off the metal struts. Drake saw the pilot clenching his teeth in a mix of anger and fear. A hyper-quick glance back showed the SAS team also sighting on the chopper—a good sign? Maybe not. They wanted the weapon of war for themselves.

Or for somebody highly placed in their government.

A volley of shots peppered the bird, making it dip and yaw. Dahl took advantage of the last solid hundred meters of wall to drop and slide whilst firing, but he didn't get far. The surface was too rough. Still, his actions sent another salvo into the chopper, finally making the pilot give up the ghost and pull the bird away from the action.

Alicia managed a faint cheer.

"Not out of this yet." Drake leapt the crenellations one at a time, landing safely and taking it carefully.

Lauren's voice slashed apart the silence that blanketed the comms. "Helo inbound. Thirty seconds."

"We're on the wall," Alicia cried.

"Yeah, I gotcha. DC tasked a satellite to this op."

Drake took another moment to be shocked. "To help?" he asked quickly.

"Why else?" Hayden shot back instantly.

Drake almost kicked himself before realizing it was probably a bad idea given the current situation. Truth was, he didn't know who else had heard those quiet American tones and the words *SEAL Team 7*.

Clearly, not Hayden.

The chopper came into view ahead, nose down, sweeping in fast over the sea. Yorgi was already waiting at the end of the battlements where a small round turret looked out over the narrow beach. Dahl soon reached him and then Hayden. The chopper approached.

Drake let Alicia go, and then helped Kinimaka past. Still moving slowly, he made a point of holding out a trailing hand, signaling the SAS. Thirty feet up from the turret, he stopped.

The SAS stopped too, another thirty feet above.

"We don't want casualties," he shouted. "Not between us. We're on the same bloody side!"

Guns sighted on his body. From below he heard Dahl's bellow: *"Stop being a—"*

Drake tuned him out. "Please," he said. "This is not right. We're all soldiers here, even the friggin' French."

That brought an anonymous chuckle. Finally, a deep voice said, "Orders."

"Mate, I know," Drake said. "Been where you are. We got the same orders, but we're not about to fire upon friendly Spec Ops . . . unless they fire first."

One of the five figures rose slightly. "Cambridge," he said.

"Drake," he replied. "Matt Drake."

The ensuing silence told the story. Drake knew the stand-off was over . . . for now. At the very least he'd earned another reprieve at the next confrontation and maybe even a quiet conversation. The more of these elite soldiers they could draw together the safer it would be.

For everyone.

He nodded, turned, and walked away, reached up for the hand that helped pull him inside the helicopter.

"They cool?" Alicia asked.

Drake settled himself as the chopper banked away. "We'll find out," he answered. "The next time we come into conflict."

Surprisingly, Lauren sat opposite him. "I came with the chopper," she said by way of explanation.

"What? As like—an option?"

She smiled tolerantly. "No. I came because our work here is done." The helicopter rose high above the sun-dappled waves. "We're heading out of Africa and toward the next corner of the world."

"Which is where?" Drake snapped his seat-belt shut.

"China. And boy, do we have a lot of work to do."

"Another Horseman? Which one this time?"

"Arguably the baddest of them all. Buckle in, my friends. We're about to follow in the footsteps of Genghis Kahn."

CHAPTER TWELVE

Lauren told the team to get as comfortable as they were able in the back of the large cargo chopper and shuffled a sheaf of papers. "First, let's get the weapon of war and Hannibal out of the way. What you found in the box are the plans to build and erect Project Babylon, a one hundred meter long, two ton supergun. Commissioned by Saddam Hussein, it was based on research from the '60s and designed in the '80s. The entire affair had a Hollywood feel to it. Superguns that could send a payload into space. Assassinated generals. Assassinated civilians. Various purchases from a dozen countries to keep it quiet. Later schemes show that this space gun might have been adapted so that it could hit any target, anywhere, just once."

Dahl was leaning forward with interest. "Once? Why?"

"It was never intended as a portable weapon. To fire it would leave a signature, which the various powers would see instantly and then obliterate it. But . . . the damage might already have been done."

"Depending on the target." Kenzie nodded. "Yes, many models have been built around the idea of a one-strike world war. A way to force a nuclear power into inexorable action. With modern day technology, however, the idea becomes more and more moot."

"Okay, okay," Smyth rasped, still stretching muscles and checking bruises after the long, hard run. "So the first Horseman's tomb held the plans to a massive space gun. We got that. The other countries didn't. What's next?"

Lauren rolled her eyes. "First, the delineation specifically says 'resting places.' You will hopefully remember that

Hannibal was laid in an unmarked grave and may not even be there anymore. To look would be disrespectful to many. To leave it unturned is disrespectful to others."

Hayden sighed. "And so it goes on. Same story, different agenda, throughout the entire world."

"Imagine if terrorists had gotten their hands on the info. Now, I would say all of the countries currently chasing the Horsemen could build a supergun of their own, no problem. But..."

"It's who certain factions of that government sell the plans to," Drake finished. "Since we're still unsure every team is officially sanctioned." He didn't need to add *even if they think they are.*

The chopper flew through clear blue skies, free of turbulence and comfortably warm. Drake found himself able to relax for the first time in about a day. It was hard to believe that, just last night, he'd been kneeling in the resting place of the great Hannibal.

Lauren turned to the next file. "Remember the Order of the Last Judgment? Let me refresh you. 'At the Four Corners of the Earth we found the Four Horsemen and laid with them the blueprint of the Order of the Last Judgment. Those who survive the Judgment quest and its aftermath will rightly reign supreme. If you are reading this, we are lost, so read and follow with cautious eyes. Our last years were spent assembling the four final weapons, the world revolutions — War, Conquest, Famine and Death. Unleashed together, they will destroy all governments and unveil a new future. Be prepared. Find them. Go to the Four Corners of the Earth. Find the resting places of the Father of Strategy and then the Khagan; the Worst Indian Who Ever Lived and then the Scourge of God. But all is not as it seems. We visited the Khagan in 1960, five years after completion, placing Conquest in his coffin. We found the

Scourge who guards the true last judgment. And the only kill code is when the Horsemen arose. The Father's bones are unmarked. The Indian is surrounded by guns. The Order of the Last Judgment now live through you, and will forever reign supreme.'"

Drake tried to glean the relevant points. "Kill code? I really don't like the sound of that. And the 'true last judgment.' So even if we neutralize the first three, the last will be a true humdinger."

"For now," Lauren said, referring to the research in front of her. "The DC think tank has come up with a few ideas."

Drake tuned out for just a second. Every time he heard a reference to research, every time the think tank was mentioned, just two words flashed through his brain like billboard-sized, red neon lights.

Karin Blake.

Her continued absence did not bode well. Karin might well have to be their next mission. He pushed the worry gently aside for now.

". . . the second Horseman is Conquest. The second description mentions the Khagan. From this we deduce Genghis Kahn is Conquest. Genghis was born in 1162. He is, literally, conquest. He conquered most of Asia and China as well as lands further afield, and the Mongol Empire was the largest contiguous empire in history. Kahn was a reaper; he swept through most of the ancient world and, it's been said before, one out of every two hundred men alive today is a relative of Genghis Kahn."

Mai clucked. "Wow, Alicia, he's like the male version of you."

Drake nodded. "The guy sure was proliferate."

"The man's real name was Temujin. Genghis Kahn is an honorific. His father was poisoned when the boy was only nine, leaving their mother to raise seven sons alone. He and his young wife were also abducted and both spent time as slaves. Despite all this, even by his early twenties, he was established as a fierce leader. He personified the phrase 'keep your enemies close', as most of his greatest generals were former enemies. He never left a score unsettled and was supposedly responsible for the deaths of 40 million people, reducing the world's population by 11 percent. He embraced diverse religions and created the first international postage system, using post houses and way stations located throughout his empire."

Drake shifted in his seat. "A lot of information to take in there."

"He was the first Khagan of the Mongol empire."

Dahl turned from staring out the window. "And his resting place?"

"Well, he was buried in China. In an unmarked grave."

Alicia snorted. "Yeah, shit, of course he was!"

"So first Africa and now China represent two of the four corners of the earth," Mai wondered aloud. "Unless it's Asia, and we're talking continents."

"There are seven," Smyth reminded her.

"Not always," Lauren replied cryptically. "But we'll come to that. The questions are: What is the weapon of conquest and where is Genghis's resting place?"

"I'm guessing one of the answers is China," Kenzie murmured.

"Genghis Kahn died in mysterious circumstances around 1227. Marco Polo stated it was through infection, others poison, still others by a princess taken as war booty. After death his body would have been returned to his birthplace, Khentii Aimag, as was custom. It is believed he was buried at the Burkhan Khaldun mountain near the Onon River. However, legend states that anyone that came into contact with the funeral procession was slaughtered. After that a river was diverted over the Kahn's grave and all the soldiers that made up the procession were then also killed." Lauren shook her head. "Life and living had little value back then."

"As, in some places of the world, it does now," Dahl said.

"So we're diving again?" Alicia scowled. "Nobody said anything about diving again. It's not my best talent."

Mai somehow managed to swallow the remark that looked set to come out of her mouth, coughing instead. "Not diving," she finally said. "It could be on the mountain too. Wasn't a particular area sealed off by the Mongolian government for hundreds of years?"

"Very true, and so we've set a course for China," Lauren said. "And the grave of Genghis Kahn. Now, to keep you up to date, the NSA and CIA are still using dozens of methods to glean information about our rivals. The French did indeed lose a man. The British departed at the same time as us. The Russians and the Swedes later, caught up in a quicker than expected Turkish sweep of the area. We're not sure about Mossad or the Chinese. Orders remain the same. One thing though . . . I do now have Secretary Crowe on the line."

Drake frowned. It hadn't been at the forefront of his mind that Crowe might be listening in to their conversations with Lauren, but it should have. Their team, their family, had secrets like any other. As he looked around it was clear that the others felt the same, and that this was Lauren's way of making them aware.

DC *always* had its own agenda.

Crowe's voice came across strongly. "I won't pretend to know more than you about this particular mission. Not on the ground. But I *do* know it's a political minefield, with twist and sub-twist and schemes at the very highest levels of some of our rival nations."

Not to mention the US, Drake thought. *What . . . never!*

"Frankly, I'm surprised at some of the administrations involved," Crowe said openly. "I thought they might work with us, but as I mentioned, all may not be as it seems."

Again Drake considered her words in a different way. Was she talking about the Horseman quest? Or something more personal?

"Is there a reason, Madam Secretary?" Hayden asked. "Something we don't know?"

"Well, not that I've been apprised of. But even I don't necessarily know the whole of it. Unabridged is a rare word in politics."

"Then it's the weapons themselves," Hayden said. "This first supergun. If built, if sold to terrorists, it could have held the world to ransom."

"I know. This . . . Order of the Last Judgment—" she spoke the title distastefully "—clearly worked out a master plan, leaving it for future generations. Luckily, the Israelis shut them down long ago. Unluckily, they didn't find this particular blueprint. This scheme."

So far, Drake saw no purpose to the call. He sat back, eyes closed, listening to the conversation.

"You have a leap on some of the others. Only Israel and China are MIA. The usual rules apply, but get to that weapon and get it first. America cannot trust it falling into the wrong hands, *any* hands. And watch your backs, SPEAR. There is more to this than meets the eye."

Drake sat up. Dahl leaned forward. "Is that a warning of a different kind?" he whispered.

Drake studied Hayden, but their boss showed no signs of disquiet. *Watch your backs?* If he hadn't heard that American twang earlier he too would think nothing of the phrase. His thoughts turned to Smyth and the death of Joshua in Peru. It measured the depth of their insubordination. As a normal soldier, and with a soldier's outlook, he'd be mightily worried. But they were no longer soldiers—they were forced to make the hard choice every day, out in the field, under duress. They bore the weight of thousands of lives on their shoulders, occasionally millions. This was no ordinary team. Not anymore.

You're only as good as your last mistake. You're only *remembered* for your last mistake. Workplace ethics the world over. His preference was to keep working, keep fighting. Head above water—because there were millions of sharks in the world constantly circling, and if you stood still you'd either drown or be torn to pieces.

Crowe signed off with a strained pep talk, and then Hayden turned to them. She touched her comms and made a face.

"Don't forget."

Drake nodded. *Open channel.*

"I am thinking this is going to be very different from the usual tomb raider stuff." Yorgi spoke up. "We face government soldiers, experts. Unknown factions, possibly traitors. We search for men lost in time, born years apart. We chase some old war criminal's prophecy, exactly how he wanted us to." He shrugged. "We are not in control."

"I'm about as close to a tomb raider as you'll ever get," Kenzie said with a smirk. "This . . . is completely different."

Alicia and Mai stared at the Israeli. "Yeah, we tend to forget about your nasty little criminal past, don't we . . . *Torsty*?"

The Swede blinked. "I . . . umm . . . I . . . what?"

Kenzie stepped in. "And I guess circumstance never forced you into any compromising positions, eh Alicia?"

The Englishwoman shrugged. "Depends if we're still talking criminal. Some compromising positions are better than others."

"If we're still awake and alert," Hayden said, "could we

start to read up on Genghis Kahn and the location of his grave? A think tank back in DC is all well and good, but we're on the ground and we'll see things they won't. The more information you can absorb, the better chance we have of finding the second weapon."

"And coming out of this alive," Dahl agreed.

Tablets were passed around, barely enough to share. Alicia shouted up first about checking her emails and Facebook page. Drake knew she didn't even have an email address let alone the first clue about social media, and gave her the look.

She pouted. "Serious time?"

"That, or get some rest, love. China ain't exactly gonna welcome us with open arms."

"Good point." Hayden sighed. "I'll get on to the local teams, and ask them to ease our entry. Everyone good with the plan so far?"

"Well," Dahl spoke off-handedly. "I never thought I'd be chasing down Genghis Kahn in China whilst trying *not* to get into a fight with half-a-dozen rival nations. But hey," he shrugged, "you know what they say about trying something different."

Alicia looked over, then shook her head. "No comment. Too easy."

"Right now," Drake said, "I'd prefer to have a bit more information."

"You and me both, Yorkie." Dahl nodded. "You and me both."

CHAPTER THIRTEEN

The hours slipped by. The chopper was forced to refuel. The lack of news about the other teams became frustrating. Hayden found her best recourse was to lose herself in the wealth of information pertaining to Genghis's tomb, but found it hard to discover anything new. The others clearly tried the same for a while, but a few grew tired and chose to grab a little rest, whilst others found it easier to turn to their personal concerns.

In their close quarters it was impossible to tune it out, and truth be told, by now the team were close and familiar enough to take it all in their stride.

Dahl called home. The kids were happy to hear from him, causing Dahl to break out into a big smile. Johanna asked when he would be home. The strain was clear, the upshot not so much. Hayden took a moment to watch Kinimaka whilst the big Hawaiian swiped at a tablet's screen. She smiled. The device looked like a postcard in his large hands and she remembered those hands touching her body. Gentle. Stirring. He knew her so well, and that enhanced their intimacy. She stared down now at the ruined tip of her finger, the one she'd been forced to ingest during their last mission. The shock of the situation had opened her eyes. Life was infinitely too short to battle wills against someone you loved.

She caught her breath a little, unsure if she really believed it. *Damn, you don't deserve it. Not after all you said.* She didn't justify a way back, and had no real clue where to start. Maybe it was the battle, the situation, the job. Maybe it was each and every moment of the history of her life.

People made mistakes. They could atone.

Alicia's done it.

The notion sent her gazing in the Englishwoman's direction as the chopper barged its way through the skies. Sudden turbulence made her clutch a strap tighter. A second of free fall sent her heart into her mouth. But it was all good. It imitated life.

Hayden's instincts were always to lead, to get the job done. She saw now that those instincts were getting in the way of other, important, aspects of her life. She saw a bleak future.

Drake and Alicia were happy, smiling, tapping at a shared tablet. Mai was letting Kenzie borrow hers, the two women taking it in turns. It was interesting how uniquely different individuals handled similar situations.

Smyth had moved in close to Lauren. "How ya doing?"

"As good as can be, you smooth bastard. This isn't the time, Smyth."

"You think I don't know that? But tell me. When *is* the time?"

"Not now."

"Not ever," Smyth said sulkily.

Lauren growled. "Seriously? We're at an impasse, man. You hit a brick wall and can't get past it."

"A wall?"

Lauren snorted. "Yeah, it has a name."

"Oh. That wall."

Hayden saw the way they were both skirting the issue. It wasn't for her to judge or interfere but it did make clear how any kind of impediment could derail and damage any relationship. Smyth and Lauren were an unorthodox pair to say the least, so unusual that they might work well together.

And yet the most untraditional of obstacles now stood in their way.

Smyth tried a different tack. "Okay, okay, so what has he given you lately?"

"Me? Nothing. I don't go there for information. That's the job of the CIA, or FBI or whatever."

"Then what do you talk about?"

It was a step forward for Smyth. An open, non-confrontational question. Hayden felt a little proud of the soldier.

Lauren hesitated just a little. "Crap," she said. "We talk crap. TV. Movies. Books. Celebrities. The news. He's a builder so he asks about projects."

"What projects?"

"From all that you ask the guarded question. Why not which celebrities, or which movies? Are you interested in buildings, Lance?"

Hayden wanted to tune it out, but found she couldn't. The cabin was too confined; the question too serious; the mention of Smyth's first name too engaging.

"Only if someone wants to damage them."

Lauren waved him away, conversation dead. Hayden wondered if Lauren might be breaking some law, slipping away to converse with a known terrorist, but couldn't quite decide how to phrase the question to Lauren. Not yet anyway.

"Less than an hour out." The pilot's voice came over the comms.

Drake looked up. Hayden saw the determination in his face. Same with Dahl. The team were fully invested, always enhancing and perfecting their skill sets. Look at the last op for example. They had all come through a violently different mission, faced evil incarnate, with nary a scratch.

On a physical aspect, at least. The mental scars—her own in particular—would never heal.

She spent a moment rifling the papers before her and

trying to absorb a little more of the history of Genghis Kahn. She looked over the Order's text, singling out the lines: *Go to the Four Corners of the Earth. Find the resting places of the Father of Strategy and then the Khagan; the Worst Indian Who Ever Lived and then the Scourge of God. But all is not as it seems. We visited the Khagan in 1960, five years after completion, placing Conquest in his coffin.*

Four corners of the earth? Still a mystery. Luckily, the clues to the identity of the Horsemen had, so far, been distinct. But had the Order found the tomb of Genghis Kahn? It seemed so.

As the chopper continued to blast through the thin air, Yorgi rose and then stepped forward. The thief's face looked drawn, the eyes hooded, as if he hadn't slept a wink since his outburst in Peru. "I told you I was a part of Webb's statement, his legacy," the Russian said, his tone revealing he was terrified of what he was about to say. "I told you I was the worst of all those mentioned."

Alicia tried to lift the sudden atmospheric dampener with a huffy grunt. "I'm still waiting to hear who the bloody lesbian is," she said brightly. "Truth be told, Yogi, I was hoping it'd be you."

"How . . ." Yorgi stopped mid-sentence. "I am male."

"I'm not convinced. Those tiny hands. That face. The way you walk."

"Let him speak," Dahl said.

"And y'all should know that *I'm* the lesbian," Lauren said. "It's not a bad or shameful thing to be, you know."

"I know," Alicia said. "You should be whomever you want to be, and embrace it. I know I do. I was just hoping it'd be Yogi, that's all."

Smyth was staring at Lauren with a confused but otherwise unreadable look upon his face. Drake thought the reaction was admirable, considering the surprise.

"So only one remains," Kinimaka said.

"Someone who is dying," Drake said, staring at the floor.

"Shall we let our friend speak?" Dahl urged.

Yorgi attempted a smile. He then clasped his hands in front of him and glared at the cabin roof.

"It is not a long story," he said, accent thick. "But it is a hard one. I . . . I killed my parents in cold blood. And I am thankful every single day. Thankful that I did."

Drake held up a hand to catch his friend's eye. "You don't have to explain a thing, you know. We're family here. This won't cause an issue."

"I understand. But it is for me also. Do you understand?"

The team, to a person, nodded. They understood.

"We lived in a small village. A *cold* village. Winter? It was not a season, it was a mugging, a pounding, a thrashing from God. It beat our families down, even the children. I was one of six, and my parents, they could not cope. They could not drink fast enough to make the days go easier. They could not knock back the right amount to make the nights survivable. They could not find a way to cope and care for us, so they found a way to rearrange the picture."

Alicia couldn't keep a lid on her feelings. "I hope that's not meant the way it sounds."

"One afternoon we all bundled into the car. A promise of a trip to the city, they said. We had not visited city in years and should have questioned but . . ." He shrugged. "We were kids. They were our parents. They drove away from the little village and we never saw it again."

Hayden saw the faraway sadness on Mai's face. Her younger life may have been different to Yorgi's, but it held a sad similarity.

"The day outside the car grew colder, darker. They drove and drove and did not speak. But we were used to that. They had no love for life, for us, nor for each other. I think we never knew love, not in the way it should be. In the darkness they stopped, saying the car had broken down. We huddled, some wept. My youngest sister, she was only three years. I was nine, the oldest. I should have . . . should have . . ."

Yorgi fought the tears, glaring at the roof as if it held the power to change the past. He thrust out a firm hand before anyone could rise to go to him, but Hayden at least knew this was something he had to get through alone.

"They coaxed us out. They walked for a while. The ice was so hard and cold, it sent out thick deadly waves. I couldn't understand what they were doing, and then I was too cold to think straight. I saw them turn us around again and again. We were lost and weak, already dying. We were children. We . . . trusted."

Hayden closed her eyes. There were no words.

"Obviously, they found car. They drove away. We . . . well we died . . . one by one." Yorgi still could not clearly articulate the details. Only the heartbroken misery scored into his face revealed the truth of it.

"I was only survivor. I was strongest. I tried. I carried and dragged and cuddled, but I failed. I failed them all. I saw life leaving every one of my brothers and sisters and I vowed to survive. Their deaths gave me strength, as if their departed spirits joined mine. I hope they did. Still do. I believe they're still with me. I survived a Russian prison. I survived Matt Drake," he managed a weak smile, "and breaking him out."

"How did you make it back to the village?" Kinimaka wanted to know. Hayden and Dahl gave him the discreet look, but it was also clear Yorgi needed to vent.

"I wore their clothes," he hissed in an achingly low voice. "Shirts. Jackets. Socks. I stayed warm and I left them all alone in the snow and ice and I made it to road."

Hayden couldn't imagine the heartache, the assumed guilt that should not be his.

"A car passed by, helped me. I gave them a story, returned to the village a few days later," he took a deep breath, "and let them see the ghost of the sorrow that they wrought. Let them see and feel how deep his anger was. So yes, I murdered my parents in cold blood."

A silence fell that should never be broken. Hayden knew the bodies of Yorgi's brothers and sisters lay in the place they fell right now, forever frozen, never laid to rest.

"I turned thief." Yorgi eased apart the heartbreaking resonance. "And later was caught. But never tried for murder. And here we are."

The pilot's voice came over the airwaves. "Thirty minutes to Chinese airspace, kids, and then it's anyone's guess."

Hayden was pleased when Lauren called up the DC think tank at that point. A diversion was the only way forward.

"We're close," she said by way on introduction. "Anything new?"

"We're working the four corners, the Horsemen's birth date references, Mongolia, the Khagan and the Order themselves, which do you want first?"

CHAPTER FOURTEEN

"Ooh, ooh," Alicia said excitedly, acting the part. "Let's hear the birth date numbers thing. I just love figuring numbers out."

"Cool. Good to hear it from a field grunt." The voice went on happily, raising a few eyebrows around the cabin but blissfully unaware, "So, Hannibal was born in 247 BC, died around 183 BC. Genghis Kahn 1162, died 1227—"

"That's a lot of numbers," Alicia said.

"Problem is—" Dahl said. "You've run out of fingers *and* toes."

"Not sure what that means," the geek continued. "But these wacko cults do love their number games and codes. Bear it in mind."

"So Hannibal was born 1400 years before Genghis," Kenzie said. "We get it."

"You'd be surprised at the number of shitbirds that don't," the geek said conversationally. "Anyway—"

"Hey, pal?" Drake interrupted quickly. "You ever been punched in the face?"

"Well, as a matter fact, yes. Yes, I have."

Drake settled back. "Good," he said. "Now you can carry the fuck on."

"We sure can't work with these figures yet since we don't know the other Horsemen. Though, I'm guessing even you guys can figure out the fourth? No? No takers? Oh, well. Now, there sure is an awful lot of firepower heading for the Mongolian Republic at this point, folks. Seven, or is it six? Yeah, six teams of elite soldiers representing six countries chasing down the Horseman of Conquest. Am I right? Ooorah!"

Drake stared over at Hayden. "This guy's the best spokesperson in DC?"

Hayden shrugged. "Well, at least he wears his emotions on his sleeve. Not hidden beneath the many folds of a deceitful cloak like most of Washington."

"On to the Horseman of Conquest. Clearly the Order have their own agenda, so conquest could be anything from a kid's toy to a video game . . . ha ha. World domination can come in many forms, am I right?"

"Just get on with the briefing," Hayden said.

"Sure, sure. So let's get straight to the Order, shall we? Though the Israelis were oddly reluctant to furnish us with any information on the Nazi war criminal cult they wiped out in Cuba, we found out what we needed to know. Once the dust settled, the Nazis clearly decided they were the ones hard done by, and came up with this elaborate idea to control the world. They created an Order, along with a crest of arms, secret codes, symbols and more. They worked out a plan—quite probably one they'd been working on for years under the Reich. They buried the four weapons and came up with this puzzle. Maybe they meant to make it more obscure, who knows? But Mossad took 'em out without a trace and a little too quickly, I think. The hidden bunker lay undiscovered for thirty years."

"Fifteen minutes," the pilot said laconically.

"And these weapons?" Hayden asked. "Where did they get them from?"

"Well, the Nazis were about as well connected as anyone is ever going to get. The big gun is an old design, updated for space and accuracy. They could absolutely get their hands on anything from the forties to the eighties. Money was never an impediment, but movement was. And trust. They wouldn't trust a soul to do this for them. Probably took the little weasels years to hide all four weapons and a few dozen favors. Trust factors in also as one of the reasons they hid the weapons in the first place. Couldn't keep them in Cuba now, could they?" The DC man burst into laughter, then somehow managed to sober.

Alicia rolled her eyes and grasped both hands together as if they might be around somebody's scrawny neck.

"Anyhoo, you guys still with me? I realize time is short and you're itchy to get into the muddy field and shoot something, but I do have a little more information. Just came in . . ."

A pause.

"Now that's interesting."

More silence.

"Care to share?" Hayden prodded the man, staring toward the solid side of the chopper as if she could see their landing point approaching.

"Well, I was gonna get into the four corners of the earth—or at least the way *we* see it—but I see we're running out of time. Look, give me five, but whatever you do—" he paused "—do not land!"

The connection was severed abruptly. Hayden glared first at the floor and then around the chopper's interior.

Drake held both hands up. "Don't look at me. I'm innocent!"

Alicia laughed. "Yeah, me too."

"Don't land?" Dahl reiterated. "What on earth does that mean?"

Alicia cleared her throat as if to explain, but then the pilot's voice barked over the speakers. "Two minutes, folks."

Hayden turned to the old faithful for help. "Mano?"

"He's an ass, but still on our side," the big Hawaiian rumbled. "I'd say take him at his word."

"Best decide quick," Smyth put in. "We're descending."

Instantly, the comms blared into life. "What did I say? *Do not land!*"

Drake rose and keyed the chopper's internal comms to

life. "Back off, pal," he said. "New intel on the way."

"But we're *inside* Chinese airspace. No telling how long before they spot us."

"Do what you can but don't land."

"Hey bud, I was told this was going to be a quick in and out mission. No bullshit. You can be sure if we hang around for more than a few minutes we're gonna have a couple-a J-20s up our ass."

Alicia leaned in to Drake and whispered, "Is that a bad—"

The Yorkshireman cut her off, seeing the urgency of the situation. "Well, clearly the knobend from DC can hear us even when the comms are off," he said with a meaningful stare at Dahl. "Ya hear that, knobend? We've got about sixty seconds."

"This is gonna take longer," the man came back. "Be brave, people. We're on the case."

Drake felt his fists clench. Such a condescending manner only provoked confrontation. Maybe that was the intent? Ever since they found Hannibal's gravesite Drake felt that there had been something off about this mission. Something undisclosed. Were they being vetted? Were they under surveillance? Was the US government evaluating their actions? If so, it came down to what happened in Peru. And if so, Drake wasn't unduly worried about their performance.

He was worried about the plots and intrigues and conspiracies those listening might cook up after the review. Any country governed by politicians was never as it seemed, and only those behind the people in the seats of power knew what was really going on.

"Fifty seconds," he said aloud. "Then we're outta here."

"Trying a trick," the pilot told them. "We're already so low you could step out of the door onto a tree, but I'm ducking the bird inside a mountain valley. If you hear anything scraping the bottom it'll either be rock or a yeti."

Alicia gulped loudly. "I thought they hung out around Tibet?"

Dahl shrugged. "Vacation. Road trip. Who knows?"

At last, the comms fired into life again. "All right, people. We still alive? Good, good. Well done. Now . . . remember all the controversy regarding the resting place of Genghis Kahn? He personally wanted an unmarked grave. Everyone who built his tomb was massacred. The gravesite was stampeded by horses, planted with trees. Literally, it is unobtainable, save for chance. One tale, which I find poignant because it so simply undoes all these madcap schemes, is that Kahn was buried with a young camel—and the site was then pinpointed when the camel's mother was found weeping at the grave of her young."

The pilot cut through harshly. "We're almost at the point of no return, bud. Thirty seconds and we either chase our tails outta here like they're on fire or send the kids in."

"Oh," the DC man said. "Forgot about you. Yeah, get out of there. I'll send you the new location."

Drake winced, sharing the pilot's pain, but shot back, "Jesus, man. Are you trying to get us captured or killed?"

He was only part-joking.

"Hey, hey. Calm down. Listen—these Nazis—the Order of the Last Judgment—were looking for the Horsemen—the resting places—between the fifties and the eighties, yeah? Clearly, they found them all. Something tells me they did not find the tomb of Genghis Kahn. I do believe more would have been made of such a find. Then there is the Order itself and the words: 'But all is not as it seems. We visited the Khagan in 1960, five years after completion, placing Conquest in his coffin.' For certain, Kahn didn't have any tomb built in 1955. But, largely because of the lack of a tomb and to assist worshippers and increase the tourist trade—China did build him a mausoleum."

"Is it in China?" Hayden asked.

"Sure, it's in China. You're thinking through the whole four corners thing, aren't you? Good, keep the gray matter active. There may even be a job here for you one day."

Hayden swallowed a choking sound. "Just explain your theory."

"Right, cool. Genghis Kahn's mausoleum was built in 1954. It's a large temple built along a river in Ejin Horo, in southwestern Inner Mongolia. Now, the mausoleum is in fact a cenotaph—it contains no body. But it *is* said to contain a headdress and other items belonging to Genghis. Always associated with this mausoleum idea rather than a known tomb and gravesite, Genghis was initially worshipped from eight white yurts, the tent palaces where he originally lived. These portable mausoleums were protected by the Darkhad, the kings of Jin, and later distinguished as a symbol of the Mongol nation. Eventually, it was decided to abolish the portable mausoleums and move the ancient relics to the new, permanent one. The timeline fits the Order's to perfection. Whatever weapon they chose as Conquest is inside Genghis's coffin, in that mausoleum."

Hayden measured his words. "Dammit, mutt," she said. "If you're wrong . . ."

"Mutt?"

"It's the best you're gonna get."

"The Order had access," Dahl said. "It explains the line in the text."

Hayden nodded slowly. "How far out are we?"

"Twenty seven minutes."

"And the other teams?"

"No way to tell if they're as clever as yours truly, I'm afraid. It's probable they have a whizz-tech advising them." A pause for appreciation.

"Fucking mutt," Alicia growled.

"No." Hayden kept her temper. "I meant—what's the latest on the internal chatter?"

"Oh, right. Chatter is loud and proud. Some teams got their asses handed to 'em by higher-ups. Some were tasked to dig around Hannibal's site again. I know the Russians and the Swedes were headed to Burkhan Khaldun, as you initially were. Mossad and the Chinese are pretty quiet. The French? Well, who knows, right?"

"You'd better be right on this," Hayden said in a voice laced with venom. "Because if you're not . . . the world will suffer."

"Just get to that mausoleum, Miss Jaye. But do it fast. The other teams may already be there."

CHAPTER FIFTEEN

"Ejin Horo Banner," the pilot said, still nervous. "Eight minutes out."

Arrangements had been made for the team to drop outside the town and trek in. A local archaeologist had been procured to help them, and would lead them into the mausoleum. Drake assumed she had no idea what would then likely happen.

To this end the chopper would remain hot and ready, despite the pilot's continued misgivings about Chinese stealth jet fighters.

A bounce and a curse and then the chopper stood stationary, allowing the team time to jump off. They found themselves amid a cluster of brush, a tangle of dying forestation, but easily saw the way forward.

Downhill, a mile or so, the outskirts of the large city sprawled. Hayden programmed her satnav for the right coordinates and then the team made themselves as presentable as possible. The Chinese wanted tourists, so today they had gained nine more. Lauren was persuaded to stay with the chopper and pick through the unremitting chatter.

"Next time," she called as the team hustled to depart, "Alicia can do the networking bit."

The Englishwoman huffed. "Do I look like a bloody secretary?"

"Umm, do I?"

Drake nudged Alicia and whispered, "Well, you did last week, remember? For the role play?"

"Oh yeah," she smiled brightly, "that was fun. I doubt Lauren's role will be quite the same."

"Let's hope not."

The two shared a warm smile as they exited the makeshift shelter and headed down the slow-rolling hill. Sparse foliage and desert soon gave way to roads and buildings, and in the distance several high-rise hotels and office buildings began to take shape. Reds, greens and pastel shades warred with the blue skies and pale clouds. Drake was immediately struck by how clean the streets and the city were, how wide some of the thoroughfares. Future proof, as they said.

Appearing odd at first but unable to help it, the tourists made their way to the rendezvous, making sure their hands were never far from their overlarge backpacks. The archaeologist greeted them in the shadow of a large black statue depicting a man riding a horse.

"Fitting." Dahl nodded at the horseman.

A spare, tall woman with scraped back hair and a direct gaze confronted them. "You are the tourist party?" She spoke carefully, picking her words. "Excuse my English. It is not good." She laughed, her small face scrunching up.

"Not a problem," Dahl said quickly. "It's more understandable than Drake's version."

"Funny fu—"

"You do not look like tourists," the woman said, stopping him. "You have experience?"

"Ah, yes," Dahl said, taking her arm and leading the way with a magnanimous gesture. "We travel the world, seeking new sights and cities."

"Wrong way," the woman said quite graciously. "Mausoleum is that way."

"Ah."

Drake laughed. "Forgive him," he said. "Normally, he just carts the luggage."

The woman led the way, back stiff, hair hanging straight

in its tight wrap. The team spread out as best they could, again not wanting to cause a stir or leave any lasting memories behind. Dahl discovered the woman's name was Altan and that she had been born nearby, leaving China in her youth and then returning only two years ago. She led them directly and courteously, and soon indicated that they were nearing their goal.

Drake saw the top of the mausoleum rising ahead, the statues and steps and other iconic elements all around. Death could crouch anywhere. Working together, the team slowed the woman down as they checked for other teams and other soldiers, all the while pretending to admire the sights. Smyth checking behind bins and benches might have fazed Altan, but Drake's description of him as a 'very limited edition' only served to increase her curiosity.

"Is he special?"

"Oh yeah, he's one of one."

"I can hear you through the fucking coms," Smyth snarled.

"In what way?"

"In car terms he's the Pagani Huayra Hermes edition, designed for Manny Koshbin by Pagani and Hermes."

"I'm sorry. I don't know what all that means."

"Understood." Drake sighed. "Smyth is one of a kind. But tell me your favorite hobby."

"I do enjoy camping. There are some lovely places in the desert."

"In camping terms imagine Smyth is that wonky tent pole. The one that constantly causes you problems but still works well once you kick it into shape, and always, but always, manages to piss you off."

Smyth spluttered through the comms, having completed his recce. Lauren fell into an uncontrollable giggling fit.

Altan regarded the Yorkshireman with suspicion, a look

she then turned upon the rest of the team. Mai, in particular, shied away from the woman as if trying to hide her own heritage. Drake understood where others would not. One thing led to another and Mai did not want to be discussing where she came from and how she ended up here. Altan gestured toward a set of steps.

"That way. The mausoleum is up there."

Drake saw an incredibly wide, incredibly long concrete walkway leading straight ahead toward a long, steep set of concrete steps. Just before the steps began, the path widened out into a vast circle, at the center of which stood an unmistakable statue.

"Well, the dude was definitely a horseman," Kinimaka pointed out.

Genghis Kahn, atop a cantering horse, stood atop a hefty slab of stone.

"The second Horseman," Yorgi said. "Conquest."

Altan must have heard the last bit, for she turned and said, "Yes. The Khagan conquered much of the known world before his death. Arguably a genocidal king, he also politically unified the Silk Road during his lifetime, increasing trade and communication through the entire western hemisphere. He was a bloody, terrible leader, but he treated his loyal soldiers well and included them in all of his plans."

"Can you tell us a little of what's in the mausoleum?" Drake wanted to be prepared. Speed counted for everything with these missions.

"Well, it is nothing but a rectangular cemetery, adorned with external finery." Altan now sounded as if she were quoting a tourist guide. "The main palace is octagonal and contains a five-meter-high, white jade statue of Genghis. There are four chambers and two halls, which appear like three yurts externally. In the Resting Palace there are seven coffins. The Kahn, three consorts, his fourth son and that son's wife."

"The Resting Palace," Smyth said. "Also sounds like the resting place."

"Yessss." Altan drew it out, staring at Smyth with patience and knowing nothing about the text they were following.

"The mausoleum is guarded by the Darkhad, the privileged ones. It is extremely sacred to many Mongols."

Drake let out a deep, worried breath. If they were mistaken and this wasn't the resting place of the second weapon . . . He dreaded even to imagine the consequences.

Life in a Chinese prison would be the least of their problems.

The long walk continued, first the pilgrimage along the extensive path and then a dissection of the sphere, a cursory glance up at the face of the ancient general, and then the endless ascent of the stone steps. The team stayed in position, rarely losing a step, and kept a constant vigilance. Drake was pleased to see relatively few visitors to the mausoleum today, which aided them greatly.

At last the impressive structure came into sight. The team paused as they reached the top of the steps to take it all in. Altan waited, probably used to tourists caught in moments of awe. Drake saw a vast edifice with relatively small domes at each end and a much larger one in the middle. Their roofs were bronze, patterned. The front of the building held many red windows and at least three large entrances. A low stone wall fronted the structure.

Altan walked ahead. Dahl glanced back at the team.

"Straight to the coffin," Hayden said. "Get it open, find the box and get out. Luckily, there's no body to contend with. As our pilot says—no bullshit."

Drake listened as Lauren chimed in with an update on the chatter.

"I'm getting a big, fat zero here now, folks. Pretty sure the Israelis and the Russians are out of it, pointed the wrong way by the text. DC thinks the French are closing in, maybe a half hour behind you. It's getting much tougher now, the listening. We're down to other resources and just a few tricks the NSA won't ever reveal. Swedes, Chinese and Brits are unknown. Like I said, it's a struggle."

"Anyone else?" Drake nudged.

"Funny you should mention that. I'm getting ghost static from an unknown source. No voices, no way to confirm, but it also feels as if, sometimes, there's another presence on the system."

"Do *not* mention ghosts," Alicia said. "We had enough horror shenanigans on the last op."

Altan stopped and turned. "Are you ready? I'll take you inside."

The group nodded and moved forward. And that's when Drake saw the Chinese soldiers exiting the mausoleum, a large box tucked under one man's arm, archaeologists threaded among them.

The Chinese carried their guns, and now the lack of tourists was firmly in their favor.

It was only a moment before their leader set eyes upon them.

CHAPTER SIXTEEN

Drake saw Dahl take hold of Altan and drag her backward, taking a long leap down the steps until they were sheltered from the Chinese soldiers. He flung his backpack to the ground and quickly unzipped the outer pocket. Working fast and not once glancing up at the Chinese, nevertheless he felt safe. Hayden, Smyth and Mai carried handguns.

Weapons were raised in the square outside the mausoleum of Genghis Kahn, rivals facing off. The man carrying the box looked nervous. The Chinese team were five strong, and were already ordering the brooding set of archaeologists aside. Drake hefted his small machine pistol and waited. To his side, the rest of the team spread out.

"All we want is the box," Hayden called out. "Lay it on the ground and walk away."

The leader of the Chinese team had eyes of gray slate. "It is you who should walk way whilst you still have chance."

"We want the box," Hayden reiterated. "And we will take it."

"Then try." The leader translated and all five Chinese started walking forward in unison.

"Whoa. We're on the same friggin' side."

"Ah, a joke. Funny. America and China will *never* be on the same side."

"Maybe not," Drake spoke up. "But we—soldiers fighting for the people—*are*."

He saw the hesitation in the leader's stride, the slight uncertainty cross his features. It must have affected them all, for the Chinese team came to a full stop. Hayden lowered her own weapon and closed the gap still further.

"Can't we find some common ground?"

A nod. "Yes, we could. But government and political leaders, terrorists and tyrants will always get in the way."

Drake saw the sadness in the man's face, and the absolute belief in his own words. Not a single gun, not a single barrel, was raised as the rival teams clashed hard. This was all about respect.

Drake rose, left his machine pistol on the rucksack, and met a charge head on. Fists connected with his chest and his upraised arms. A knee plowed hard into his ribs. Drake felt the air explode from his body, and fell to one knee. The assault was relentless, knees and fists hitting hard and raining down, the ferocity designed to allow him no chance of retaliation or relief. He took the pain and bided his time. Other scenes flashed by as he twisted and turned. Alicia struggled with a tall man; Hayden and Kinimaka engaged with the leader. Mai sent her opponent over her shoulder and then came down painfully on his sternum.

Drake saw the chance and seized it. Behind, he heard Torsten Dahl make the usual entrance, leaping over the top of the stairs; a big presence and impossible to ignore. Drake's attacker paused for just an instant.

The ex-SAS man was scrambling across the ground, swinging his legs and catching his opponent at the back of the knee. He tumbled forward, falling to his knees. As he fell to Drake's level, the Yorkshireman delivered a massive head-butt. A yell and a widening of the eyes signified how hard he'd hit. The Chinese special ops man wavered and held himself up on one hand. Drake rose and returned the favor in full—striking with knees and jabs to the head. Bruises appeared and blood flowed, but nothing life threatening.

Dahl rushed past, targeting Alicia's opponent. The Swede hit like a bull just as Alicia struck out. Her attacker flew off his feet and came down hard on the back of his neck, shuddering, stunned. The two turned in time to see Mai knock her own opponent unconscious and then located the man with the box.

"Hey!" Alicia cried as he set eyes on them and started to run.

They took off at a sprint, but Smyth and Yorgi had already circumvented the battle. "Y'see?" Alicia said. "We have strength in numbers. I knew there was a reason we suffered so many in this bloody team."

Up ahead, Kenzie blocked the man's only other route—back into the mausoleum. With a grim glare now and a resigned stance, he took out the weapon he'd earlier stored away.

Drake checked the area, and saw Hayden finally subduing the team leader.

"Don't do it!" he cried at the man. "You're way outnumbered, pal."

Hayden glanced up, took in the situation, and then wiped blood from her cheek. Drake now saw Altan creeping back up the steps to take a look and sighed to himself. *Curiosity* . . .

The gun remained steady, the box still held tightly, almost in a death grip. Hayden rose and held up a hand, palm out. The tall incense burner stood between herself and the man, but she moved until she had a clear line of sight.

Kenzie advanced from the rear. Smyth and Kinimaka from the side. There were no signs of panic in the soldier's eyes, only resignation.

"Nobody died." Hayden indicated the unconscious and groaning Chinese soldiers. "Nobody has to. Just leave the box."

Alicia caught his attention. "And if you need a slap just to make it look good," she said. "I'm here."

A soldier's mentality did not include giving up. And this

guy had nowhere to go, no route of escape.

"The gun," Drake said, "is a false hope. You know it is."

The comment struck home, the gun hand wavering for the first time. A heavy silence stretched and Drake noticed a couple of the downed men starting to stir. "You gotta decide, pal," he said. "Clock's ticking."

Almost immediately the man slipped his gun away and started to run. He aimed for Hayden and then, close to the incense burner, threw an arm against the top, hoping to topple it toward her. A dull clunk and a groan was his only reward as the object proved to be solidly fixed, but he kept on running.

Hayden waited, keeping his attention.

Alicia sprinted in from the blind side, diving and taking him in a rugby tackle around the waist. The man folded, almost broken in two, head striking Alicia's shoulder and the box tumbling away. Hayden made a scramble for it, catching it up before too much damage was done. A quick glance affirmed the Order's crest.

Alicia patted the unconscious man. "Told you I'd be there for you."

The team evaluated. The Chinese were already moving. The French had to be close. A word from Hayden brought Lauren back on the line.

"Bad news, guys. The French have eyes on you and the Russians have eyes on them. Get moving!"

Bollocks!

Drake stared all the way back down the steps and along the straight path that led to the mausoleum. He saw running men, a team of four that almost certainly had to be the French. "They're bloody good," he said. "In real terms, that's twice they've gotten to us first."

"We should go," Smyth said. "They'll be on us in minutes."

"Go where?" Alicia asked. "They're hogging the only exit."

Drake spied trees to the sides and lawns to the front. In real terms, the choice was limited.

"C'mon," he said. "And Lauren, send in the chopper."

"On its way."

"Make it quick," Smyth said. "Those French are fast on their feet."

Drake took off, leading the way, assuming the Russians couldn't be too far behind. Sadly, it couldn't be long before somebody started shooting. They had fared well so far, seeing the best of soldier-to-soldier and man-to-man values, but the chances of such a fragile truce lasting were minimal.

Let's face facts, if these countries wanted to work together and share the rewards, the men and women in the seats of power know full well it would be the easier way—and yet still they fight.

He slipped among the trees. The team rushed in his wake, Hayden clutching the ornate box with its so-far undiscovered secret. Dahl loitered at the back, tracking the progress of the French.

"Five minutes behind us. No sign of the Russkies. And the Chinese are waking up. Good, that might hold them all up a bit."

"Chopper ten minutes," Lauren informed them.

"Tell him to get his foot down," Alicia said. "This guy's supposed to be hot."

"I'll pass that on."

Drake took the most direct route, hoping for a nice swathe of cover. The trees stretched to all sides, the ground soft and loamy, and smelling richly of the earth. Kenzie picked up a thick branch, shrugging as she ran as if to say, 'this will have to do.' First a long dip and then a sharp incline, and the route behind them vanished. The skies were barely visible and all sound was muted.

"I just hope nobody's waiting for us up ahead," Dahl said.

Kinimaka grunted, pushing hard. "Trust the listeners," he said, clearly harking back to his CIA days. "They're better than you think."

Drake also saw that they were not here, on the ground, and possessed little field instinct. He scanned every horizon, confident that Dahl would be doing the same from the back. After four minutes, they briefly paused to listen.

"Bearings on that chopper?" Hayden whispered to Lauren.

The New Yorker could see their position as blinking blue blobs on a scanner. "Dead ahead. Keep going."

All around was silent; they could be the only people in the world. Drake continued after a while, picking his steps carefully. Alicia crept along at his side, Hayden a step behind. The rest of the team now spread out to maximize their range. Weapons were drawn and held loosely.

Ahead, the trees were thinning. Drake stopped near the outer perimeter, checking the lay of the land.

"Short slope down to a flat field," he said. "Perfect for the chopper. Shit, even a Swede could hit a target that big."

"Three minutes to rendezvous," Lauren said.

Hayden leaned close to Drake. "How's it looking?"

"No sign of enemies." He shrugged. "But considering who we're dealing with why would there be?"

Dahl approached. "Same here. They're out there all right, but well hidden."

"And you can be sure they're heading this way," Mai said. "Why are we waiting?"

Dahl eyed Drake. "The Yorkshire Pudding needs a breather."

"One day," Drake said, giving the terrain a final glance. "You're gonna say something really surprisingly hilarious, but until then please, just speak when you're spoken to."

They eased out of the tree line, advancing down the sharp, grassy slope. A warm breeze greeted Drake, a pleasant sensation after the cloying stand of trees. The entire area was empty and fenced off close to where it ended at a stretch of tarmac far ahead.

"Move it now," Drake said. "We can set up a perimeter on the flat land."

But then the peace and emptiness of the entire area was shattered. The SPEAR team raced downhill, whilst to their left the Russians poured from where they'd been concealed. Ahead of both of them, sheltered by a far copse, the French also burst into view.

At least, that was Drake's take on things. They weren't exactly wearing name tags, but the features and bearings were strikingly different.

At the same time, their chopper appeared in the skies above.

"Oh shit."

To his left, a Russian dropped to one knee and steadied a rocket launcher across one shoulder.

CHAPTER SEVENTEEN

Drake spun mid-step, and opened fire. His bullets tore up the grass around the elite soldier but didn't spoil his preparations. The rocket launcher never wavered; the arm balancing it remained firm. His comrades fanned out all around him, returning fire. Drake suddenly found himself in a world of danger.

The French ran hard straight for the landing chopper. Drake, along with Dahl and Smyth, kept the Russians at bay and wary. The pilot's face was visible, focused on a place to land. Alicia and Mai didn't slow one bit, and waved to catch his attention.

Bullets laced the air.

Drake winged one of the Russian, sending him to one knee. Hayden's voice thundered across the comms.

"Pilot, evade! Lauren tell him, they have rockets!"

Drake, Dahl and Smyth battered the Russian contingent, but they remained too far away to line up properly, especially whilst moving. The pilot looked up, face stricken.

The RPG fired, the missile shooting out with a whoosh of air and a hefty clap. Drake and the others could only watch helplessly as it left a trail in the air and flew unerringly straight toward the chopper. Panicking hard, the pilot made a jerky evasive maneuver, banking the helicopter, but the streaking rocket was too fast, impacting with the underside and exploding in a billow of smoke and flame. The chopper lurched and fell, pieces falling away and hurtling beyond its flight path.

It was only then, as he stared in disbelief, distress and grim anger that he saw where its terrible trajectory would take it.

The French saw it coming and tried to scatter, but the devastated helicopter smashed to the ground among them.

Drake hit the ground, burying his head inside a divot. Red and orange flames shot upward and outward, and black smoke billowed up at the sky. The bulk of the chopper landed on one man; he and the pilot dying instantly. A rotor blade sheared away and passed clean through a third unfortunate, so fast and sudden he knew nothing about it. Drake looked up to see another struck by an enormous chunk of burning debris. The force of the blow knocked him off his feet and a dozen steps backward, after which he ceased all movement.

Only two Frenchmen remained alive; the bulk of the team devastated in one unfortunate incident. Drake saw one of them crawling away from the raging fire, his arm singed, and the other staggering over. Somehow, the second managed to cling to a weapon and help his comrade away at the same time.

Drake swallowed his rage and kept a tight hold on his focus. Their only method of extraction was down, destroyed. Hayden still held the box, but now the Russians were rushing at them, intentions absolutely apparent. The man with the RPG was still aiming at the wreckage as if considering a second strike.

Drake rose and the team rose with him. Moving away from the Russians and toward the fire, they laid down a net of cover that forced their enemies to lie low. Drake and Dahl both struck men in their vests, sending them sprawling. The seething flames reached for them as they came closer, sharp pops and heavy creaks bursting from within. Drake felt the wash of it across his face and then ducked around the blind side. The remaining French were already far away, struggling with their wounds and losses, and clearly out of the conflict for now.

Drake spun on one knee, keying the comms.

"Chopper down," he said to confirm with Lauren, then: "We need another mode of evac right now."

The reply was subdued. "On it."

The team continued to back away, putting some distance between the flaming obstacle and the oncoming enemy. Incredibly, and callously, the Russian with the RPG loosed another missile at the already demolished chopper, sending further gouts of flame and shrapnel into the air.

Drake felt a chunk of metal glance off his shoulder and spun around with the impact. Dahl glanced over but the Yorkshireman nodded—*I'm okay.*

Alicia pointed them toward the far fence. "That road's the only option. Hoof it, people!"

Hayden steadied the box and ran. Smyth and Kinimaka stayed at the back, keeping the fire between themselves and the Russians. Drake scanned the ground ahead, always ready for more surprises and expecting the worst. The Chinese were somewhere, and the Israelis, Swedes and Brits were in the wind.

Their speed distanced them from the pursuing Russians and they arrived at the fence with time to spare. Alicia and Mai cut a way through and then they were standing on the other side, next to a two-lane stretch of blacktop that vanished both ways into a seeming wilderness. Lauren hadn't come back to them as yet, but they left her to her devices, knowing DC would be helping.

Drake wasn't filled with a huge amount of confidence. He didn't blame Lauren—the New Yorker was treading fresh waters, but nothing so far on this mission told him the men and women sitting safe and warm in the Capitol fully had their backs.

Alicia set out at a jog. It was an increasingly odd scenario. Drake knew the Russians had to have some kind of backup. Maybe it was on its way.

"Look there," Kenzie spoke up.

Approximately half a mile ahead, a black SUV had stopped to pick up the struggling Frenchmen. As they watched it made a fast one-eighty in the road, loaded the two operatives and then screeched away.

"Poor bastards," Dahl said.

"We should worry about ourselves," Smyth said. "Or we're gonna end up the 'poor bastards' too."

"Grumpy has a point," Alicia said, scanning all directions. "Seriously, we have nowhere to go."

"Bury the box." Kinimaka indicated a stand of trees close to the road. "Come back for it later. Or ask Lauren to send another team."

Drake looked at Dahl. "Shouldn't be too difficult, eh?"

"Too risky," Hayden said. "They could find it. Intercept the message. Besides, we need this information. The other teams might already be headed for the third Horseman."

Drake blinked. He hadn't thought of that. A knot of stress began to pulse right in the middle of his forehead.

"Never thought I'd be stranded in friggin' China," Alicia complained.

"It *is* one of the four corners of the earth," Dahl told her. "So take comfort in that."

"Oh, thanks dude. Thanks for that. Maybe I'll buy a condo."

The Russians had already reached the road. Drake could see one of them shouting into a radio. His eyes then moved past the Russians and tried to focus on something moving in the distance.

"Could be their transport," Dahl said, running and staring backward at the same time.

Yorgi laughed, eagle-eyed. "I hope so. And ten years ago you might have been correct."

Drake squinted. "Hey, it's a bus."

"Keep running," Hayden said. "Try not to look interested."

Alicia laughed. "Now you've done it. I can't stop looking. You ever do that? You know you shouldn't stare at someone and find you can't bloody look away?"

"I get it all the time," Dahl said. "Naturally."

"Well, a skin-covered muppet is a rare sight," Drake put in.

The bus was bright yellow and modern, and sped past the Russians without slowing. Drake considered its speed, its driver and the passengers, but knew they had no choice. They were a good few miles from any large city. As the bus approached and the Russians stared, the SPEAR team blocked the road.

"Slow down," Alicia mouthed.

Smyth barked out a laugh. "This ain't Kansas. He ain't gonna understand you."

"Universal language then." Alicia held up her weapon despite Hayden's glare.

"Quick," Dahl said. "Before he jumps on the radio."

The bus slowed and swerved a little, wide front end moving to the offside. Already the Russians were running. Drake nudged the door, motioning for the driver to open it up. The man's face was scared, eyes wide and flitting between the soldiers and his passengers. Drake waited for the door to open and then stepped up, holding out a hand.

"We just want a ride," he said as comfortingly as he could.

The team filed down the center of the bus. Dahl jumped up last and tapped the driver on the arm.

"Go!" He pointed down the road.

The Russians were no more than a hundred yards behind, weapons raised as the driver mashed his foot to the floor. Clearly, he'd been watching his side mirrors. The bus lurched into action, the passengers jerking backward. Drake held on. Alicia strode down to the rear of the bus to gauge the pursuit.

"They're gaining,"

Drake waved at Dahl. "Tell Keanu to get a bloody move on!"

The Swede looked a little confused, but spoke to the bus driver. The vehicle picked up speed slowly. Drake saw Alicia wince and then turn quickly, shouting at the bus passengers.

"Get down! Now!"

Fearing the RPG, Drake dropped too. Luckily, only bullets spattered the back of the vehicle, all wedging into the chassis. He sighed with relief. Clearly, the Russians had been warned against civilian casualties. That was something at least.

Again, the political machinations behind each elite team's agenda came to mind. No way was every team state-sponsored; nor were some leaders even aware of what was happening. Again, his mind went to the French—and the soldiers that had died.

Doing their job.

The bus pulled away from the Russians, speeding down the road, its entire frame juddering. Drake relaxed a little, knowing they were headed back toward Ejin Horo by the direction they were taking. The driver negotiated a wide sweeping bend. Drake turned as Alicia let out a low squawk from the back seat.

And saw a black chopper that belonged to the Russians swooping down to pick them up.

Hayden's voice filled the comms. "They won't attack."

Drake pursed his lips. "Fluid op. Orders change."

"And they might still force the bus off the road," Dahl replied. "How long to the city?"

"Eight minutes," Lauren responded.

"Way too long." Dahl strode down the aisle toward the back of the speeding coach and began explaining to passengers that they should move toward the front. A few moments passed and then he joined Alicia.

"Hey Torsty. And I always thought back seats were just for kissing."

The Swede made a choking sound. "Are you trying to make me travel sick? I know where those lips have been."

Alicia blew him a kiss. "You don't know *everywhere* they've been."

Dahl suppressed a smile and made the sign of the cross. The Russian chopper touched down briefly whilst the soldiers climbed on board, hovering over the tarmac. The bus put some distance and the bend between them, and Alicia and Dahl scanned the air.

Drake kept an eye up front for the escaping Frenchmen, but was in two minds if they'd attempt an assault. They were undermanned and struggling with losses. They were re-evaluating. It made more sense that they'd jump straight onto the third clue.

Still, he watched.

Lauren's voice came over the comms. "Six minutes. You guys have time to talk?"

"About what?" Smyth growled, but refrained from adding anything inflammatory.

"The third Horseman is a mystery, someone the Order threw in there to muddy the waters. Famous Indians include Mahatma Gandhi, Idira Gandhi, Deepak Chopra, but how do you find the *worst* that ever lived? And was famous." She sighed. "We're still checking. The think tank back in DC is stumped so far though. I told them it might not be a bad thing."

Drake breathed easier. "Aye, love. Not the worst thing that could have happened," he said. "It should slow down the other nations."

"It sure will. In other news, we think we've cracked the four corners of the earth."

"You have?" Mai said. "That's good news."

Drake loved her typical understatement. "Steady on, Mai."

"Yeah, don't wanna blow your socks off with excitement," Alicia added dryly.

Mai didn't deign to respond. Lauren went on as if nothing had been said: "Wait a moment, guys. I've just been told the Chinese are back at it. That's at least two choppers headed your way."

"We're in a Chinese bus," Yorgi said. "Won't we be safe from them, at least?"

"That's a bit naïve," Kenzie said. "Governments don't care."

"Despite the over-generalization," Hayden added. "Kenzie is right. We can't assume they won't hit the bus."

Prophetic words, Drake thought, as a black speck grew in the blue skies that stretched in front of the bus.

Alicia said, "The Russians are here."

This just got a whole lot harder.

CHAPTER EIGHTEEN

Choppers swooped in from front and back. Drake watched the Chinese bird dive almost to the tarmac before leveling and coming straight at the bus.

"They're forcing us to crash," he said, then gestured at the scared-looking driver. "No, no. keep going!"

The bus's engine roared, the tires thundered against the ground. Some people, clustered at the front, had already started to scream. Drake knew the Chinese wouldn't deliberately crash the chopper, but it was hard to convey his knowledge to the passengers.

The driver closed his eyes hard. The bus veered.

Drake swore and pulled the man away from his perch, grabbing hold of the wheel. Smyth assisted and manhandled the man into the aisle. Drake jumped behind the wheel of the bus, foot on the gas pedal and hands firmly on the wheel, keeping it in a dead straight line.

The chopper's nose pointed directly at them, the gap closing at a rapid rate.

Screams erupted from behind and to the sides. Smyth now had to hold the driver down. Drake held on.

The comms crackled. "C'mon, my rough-arsed Keanu," Alicia breathed. "The Russkies are practically up our—"

"Bitch," Kenzie snapped back. "Be quiet. Have you looked out the front?"

An Alicia squeal resonated around the inside of the bus.

"Thoughts?" Drake asked at the last second.

"This ain't exactly a board meeting!"

Drake held fast to his faith, his experience and the steering wheel. Loud protests filled his ears. Bodies hit the floor of the bus. Even Smyth cringed. At the very last moment the Chinese chopper banked right and the Russian chopper pulled up, skids almost brushing the back end of the bus. Alicia whistled and Dahl cleared his throat.

"I do believe we won that round of chicken."

Drake forged on, seeing another wide sweeping bend ahead. "And the bonus is—we're not fried and crispy."

"Quit it," Kinimaka said. "I'm already hungry."

Alicia coughed. "That is one crazy Chinese chopper."

"They're coming back," Hayden said.

"You guys are approaching the city outskirts right now," Lauren said. "But still three minutes from any decent population areas."

Drake jumped on the comms. "C'mon, people! You have to make 'em fear it!"

Kenzie approached the rear set of doors, shouting, "Anyone on here got a katana?"

Blank looks met her words, two or three people offering up their seats. An old man, wide-eyed, extended a shaking hand holding a bag of sweets.

Kenzie sighed. Drake flipped a switch to open the doors. In a moment the Israeli had swung her body out, gripped the lip of a window, then the roof, and hauled herself onto the top of the bus. Drake kept it as steady as he could, avoiding a large pothole, breathing deeply as he understood his own responsibility arising from Kenzie's action.

Then, in the rearview, he saw Dahl leap over to join her.

Oh shit.

Concentrating hard, he kept it steady.

Dahl swung himself up onto the top of the bus. Kenzie extended a hand but he nodded past her.

"Quick!"

The Russian chopper had banked above and was now swooping again, this time coming from a three-quarter front angle. He could see a man hanging out of each side, weapons aiming, probably targeting the wheels or even the driver.

Instantly, he whirled, seeking the Chinese helo. It wasn't far away. Diving in from the left, it too had men pointing weapons out of the doors. The fact that the Chinese weren't firing heavily on their own bus, whilst heartening at first, was tempered by the knowledge that they needed the box that Hayden held, and they needed it intact.

Kenzie steadied herself atop the bus, gauging for wind and movement, and spread her knees. Then she raised her weapon, focusing on the chopper. Dahl hoped she wouldn't even try to take it down, just deter the shooters. The Russians had exhibited no such restraint, but Kenzie was desperate to change.

Dahl judged the incoming helicopter. Packed full, it was less than nimble, but lethal. The last thing he wanted was to cause any kind of accident, let alone one that might send it crashing into the bus.

The front wheels bounced over a pothole, eliciting a "sorry" from Drake. Dahl heard nothing more except the rushing air and the roar of the helicopter. A shot glanced off the metal close to his right foot. The Swede ignored it, aimed, and fired.

The bullet must have hit true, for a man dropped his gun and withdrew. Dahl didn't let it upset his concentration though, just fired another shot through the open doorway. The chopper veered straight at him, coming fast, and this time Dahl knew it would be a bad idea to play chicken.

He flung himself to the roof of the bus.

The chopper screamed overhead, slicing through the space he'd just vacated. It didn't have the maneuverability to swing around at Kenzie, but passed close enough to send her stumbling to the side.

Toward the edge of the bus's roof!

Dahl slipped and slithered along, trying to reach her in time. Kenzie arrested her fall, but lost her grip on her weapon; still the momentum sent her tumbling off the speeding bus and toward the ungiving road far below.

The Chinese bird banked hard, coming around. The Russian shot overhead, a stray bullet puncturing the metal close to Dahl's right thigh. Kenzie's body slipped over the side of the bus and he thrust his entire frame into a last desperate leap, arm extended.

He managed to clamp his right hand around her flailing wrist; took firm hold and waited for the inevitable wrench.

It came, but he held on, stretched to the limit. The shiny, smooth metal worked against him, allowing his body to slide toward the edge, Kenzie's weight dragging them both down.

Shouts came over the comms. The team could see Kenzie's feet thrashing around outside one of the side windows. Dahl held on beyond endurance, but every moment that passed sent his body slipping closer and closer toward that hard edge.

Atop the bus there was no grip, and *nothing* to grip. He could hold on, he would never let go, but he couldn't find any purchase to pull her up either. Drake's voice came over the comms.

"Do you want me to stop?" Loud, unsure, a little anxious.

Dahl read the emotions well. If they stopped they'd be hit hard both by the Russians and the Chinese. No telling what the outcome would be.

Lauren's voice interrupted. "Sorry, I just got word the Swedes are coming at you. It's now a four-way spread, people."

Dahl felt the weight stretching his muscles. Every time the bus bounced, another inch of him slipped toward the edge and Kenzie dropped a little further. He heard the Israeli's voice from down below.

"Let go! I can make it!"

No way. They were traveling at sixty miles per hour. Kenzie knew he wouldn't let go and didn't want both of them to fall. Dahl felt even more respect for her. The heart he knew was deeply submerged had just risen a little closer to the surface.

The sound of her boots drumming against the windows caused his own heart to beat faster.

They slipped together; Kenzie down the side and Dahl across the top of the bus. He tried to grip a rough lip that ran down the edge but it was too tiny, and cut through his flesh. Not seeing any hope he hung on as long as he could, risking everything.

His chest moved toward the drop, sliding inexorably. His eyes met Kenzie's, staring up. Their exchange was wordless, expressionless but profound.

You should let me go.

Not a chance.

He hauled once more, only to slip past the point of no return.

Strong hands clamped down onto both of his calves, hands that could only belong to Mano Kinimaka.

"Gotcha," the Hawaiian said. "You guys ain't going nowhere."

The Hawaiian steadied Dahl and then slowly dragged him back from the drop. Dahl kept tight hold of Kenzie. Together, they inched toward safety.

Above, the choppers plunged for a final time.

Drake knew Kinimaka had firm hold of his friends, but still didn't dare to swerve the bus too sharply. The Russians and Chinese were coming in hard from different directions, no doubt aware this would be their final pass.

The sound of windows being smashed told him the others weren't standing idle. They had a plan.

Behind, Alicia, Smyth, Mai, Hayden and Yorgi each took a window on separate sides of the bus and smashed it through. Targeting the oncoming choppers, they laid down a spread of fire that forced them to quickly veer away. The tree line ended and Drake saw buildings ahead.

A network of roads, a roundabout. Gunfire resounded behind him, filling the bus; the black choppers lifted away into the skies.

He sighed with relief.

"We survive," he said. "To fight another day."

Lauren interrupted. "The Swedes have pulled back too," she said. "But I'm still getting a kind of ghosting on the signal. Something between DC, the field and me. It's odd. Almost as if . . . as if . . ."

"What?" Drake asked.

"As if there's another set of communications going on. Something else at play. Another . . ." she hesitated.

"Team?" Drake finished.

Hayden grumbled out loud. "That sounds ludicrous."

"I know," Lauren replied. "I really do, and I'm no expert. If only Karin were here, we'd have something better, I'm sure."

"Can you catch any dialogue?" Hayden asked. "Even a little?"

Drake recalled the earlier mention of SEAL Team 7, heard only by Dahl and himself. It occurred to him again that all communications were being monitored.

"Can we shelve it for now?" he asked. "And find us the best way out of here?"

Lauren sounded relieved. "Sure, sure," she said. "Give me a minute."

CHAPTER NINETEEN

Hayden Jaye waited several hours until the team were safe, stuffed into a small satellite safe house in Taiwan, before leaving the cramped space to make a call.

Her objective: contacting Kimberly Crowe.

It took a while, but Hayden persevered. She found a quiet corner around the back of the house, crouched down, and waited, trying to keep her head from spinning. It was hard to find something permanent in her life, something to cling to, outside the team. SPEAR had become her life, her reason for living and, as a consequence of that, she simply had no personal bonds, nothing outside of work. She thought back through the whirlwind of adventures they'd shared—from the Odin thing and the Gates of Hell, all the way through Babylon and Pandora, the nuke that almost decimated New York City, her old break up with Ben Blake and her recent split from Mano Kinimaka. She was strong, too strong. She didn't need to be that strong. The most recent incident with the Inca treasures in Peru had affected her both mentally and physically. Never before had she been so rocked to her core.

Now, she quietly reevaluated. Bridges may have been burned, and that had to be fine. But if she did want to change, if she wanted *more* in her life, she had to be damn sure before taking the plunge and risking hurting anyone ever again. Be that Mano, or anyone else.

I care. I really do. And next time, I need to be sure that I'm being true to what I ultimately want.

Out of life. Not out of work. The SPEAR team gelled and worked well, but nothing lasted forever. A time would come—

"Miss Jaye?" a robotic voice said. "I'm putting you through now."

Hayden pulled it together. The next voice on the line belonged to the Secretary of Defense.

"What's the problem, Agent Jaye?" Curt, quiet, detached. Crowe sounded on edge.

Hayden had taken the time to figure out how to phrase her main question. She'd decided to bury it in bullshit and see what Crowe picked up on.

"We're out of China and have secured the second box. The team is checking it out now. Reports soon, no doubt. No casualties, though plenty of cuts and bruises. Not all of the opposing teams are hostile . . ." She let that hang for second, wondering if Crowe might bite, then went on: "Some countries are more aggressive than other. The French lost at least three. One Russian wounded. Could there be another, more covert team along? We've heard snatches of furtive American chatter, which proves nothing, of course. The Brits are on our side, at least they appear to be and Drake has some sway with them. We're now in a safe house awaiting the think tank to figure out the location of the third Horseman."

Now she stopped, and waited.

Crowe kept her reserve. "Anything else?"

"I don't believe so." Hayden felt disappointment as her efforts came to nothing. She wondered if she should be more direct.

"I am in constant contact with the DC people," Crowe said. "It isn't necessary to keep me informed."

"Ah, okay. Thank you."

Hayden started to sign off. It was only then that Crowe sent a seemingly innocent word of enquiry down the line.

"Wait. You said you thought somebody might be impersonating Americans? Out in the field?"

Hayden hadn't said anything of the sort. But from all that pertinent information Crowe had picked up on only one thing. She forced a laugh. "It appears so. We heard it on the ground." She kept Lauren's involvement out of it. "Of course, we know there's no second team so maybe it's one of the other countries using ex-US Spec-ops, or even mercenaries."

"A fringe foreign government element using United States' personnel?" Crowe hissed. "Could be, Agent Jaye. You may be right. Of course," she laughed, "there's no second team."

Hayden listened to more than words. "And when we return? What do we return to?"

Crowe was silent, which told Hayden she knew exactly what was being asked. "One thing at a time," she eventually said. "The Order's so-called Horsemen must be found and neutralized first."

"Of course." Hayden also knew this was her last chance to talk directly with Crowe, so took it a little further. "And if we hear the American chatter again?"

"What am I—a field agent? Deal with it."

Crowe killed the call, leaving Hayden to stare hard at the cellphone screen for several minutes, now not only reevaluating herself, but the intentions of her country too.

Drake took the chance to relax whilst Yorgi, Mai and Kinimaka dealt with the new box. The fact that it came from Genghis Kahn's mausoleum and had lain among the legendary figure's personal possessions only added to the reverence with which they handled it. The clear, repugnant symbol on the top proved that it once belonged to the Order of the Last Judgment.

Kinimaka studied the lock. "I'm sure the Order once had a plan to hand out keys," he said. "But life got in the way." He smiled.

"Death," Mai said quietly. "Death got in the way."

"Want me to finesse it open?" Yorgi asked.

"Yeah, let's see some of those thiefy skills, Yogi." Alicia spoke up, sitting with her back against a wall at Drake's side, water bottle in one hand, pistol in the other.

"No point." Kinimaka snapped the lock with a meaty paw. "It ain't exactly art."

Kenzie crawled over as Mai lifted the lid. It was an odd scenario, Drake thought, soldiers crammed into a tiny room with nowhere to sit and nowhere to communicate from, or make food. Just a mini-fridge packed full with water, and a few boxes of biscuits. The windows were draped, the door massively barred. The carpet was worn, threadbare, and smelled of mold but the soldiers had experienced worse. It was good enough to get some rest.

Hayden was let back in by Smyth, who guarded the door, entering just as Mai reached inside the box. Drake thought the boss looked worn and worried, on edge. Hopefully, later, she would elaborate on her conversation.

Mai shuffled around for a few seconds before pulling her hands out. She held a thick wad of papers covered by a thick binder and secured by a knotty length of twine, which made some members of the team raise their eyebrows.

"Really?" Kinimaka sat back on his haunches. "This is a weapon that could endanger the world?"

"The written word," Kenzie said, "can be pretty powerful."

"What is it?" Lauren asked. "We have all the DC guys waiting."

Time continued to work against them. As ever, it was the key to staying ahead of the game and in particular—the race. Drake saw two ways of moving forward. "Mai, Hayden and Dahl, why don't you figure out what that is? Lauren—what do you have on the third Horseman, since we're gonna need a direction to head toward?"

Lauren had already told them she would meet them at the third location. Now, she sighed audibly. "Well, nobody is 100 percent sure, guys. To put you in the picture I'm gonna have to run you through their interpretation of the four corners of the earth."

Drake watched Mai and the others frowning their way through the weapon of Conquest. "We have time."

"Well, it is really interesting. Before the discovery of the so-called New World in the sixteenth century it was believed the earth was divided into three parts—Europe, Asia and Africa. The division between these continents was the Hellespont, which nicely integrates with the Order's plan that you've been following so far. So, Asia began beyond the Hellespont, an unknown land of exotic riches they called the Orient. Of course, later they found America and *it* then became the New World, desirable, unexplored and laden with promise. A book of emblems was published, depicting the new four corners of the world. Asia, Europe, Africa and America. It seems the Order decided to assimilate this ancient thinking into their map for unknown reasons—though probably because they still considered themselves all-powerful, relic-hunting patriarchs." Lauren took a breath.

"So it's a re-education of the world, which happened again when they found Australia, and then Antarctica?" Kenzie said.

"Yes, a gradual re-education through the ages which, some think, is still happening. But that's an entirely different story. It hasn't all been happiness and roses. The phrase, the four corners of the earth, has been possibly the most controversial expression in history. In Hebrew it is translated to *extremity*. In Numbers 15:38, it's borders; in Ezekiel, corners; and in Job, ends. It can also be translated as divisions. Obviously the Bible left itself open to ridicule right there . . ."

Drake got it. "Because it suggests the world is flat?"

"Yeah. But the Bible covered that in Isaiah, calling it a sphere. So, a deliberate reference. The point is they could have used any number of words—about a dozen—to describe a corner. It is believed the word *extremity* was used intentionally, to convey, well, exactly that. And no Jew could ever possibly misinterpret the true meaning since for 2000 years they have faced the city of Jerusalem three times a day and chanted: 'Sound the great trumpet for our freedom. Raise the banner for gathering our exiles, and gather us together from *the four corners of the earth* into our own land.'"

"So they didn't just pick the phrase at random?" Smyth asked.

"No. The book of Isaiah explains how the Messiah shall gather his people from the four corners of the earth. From every extremity, they shall gather in Israel."

Kenzie didn't move a muscle nor say a word. Drake had no clue as to her religious beliefs, if she even had any, but knew that nevertheless it would inevitably have been a large part of her life. In that moment he studied her a little more as they waited for Lauren to continue. Dahl's belief that she was inherently good, and would always come back to her moral heart, was panning out—to a degree. He still saw the edge in her—the lawless edge—but that wasn't necessarily a bad thing.

At times.

But you couldn't have it both ways. And that's what he saw in Kenzie—a ruthless slayer when they needed one and a struggling soul when they didn't. For her sake, they had to let her change.

"It makes sense, of course," Kinimaka said. "First Africa, then China. So what's next?"

Lauren responded immediately. "Yeah, we think the

Bible's meaning was *extremities*, and so did the Order. They made it hard for whomever came next. According to the text . . . well . . . I'll read out the relevant passage: 'Find the resting places of the Father of Strategy and then the Khagan; the Worst Indian Who Ever Lived and then the Scourge of God. But all is not as it seems. We visited the Khagan in 1960, five years after completion, placing Conquest in his coffin. We found the Scourge who guards the true last judgment. And the only kill code is when the Horsemen arose. The Father's bones are unmarked. The Indian is surrounded by guns . . .'"

Drake absorbed it. "The worst Indian that ever lived? And he's surrounded by guns? Surely, it could be anywhere in India. It's a country surrounded by guns."

"Back when the Order were hiding the Horsemen?"

Drake thought about it. "Well, yeah, I guess so. What is the third Horseman anyway?"

"Famine."

He let out a long breath and looked over at Alicia. "Couldn't be Fluffy Princess could it?"

Alicia waved a hand to and fro. "Maybe. I'll take it under advisement."

Drake stared. "You are freakin' impossible."

"Any preferences?"

"To what?"

"Which princess? A girl's gotta know, you know."

He studied his boots. "Well. I always had a thing for Cleopatra. I know she's not a princess, but . . ."

"A queen? Even better."

Lauren was still speaking. "As I said before, the guys and girls are still evaluating which Indian the Order could be referencing. Truth be told, it's too ambiguous. I mean, even putting yourself in their place, in their time, it could be one of a dozen."

"And they're all surrounded by guns?" Smyth asked.

"Living in India, yeah. Mostly."

"Well, at least we have a destination," Alicia said.

Drake looked over to Mai, Hayden and Dahl, who were dealing with the contents of the second box, Conquest.

"Any luck?"

Hayden wiggled her hand, signaling they were almost there. She looked up. "It appears to be a plan for a doomsday scenario. Do you remember the linchpin effect? One small event triggers another and another, each one larger?"

"Chaos theory," Dahl said. "It *is* a weapon of conquest and Genghis Kahn was a deep thinker. With this, you could conquer the world."

Drake tipped back his water bottle.

Alicia said: "A domino effect weapon?"

"Exactly. Like the assassination of Franz Ferdinand led to the star of World War 1. Potentially, this blueprint of rising chaos could start World War 3."

"And again," Drake removed his comms for a moment and spoke quietly, "that's pretty tricky. Who do we give it to?"

Everyone stared. It was a valid question. Hayden signaled that he should say no more. He knew Washington and the Secretary of Defense were already unhappy with them, and turned back to wondering about SEAL Team 7.

Coincidence?

Not a chance.

Hayden surveyed the sheets of paper for another few minutes, then shoved them inside her jacket. To the team at large she shrugged to indicate the decision was not yet made and absolutely anything could happen to the unsecured papers.

Aloud she said, "We'll sort this as soon as we can. Right

now, we need that third location. Lauren?"

"I hear you. We're still waiting."

"Now wait a minute," Kenzie said, the frown on her face from the last ten minutes still clear. "You people say there are four corners of the earth, right?"

"Well, the Bible mentions it," Lauren said. "And so have the Order of the Last Judgment."

"Well, something's off. Don't you see it?"

Drake blinked, now more confused than ever. Dahl studied Kenzie closely.

"Perhaps some explanation would help?"

"The four corners? Africa, Asia, Europe and America."

"Sure. That's what they tell me."

Kenzie spread both her arms. "And where is India?"

Hayden rose to her feet. "Crap, India is a part of the Asian continent."

"Which we've already dealt with."

Lauren was thinking on her feet. "Which leaves only Europe and America," she said. "Hey guys, are you thinking what I'm thinking?"

"Probably," Alicia moaned. "Is your arse numb from sitting on a crappy floor too?"

"Chicken," Kinimaka said. "But then I'm always thinking 'chicken.'"

"The Order are war criminals from the forties. By the time they concealed the weapons the term 'native American' was in use, but they wouldn't have thought of it that way. They were born in the twenties or earlier, for God's sake."

"Red Indians?" Drake said. "From the Wild West? Bloody hell."

"It's possible," Lauren said. "That the think tank has been looking in the wrong place."

"So who was the worst that ever lived?" Dahl asked.

"Let me get back to you on that. For now, just get on a plane."

Drake wasn't the only one that stared hard at Hayden.
Back to America?
Shit.
Hayden, in particular, watched Smyth. They had no idea what might have transpired since Peru, or what the authorities were thinking. The soldier, to his credit, immediately began to rise and check his pack.
The third Horseman? Famine? And America? Do our rivals know?
Would she ever get a moment's peace to sort her life out?
Not today, Hayden, not today. Signaling the others to remove their comms and turn them off, she made a point of standing in their midst.
"We do this," she said. "And we do it right. As we should, as we always do. But guys—I have reservations. I believe—" she paused "—that Crowe and the American government have a second team in play. SEAL Team 7, and obviously they're damn good. This team might not be in play *just* to make sure we get all of the Horsemen."
Drake frowned at that. "Sorry?"
"Well, did you think there might be a second scenario? What if they're here, essentially, to take us out?"

CHAPTER TWENTY

Karin Blake sat with her black boots resting on a table top, a cellphone tucked between her neck and chin, clicking away at a keypad with her free hands. She wore a ratty T-shirt and jeans, and had tied her hair back with a thick scrunchie. The voice speaking into her left ear was almost drowned out by Palladino's laughter.

"Shut the hell up, Dino!" she turned and shouted.

"Yeah, yeah." The soldier turned with a grin and then saw her face. "All right, all right. Jeez, who put you the hell in charge?"

Karin apologized to the speaker. "Kids are rowdy," she said. "Any more and they'll be outside on the naughty step."

The woman laughed quietly. "Oh yeah, I got me two of those."

Karin eyed the tall muscular Dino and their comrade-in-arms—the smaller, lean Wu. Both soldiers were letting off steam, bored being cooped up in the desert house for the last week, setting up various systems. What they needed was some real action.

Karin said, "And they escaped?"

"For sure. I was part of the communications unit. They got us on shifts. Team SPEAR took the box from the Chinese and managed to sneak off to Taiwan. Part luck, part reserve on the side of the other teams, I guess."

Karin knew it was much more than luck. There was no better team operating in the world today than SPEAR. Once, she had been proud to be a part of it.

"This Horseman shit doesn't mean much to me," she admitted. "I'm focusing on other things. But tell me, where are they headed next?"

"Well, I don't know yet. India, it seems. But there appears to be some disagreement. Look, I agreed to help a little because of what happened to Palladino's poor parents and because we're on the same side, but there's a limit to what I can say."

Karin sensed the growing suspicion. "We don't need much more. Just this—when I call I need to know the position of Drake's team. Whether it be tomorrow or in a month's time. Can you do that?"

The response was steady. "Yes, so long as I stay on the same unit. I guess."

"Thank you." Karin ended the call quickly before any more questions could be asked. She took a moment to appraise the room and see where they were at. Since appropriating this place from a nest of drug dealers they had cleared out anything bad, finding paraphernalia in all kinds of places, from under the floorboards to under the house, and within nooks and crannies throughout the loft space. Burning every last scrap had been an indulgence, and a desire. Still off the grid, Karin, Dino and Wu had installed computers, communications, surveillance devices and more. If the desert house was to be their HQ, it should be fortified, defendable, a castle in its own right.

Karin thought they were almost there.

A new, nagging thought now occurred to her.

She watched Dino and Wu work with the computers, attaching leads as per her own instructions and installing software, firewalls and more. She had been dynamite at this kind of thing before she took her training. Now, she was much more. Yes, they were still short of a few things, but current funds would only stretch so far. They needed some source of steady income.

Don't ignore it. You can't push it, bury it down deep.

Karin knew all about SEAL Team 7. She knew why they

were in the field, what their objectives were; their strengths and weaknesses; their agenda and ultimate, secret orders. Effectively and supportively then, she could now warn Matt Drake.

It roiled, it twisted, it made acid in her gut.

Every incident they'd been through, highlights and low times, days of utter craziness, plucked at her emotions like a bird pecking at a stubborn worm. Karin had been hurt so badly once before and had given up on life, only to find it again in the most unlikely of places. A new purpose had been granted her.

And again, totally unexpected, she'd found devastation when her brother and family died, and then love when Komodo fell for her. Perhaps that very early incident, when she was so young, ruined her and set her on a course for life.

Devastation.

Now, all she really wanted to do was destroy the good things she had. If something went right, she wanted it to fail. If something great awaited her, she would make sure it fell apart with prejudice.

If the new team started to thrive, to bond, she would tear it apart.

Self-destruction was not a new way of life for Karin Blake. *It's my chosen way of life. My comfort blanket.* She'd always wondered if it would come full-circle, right around and back to this.

So here she sat, relaxed, possessing information even the SPEAR team lacked as they traversed the four corners of the earth in their efforts to secure four nightmare weapons. The junction stood wide open at her door.

One path led to possible redemption, to friends, camaraderie, and the pain of life.

The other path would destroy all that history, all that

uncertain future, and would give her everything she needed: chaos.

Karin gathered up her things and wandered outside onto the front porch. The desert air was arid, edged with dust. A bright orb blazed high in the sky. Somewhere, far away, a super-elite American Special Forces unit called SEAL Team 7 was stalking her old comrades—Matt Drake and Alicia Myles, Torsten Dahl and Mai Kitano and the others—with an intention to kill.

Karin thought about warning them.

Then stuck her head back inside the door. "Hey losers, get your asses in gear. We have places to go and fools to see. Tyler Webb's secret stash won't stay hidden forever."

CHAPTER TWENTY ONE

Karin rode shotgun, watching Dino as he carefully weaved their Dodge Ram along the meandering snakes that made up Los Angeles' highways and byways.

"Keep it steady," she said as the young soldier overtook a red roadster. "You do remember we're being hunted?"

Dino grinned over at her with immature glee. "Just happy to be outta the house, Mom. Any case, you gotta know I'm better than you. Better in every way."

"So you keep saying."

"The Army won't let us go," Wu said. "Every time we surface, we're vulnerable."

"Tone it down, Mr. Misery. Jeez, you two could be a double act."

"We'll see how happy you are when they have your nuts connected to a car battery."

"Don't be an ass, Wu. It's the Army, not the CIA."

Karin enjoyed the constant, rolling views to both sides of the car; Los Angeles sprawling in all its glory. A moment to relax and think about precisely nothing. Thick greenery and concrete behemoths fought for precedence, and beyond those the metal high-rises that sparkled underneath the blazing sun. A light smog hovered around cloud level, dimming the day, but it was barely noticeable. People came and went, barely visible along the sidewalks and shopping malls, zipping this way and that in their cars. The Hollywood Hills passed by slowly to the right, unnoticed because at that point Dino spotted a black-and-white cruiser easing its way along the fast lane and pulled in like the good boy he was, eyes on the road, focus dead ahead.

If you didn't look at them they wouldn't notice you.

Eventually the coast road opened up and they were on their way to San Francisco.

"Beats the desert." Wu studied the glittering, rolling waves.

Karin reviewed the task ahead. Their time inside the HQ had been well spent. First, they had set up the computers, two top-of-the-line Macs with as many special toys as they could afford. The fiber cable was the hardest part, but once they'd sorted that and Karin installed a bevy of firewalls, they were ready to go. Even then, even with Karin at the keyboard and using her genius intellect, they did not have the capabilities for mad hacking. They were limited, forced to use ingenuity.

Karin was aware of Tyler Webb's innumerable secret bank accounts. She'd monitored them when working for SPEAR. She was aware of what some called his legacy; the small amount of secrets he had on her old team. And she was aware of the immense secret stash; something the world's most wealthy, avid stalker had amassed against hundreds of individuals, again including members of her old team.

Most thought, since Webb was dead, they could locate it at their leisure.

Trouble was, Karin had no such thoughts. Access to the secret stash would give her incalculable power—and at the end of everything power was where it was all at. The three of them could move forward from there; gaining money, anonymity, security and influence. Of course, if there were hundreds seeking Webb's stash it might prove particularly hard to steal.

Right now, nobody knew where it was.

Except Karin Blake.

Or so she thought. The next few hours would tell. Insider knowledge had been most helpful. She knew all about

Nicholas Bell, and how the whistleblower had been sitting inside a jail cell telling all—names, places, identities, the entire rotten shebang. She knew how Lauren Fox liked to visit. She knew the people that listened and talked to Lauren Fox.

Well, she knew them, they didn't necessarily know *her*.

Maybe a little late to the party—Karin's army training and subsequent departure had taken a while—but she made up for that with a little top-flight hacking flair. Bell's conversations were monitored. Smyth, it seemed, had the juice to regularly receive a copy of those conversations—*naughty boy*—and treat them as he wished. Who knew what the irascible, easy-to-anger soldier did with them? Protected national security, obviously.

The point was, Karin *could* hack the line that went directly to Smyth's network. For her, it was a relatively easy job. She took the time to glean the rich pickings. Tyler Webb had once owned countless offices, houses, penthouses, and even an island, around the world. Place names that resonated with her included Washington DC, Niagara and Monte Carlo. Bell had talked to Lauren, but he'd also talked to guards and lawyers, and Smyth's recordings included snippets from all of them.

Smyth does not have the brightest future, she thought.

However you spun it, the Peru incident—or incidents—had placed the SPEAR team in a world of hurt.

Karin shifted her position as a sign flashed by, stating they were 130 miles away from San Francisco. Bell had become quite vocal with Lauren—stating facts again and again that might be right, naming names, places, bank accounts. At this point Karin didn't dare tap any of the accounts for fear the authorities might be quietly monitoring them to see who popped up. They needed a foolproof action and escape plan in place first.

Hence the trip to San Francisco.

When pressed, Bell revealed how Webb used to occasionally boast about what he knew. The man had been a ritual stalker, a wealthy shadow with the resources to expose and hurt and own just about anyone in the world if he wanted to. Webb had always offered tidbits to Bell, stringing him along, but had hinted at what he called the mother lode.

This 'mother lode' had turned out to be a specific office where the deranged megalomaniac kept all the dirt he'd ever collected on anyone. Of course, he'd never told Bell where it was.

Karin considered it all though. She had the exclusive benefit of being able to view it all from the inside. And she remembered moments when Webb had stolen information from and made clandestine visits to most of the team. Her eidetic memory came into its own right there. Of course, it wasn't easy, but Karin knew Webb had worked out of a known office in DC back then and had managed to backtrack on the communications that were now a matter of record.

Large files were sent to a particular address in San Francisco on half a dozen occasions. Further investigations showed other large files being received from other known offices. So whilst the authorities trawled and crawled through a thick sludge of data, Karin was able to pinpoint exactly what she needed.

Dino guided them through the traffic, over the Golden Gate and past Fisherman's Wharf. Tourists thronged the area, cameras at the ready, stepping out into the road without much care for themselves. Dino blended in with the traffic, giving the cops no reason to notice them. A steep hill brought them further into the city and soon they were circling Union Square, passing by banks and pharmacies, ships and restaurants in the hardest quest yet—to find a good parking spot.

"Just leave it here." Wu waved at a small space near a Walgreens. "The address is a five-minute walk away."

"Five minutes?" Karin said. "Could be an age if Webb left any contingencies."

"Plus," Dino said as he inched closer to their destination, "this is a Dodge Ram. I'd be hard pressed to park my ass in that spot."

"Want me to do it? I *can* drive."

"Oh really? Well, sure, *Toretto*. Let's see how you handle—"

"Kids," Karin breathed. "Shut the fuck up. See over there?"

"We need good access for a fast getaway. We need quick access. We need . . ." Dino paused. "Shit, we're gonna need a long-stay garage ain't we?"

Karin nodded. "Right there. If we have to we go to ground for a while; we can always drive out of here another day when the dust settles."

"Crap, I hope not," Wu muttered. "Been spending enough time with you two these days."

"Is that a problem?" Karin wondered as Dino guided the Ram into the underground parking structure.

"Well, the testosterone is a bit high. You two compete like siblings, all the time. Gets a bit tiresome at times."

"Us? Compete?" Karin glared over at Dino. "Do we?"

The young soldier laughed loudly. "Only because you won't admit I'm better than you."

"I don't see it." Karin eyed him critically, then turned to Wu. "Do you see it?"

"Let me put it this way. If you two ever got blind drunk and decided to mate, you'd have to do it standing up because *both* of you would wanna be on top."

Karin laughed raucously as Dino finally found a spot to

his liking. "Blind drunk? Shit, there just isn't enough alcohol in the world to make that happen, Wu."

Dino removed the keys and cracked the door open. "Time to focus. All this mating crap isn't helping."

"Don't like girls, Dino?" Karin joined the two men around the front. "San Francisco has a zoo. We can always take you there after we're done."

Dino ignored her, pulled out his cellphone and waited until the address they wanted had loaded up. "Three minutes," he said. "We ready?"

Karin shrugged into a rucksack. "As fuck."

It was an office building, a high rise, and Webb's space was on the thirty-fifth floor. Karin thought it was unusual for him—the madman usually preferred to live at the highest levels so he could look down on everyone—but she thought he might have kept this address as unassuming and secret as possible—it was something he treasured and the elite storage facility of his entire life's work.

Every precaution, she thought.

Which made what they were about to do all the more . . .

Stupid? Naïve? Clever? Smart?

She smiled grimly to herself as she realized the answer relied on the outcome.

The trio entered through a swing door on the ground floor, spied a bank of elevators and headed over. Men and women wearing dark suits wandered to and fro. An information desk sat in the far corner, manned by two black-haired secretaries. The noise level was low, everyone keeping it down. Karin saw one overweight guard in a corner, staring out at the passing traffic and three security cameras. She steered Dino to an information board.

"Thirty five." She nodded. "One company owns the entire floor."

"Makes sense."

Wu stared at the name. "Minmac Systems?" he read. "Same old, same old."

Faceless corporations that ran the world.

Karin pushed on, reaching the elevators and re-checking. Finding a blank 35 would not have surprised her—or the number missing all together—but there it was—white and shiny just like all the others. Various floors were pressed by the occupants and Karin waited until the very last, but only she pressed 35.

They didn't wait long. She took her rucksack off, pretended to rummage inside for something. Dino and Wu also made ready. As the elevator dinged and the doors opened at 35, the trio waited just a few seconds to see what they faced.

A polished hallway ran away, doors and windows to either side. At the far end stood a wooden desk. Pictures adorned the walls, bland and boring. Karin guessed somebody was waiting from the very moment she'd pressed the button, but they were here now. They were ready, eager, young and capable.

She led the way, stepped into an odd world that somehow still belonged to a dead man. If anything, this was Webb's legacy. His mother lode.

No CCTV. No guards. The first door she tried wobbled so crazily in its frame she walked away. It was all for show, just a front. She pulled out her gun and stuffed her pockets full of magazines. The vest she wore beneath her coat had felt bulky all the way here, but now it kept her secure. The team spread out as they approached the desk, wary.

Karin paused and looked both ways down two new hallways. She was surprised when a robotic voice spoke up.

"Can I help you?"

She noted the sensor attached to the front edge of the desk. Still, she saw no cameras.

"Hello? Is someone there?" Playing the fool.

All the while, she considered the blueprint inside her head. Not only had Webb's large data stream led her to this address, she had been able to pinpoint the location of the exact terminal it arrived at by using a digital construct of the building's frame. She knew they should head left and then to the right, but wondered what the robots might do . . .

"I think we're lost." She shrugged at Dino and Wu. "Just wait, Mr. Robot, whilst we try to find someone."

It was worth a try. Karin headed left, the guys at her back. The first man-mountain appeared from the left, stepping out of an office, baseball bat held firmly in one hand, its head slapping the other. A second appeared up ahead, closely followed by a third, and then a fourth stepped up from the left, this one carrying a hammer.

Wu grunted. "Three behind."

Karin waved her gun. "C'mon guys, what am I missing?"

The first mountain, a bald-headed individual, grinned. "There's a radar, girl, and we stay under it."

"I see. So, knowing Tyler Webb as I do—a man that relishes making noise at the right time and place—this is his garden of tranquility? Meditation? Well, we're unlikely to disturb him now boys, are we?"

"A gunshot will have the cops here in ten minutes," the man said. "SWAT in twenty."

"And building security?"

The man laughed. "Whatever."

"Thanks for the info."

Karin shot him in the arm without warning, saw him stagger. She shot the next too, a round to the stomach, and waited for him to fall to the floor before leaping over his back and using his spine to push off.

A baseball bat swung close to her head, missed, and smashed through a door, shattering the glass and framework. She ignored it. Wu was behind her, with Dino dealing with the other direction. A third obesity blocked her way. She fired two shots into the general mass, ducked a hefty swing and then had no choice other than to hit the immovable bulk head on.

She bounced back, shaken.

She held on to the gun as she fell back on her spine. Looking up, she saw the enormous round face staring down at her—a numb, cruel giant with bullet holes he didn't feel, blood flows he didn't see, and the biggest razor-blade-spotted, wooden club she'd ever seen.

"Fuckin' caveman."

Karin fired upward as the club came down. Two bullets fired through the overhanging belly, striking the ceiling, but the club kept on coming down. Karin averted her skull. The club landed beside it, splintering the floor, drawing sparks from the glinting blades. For a second it lay there, then the arm holding it strained and it began to pull away from the floor.

Karin scooted back, saw the terrible face and fired straight at it. This time the owner felt it and staggered immediately, luckily falling to the right and straight through another colleague, trapping the lesser man beneath.

Wu jumped over her, firing into two more hefty bulks. These men fell to their knees. A club slapped Wu across the bicep, making him yelp. Karin turned to see the first man—the bald guy she'd shot through the leg—dragging himself alongside her, leaving a trail of blood.

"You just fucked it up real good, lady. For everyone."

"Oh, so now that I've shot you I'm a lady, yea? I take it you know what we're here for?"

He scrambled for his club, and a knife that hung at his belt.

"You kidding? There's only the one thing here, you know that."

Karin nodded. "Sure."

"But you'll never find it."

She glanced quickly at the many, many rooms full of computer terminals, all no doubt working, running some kind of program, and all the same as their neighbors.

But she knew better. "Oh, I think I might."

She also knew a man like Webb would never consider installing a kill switch. Not after all the hard work he'd put in to acquire such material, not when every sweet stalking he'd ever undertaken lived right here.

She dodged the bat, stopped the knife strike, and left the man with a second bullet hole. She jumped up and followed Wu, then glanced back to see how Dino was doing. All was well. The only problem they had now was the police.

Wu hesitated; the hallway was clear. "Where to?"

Karin ran past, the location seared into her memory. "To the lair of one of the worst monsters that ever lived," she said. "So keep it frosty. This way, boys."

CHAPTER TWENTY TWO

The room itself was obnoxious, the last vestige of Tyler Webb, crawling with external imagery manifested of a malignant inner madness. They destroyed the locks in seconds, saw the framed pictures on the walls—favored victims and stalkings, before and after shots—and a bizarre collection of spy-gadgets from all over the world, sitting on tables all around the room.

Karin ignored it as best she could, hearing sirens already through the glazed windows. Wu and Dino stood guard whilst she dashed over to the terminal.

Double-checking, she confirmed it was the very one that had received enormous streams of data, plugged in a specially formatted flash drive, and looked for a small green light that would confirm automatic download of the terminal's contents. Karin had anticipated a large amount of information might be transferred and had configured the stick accordingly. It was as fast as she could make it.

"How we doing?" She glanced up.

Wu shrugged. "All quiet here."

"Apart from the moaning," Dino said. "Plenty of that."

Part of their plan was to leave casualties. It would confuse and delay the cops. Karin was happy that they were, at the very least, thugs and deserved their upcoming new lot in life. She glanced at the flashing green light, saw it was blinking fast, and knew it was almost done.

"Get ready."

Sirens shrieked outside the window.

The light stopped flashing, signaling all was complete. She withdrew the tiny drive and zipped it inside an inner pocket. "Time to go."

Instantly, the boys moved out, stepping carefully around the fallen, bleeding men and kicking two that tried to rise up. Karin threatened them with her gun, but wouldn't have used it. There might still be some confusion as to where the gunfire had come from. Already, they would be manning the surveillance cameras and asking myriad questions. The key to escape was not to be quick, not even to be careful.

It was to be unexpected.

They unbuckled their backpacks, withdrew their contents and then threw the empty bags away. Staring at each other, they nodded.

"Officer." Wu saluted Dino.

"Officer." Dino nodded smartly at Karin.

"Sarge," she exaggerated her British accent and headed for the service elevators.

In her pocket, the key to power, to government and royal manipulation, to coup upon coup, to financial freedom and law enforcement control.

All they needed was a safe place to start it up.

CHAPTER TWENTY THREE

Another day, another plane journey, and Matt Drake was feeling seriously jet-lagged. Takeoff had happened only an hour ago and they were chasing the day toward the Atlantic, en route to the United States of America.

With no clear idea of where to go.

The third Horseman—Famine. Drake dreaded to imagine what kind of warfare the Order had dreamed up for famine. They were still highly engrossed with figuring out the first weapon—the space gun and, in particular, the second weapon—the linchpin code. Hayden still held all the information to it, but the pressure to share was immense. Only the sudden scramble and unclear destination were making her lack of action acceptable.

The linchpin code engineered events carried out across half of Europe, and finally America, to bring down the world's heads of states, the country's infrastructures, hobble their armies and free the psychos—those that wanted to send Earth back to the dark ages. It appeared frighteningly real, and frighteningly easy. Once that first domino toppled . . .

Hayden stayed quiet as she read through. Drake allowed his mind to cruise past all the recent revelations: SEAL Team 7; the Special Forces teams engaging with each other; the French losses, due mostly to the Russians; and now a Native American connection. Of course, the tribesmen had been superb horsemen—possibly the best that ever lived. But where did famine come into it all?

Alicia snored softly at his side, getting a little shut eye. Kenzie tried her best to video the event, but Dahl managed to hold her back. Drake noticed it wasn't gentle physical persuasion, but rather words that changed her mind. He wasn't sure about Dahl and Kenzie getting close. None of his business, of course, and he was essentially traveling the same train tracks but . . .

Drake wanted the best for the Mad Swede, and that was all.

Lauren sat up front, with Smyth as close as he could get without making her feel too uncomfortable. Yorgi, Kinimaka and Mai spoke in quiet tones toward the plane's rear; the cargo hold they were in not much more than a high-ceilinged, drafty, rattling shell. Just once he'd like to fly first class. Even coach beat luggage class.

Lauren concentrated on the feed they still had going between themselves and DC. The chatter was bland and unfocused right now, more a brainstorming session that a real discussion. *That many geeks though?* Drake had no doubt they would find exactly what they were looking for.

The hours passed and the States drew closer. Lauren became interested in the various feeds coming in from rival nations. The Israelis, it seemed, had worked out the American connection almost at the same time as SPEAR. The Brits too. The Chinese were silent and the French quite possibly out if it. Drake knew they'd hear nothing from the SEALs. They weren't really there, of course.

"Interesting to see if they'll fly these teams into America under the radar," Dahl said. "Or use internal teams."

"People already insinuated into society?" Hayden looked up. "I doubt it. Sleeper agents take years to build."

"And it ain't hard to fly in unseen," Smyth said. "Drug dealers have been doing it for decades."

"Any clue as to this worst Indian that ever lived?" Mai asked.

"Not from DC, and if our rivals know they're keeping the lid on it."

"Bollocks."

Drake checked the time and knew they were nearing the States. Gently, he shook Alicia awake.

"Wah?"

"Time to wake up."

Kenzie leaned in close. "I have your bottle ready, baby."

Alicia flapped at her. "Shit, fuck! Get that thing away from me!"

"It's only me!"

Alicia pulled away as far as the bulkhead would allow. "Bloody circus clown fizzog."

"What's a fizzog?" Kinimaka looked genuinely interested.

"It's English for 'face,'" Drake said. And in response to Kenzie's apparent downheartedness he said, "I don't agree. You're a reet bobby dazzler."

"Really?" Alicia growled.

"A *what?*"

"Means you're not bad to look at, love."

Kenzie frowned as Alicia began to snarl and Drake realized he'd probably overstepped the mark with both women. Well, at least with Kenzie. Quickly, he nodded at Lauren.

"No way. Are you *sure?*"

Attention switched to the New Yorker.

"Oh yeah, I'm sure." Lauren was quick enough to cover her surprise and jump straight on the comms for an update. "Give me something."

Immediately, as if by fate, some good news came back. Lauren put it on speaker. "Hey people, good to see we're all still kickin'." Mr. Obnoxious back on the line. "Well, the good news is whilst you boys have been getting your share of zees, I've been slaving away over a red hot computer. So, first the second Horseman and Conquest. Miss Jaye? The big dogs are barking."

Hayden shook her head. "Speak American, asshole, or I'll have you fired."

Drake glanced across, knowing she was still playing for time. At the end of the day the linchpin code was in their possession and the Americans knew it. A thought struck him then and he signaled for her to join him at the back of plane.

Together, quietly, they huddled.

"Would it be possible to simply *lose* one of the sheets?" he asked. "The crucial one."

She stared. "Sure, if you wanna paint a target on us. They're not that stupid."

He shrugged. "I know, but look at the alternative."

Hayden sat back. "Well, I guess we're already fucked. What harm could one more act of insubordination cause?"

"Let's ask SEAL Team 7 when they get here."

The two stared at each other for a while, both wondering just what exactly the other team's orders were. The secrecy of it all worried them. Hayden heard the obnoxious man start to speak again and turned.

"Agent Jaye, Washington wants to know the exact details of the Conquest box."

"Tell them I'll get back to them."

"Umm, really? Okay."

"Do you have anything new?"

"Yeah, yeah, we do. Give me a sec."

Hayden turned back to Drake. "Decision time, Matt. All the way in?"

Drake rocked back on his heels and offered a grin. "Always."

Hayden plucked a sheet of paper from the pile.

"You already found the right sheet?"

"I thought of this two hours ago."

"Ah."

Together, and without another second of agonizing, they destroyed a crucial clue in the linchpin chain. Hayden then tucked all the sheets back together and deposited them back in the Order's box. The rest of the team eyed them both without comment.

Together, they were as one.

"All right." The man from DC had returned. "Now we are well and truly cooking on gas. It seems the Order of the Last Judgment were spot on with their descriptions of the third Horseman—Famine. The Worst Indian Who Ever Lived and that he's surrounded by guns."

"A Native American?" Kinimaka asked.

"Oh yeah, born in 1829; that's seven hundred years after Genghis Kahn and fourteen hundred after Hannibal. Almost exactly . . ." He paused.

"Odd," Kinimaka filled the gap.

"Maybe, maybe," the geek said. "Somebody once said there are no coincidences. Well, we'll see. Anyways, I've re-routed the plane and you're now headed for Oklahoma."

"Do we know who this old horseman might be?" Drake asked.

"I'd say he's the most *famous* Native American of all, not the worst, but what do I know?"

Alicia shifted, still half-dozing. "Not a whole goddamn lot."

"Why, thank you. Well, *Goyaale,* meaning 'the one that yawns', was a famous leader of the Apache tribe. They resisted the US and Mexicans throughout his lifetime, his raids becoming a terrible thorn in America's side."

"Many Native Americans did," Mai said.

"Of course, and rightly so. But this man was revered as a superb leader and strategist, the archetype of raiding and revenge warfare. Does that sound familiar?"

Drake nodded along. "Same as Hannibal and Genghis."

"You got it, kiddo. He surrendered three times and then broke out three times. They made several movies of his exploits. He was then treated as a prisoner of war and moved first to Fort Bowie along with many others."

"And he escaped again?" Alicia looked like she'd like to think so.

"No. In his old age, Geronimo became a celebrity."

"Ah, now I see," Drake said. "Along with Sitting Bull and Crazy Horse, he's probably the best known."

"Well, yeah, and did you know those three used to get together? Pow wow around the campfire. Plot this and that? Talk about choosing your favorite celebrity to go get a coffee with—I'd choose those three."

Alicia nodded. "It'd be an experience," she agreed. "Of course, assuming Depp and Boreanaz weren't free."

"In 1850? Probably not. But that Depp guy? He never seems to age, so who knows? Remember the story about medicine men that could shift their manitous—their spirits—through time? Anyways . . . Geronimo appeared at the 1904 World's Fair and several other lower key ones. The poor guy was never allowed to return to the land of his birth and died at Fort Sill, still a prisoner of war, in 1909. He's buried at the Fort Sill Indian Cemetery and surrounded by the graves of relatives and other Apache prisoners of war."

"Guns." Dahl said. "Braves."

"Yes, and the many guns of Fort Sill itself of course, which today serves as the United States Army Artillery School. It remains the *only* active fort of the southern plains which played a part in the so-called Indian Wars and has participated extensively in every major conflict since 1869." The geek paused before adding, "The Order chose this place and this horseman for a reason."

"Apart from the guns?" Dahl asked.

"Notoriety, too," came the reply. "Initial raid on the

Indian territories were led, from here, by Buffalo Bill and Wild Bill Hickok. The fort included the 10th Cavalry, also known as the Buffalo Soldiers."

"So, to recap." Dahl sighed. "Geronimo's grave is inside Fort Sill. The Order managed to secrete the plans to a devastating weapon inside it at least forty years ago and now half a dozen of the deadliest Special Forces teams on the planet are rushing headlong toward it."

Into the deep silence the geek said cheerily, "Yeah, man, cool stuff, eh?"

CHAPTER TWENTY FOUR

As the airplane banked into its final leg of the flight to Oklahoma, the team discussed what they knew so far—most of the revelations around the four corners of the earth, the Horsemen and the deadly weapons that the Nazi war criminals had buried inside old military leader's graves. The plot was vast, complex, and necessarily so—because the Order had wanted it to be viable for a hundred years. And even now, according to the text, the fourth Horseman was the 'true last judgment'.

In light of the weapons discovered so far, what the hell could that possibly be?

Drake pondered it. First, they had to get to Fort Sill and stop everyone getting their hands on the weapon of Famine. *And worry about others heading straight for the fourth Horseman—the Scourge of God. I mean . . . what kinda title is that?*

"Can I ask a question?" he said, as the plane began to descend.

"You already did," the geek guffawed, causing Hayden, Alicia and Mai to close their eyes, their patience worn.

"How did Geronimo come by his title?"

"Geronimo was a true fighter. Even on his deathbed he confessed his regret at his decision to surrender. His final words were: 'I should never have surrendered. I should have fought until I was the last man alive.' He also had nine wives, some simultaneously."

"But the worst Indian that ever lived?"

"During his military career Geronimo was famous for his daring escapades and innumerable escapes. He would disappear into caves that had no exit, later to be seen outside. He would win consistently, though always outnumbered. There is a place in New Mexico, to this day, known as Geronimo's Cave. One of the greatest stories involve him leading a small band of thirty eight men, women and children who were terribly hunted by thousands of American and Mexican troops for over a year. So, he became the most famous Native American of all time, and earned himself the title of 'the worst Indian that ever lived', among the white settlers of the time. Geronimo was one of the very last warriors to accept the United States' occupation of their lands."

"I was once called 'the worst bitch that ever lived,'" Alicia recalled wistfully. "Can't remember who by."

"Only once?" Kenzie asked. "That's odd."

"It was most likely me." Mai gave her a small smile.

"Or me," Drake said.

Dahl looked like he was wracking his brains. "Well, I think I remember . . ."

"Fort Sill," the pilot said. "Ten minutes out. We have clearance to land and the area is hot."

Drake frowned as he made ready. "Hot? Is he reading from a redacted script, or what?"

"Must be eighty down there." Kinimaka stared out a very small window.

"I think he means—troubled," Yorgi spoke up. "Or under attack."

"Nah, he's referring to its status," Smyth told them. "Highly prepared."

The plane touched down and came to a swift stop. Almost immediately, the rear cargo doors began to open. The team, already stretching and on their feet, hurried out into the sunshine which glared hard off the asphalt. A chopper was waiting, which whisked them away toward the grounds of

Fort Sill. As they flew in, a Fort Sill colonel apprised them of the situation.

"We're on full alert here. Got every gun prepped, armed and aimed. Geronimo's gravesite too, and we're ready to roll."

"We're five out." Hayden said. "Coming in hard on the gravesite. I'm sure you're aware of all potential hostiles."

"I've been fully prepped, ma'am. This is a United States Army site, a Marine Corps site, as well as a home to Air Defense and the Fires Brigade. Believe me when I tell you we have all our angles covered."

Hayden signed off and watched Fort Sill appear below. Drake studied the area and made a final check of his weapons.

I bloody well hope so.

CHAPTER TWENTY FIVE

The atmosphere was electric, every soldier tense and expecting some kind of war. The team passed between wide brick pillars and moved among many gravestones, each one the resting place of a fallen hero. Geronimo's grave lay off the beaten track, and took them long added minutes to reach. Hayden led the way and Kinimaka brought up the rear.

Drake listened as he adjusted to his surroundings. The site of so many artillery battalions was never likely to be quiet, but today a man could almost hear a leaf blowing in a breath of wind. All around the base, men waited. They were prepared. The order had come down from on high to stand strong in the face of whatever was about to happen. The Americans would not lose face.

They walked a narrow, shale-strewn path, their boots crunching. It seemed peculiar to remain on high alert inside such a base, but the countries and teams they were up against were no doubt capable of anything.

Drake walked beside Lauren, who kept the team apprised of any new information.

"The French are still operational. Two of them for now, more on the way."

"Reports of a gunfight in Oklahoma City. Could be the Brits. No way to tell at this point."

And a reply: "Yes, we do have the Conquest weapon. It's right here. If you designate somebody on the base I'm sure we can hand it off."

Drake guessed they were probably safe from SEAL Team 7 inside here, at least. The simple fact that they'd been allowed into the United States and then the army site told him something was seriously amiss.

Who sent the SEALs?

Why?

Hayden pulled up then as their guide led them along another even narrower path. Presently he stopped before half a dozen markers.

"That one," he said, "is Geronimo's."

Of course, it was pretty much unmistakable. The marker was no ordinary gravestone, it was a cairn; a large, man-made pile of stones in the shape of a rough pyramid with a plaque mounted at the center, the name 'Geronimo' deliberately unambiguous. Incredibly old it was, and must have been spectacular in its time. It was flanked by the grave of his wife, Zi-yeh and his daughter, Eva Geronimo Godeley.

Drake felt a kind of spiritual reverence upon seeing the great warrior's grave, and knew the others felt the same. The man had been a soldier, at war mostly with the Mexicans and fighting for his family, his lands and his way of life. Yes, he had lost, just as Cochise and Sitting Bull and Crazy Horse had lost, but their names lived on through the years.

A small digger stood poised.

Hayden nodded at the base commander, who nodded to the digger driver. Soon, the large digger was at work, turning up huge chunks of soil and depositing them on the ground nearby. Drake was also aware of the desecration, and accusations that might be leveled at the military but the presence of so many soldiers nearby meant it was unlikely anyone would know. They would probably shut Fort Sill down from the public for a while.

How did the Order do this?

Interesting . . . all those years ago? Perhaps access was

easier back then. Hayden told the digger driver to take it easy as he delved, no doubt remembering Hannibal's shallow grave where no coffin had been buried. The team watched as the hole grew deeper and the mound of earth grew higher.

At last, the digger stopped and two men jumped into the hole to remove the last scraps of earth.

Drake inched toward the rim of the hole. Alicia stole along with him. Predictably, Kinimaka hung back, not wanting to end up at the bottom. The two men cleared earth from the top of the coffin and shouted up for lifting ropes to be attached to the digger's bucket. Soon, the coffin was rising slowly, and Drake took another look around.

Stoic, hard-faced individuals stood all around, and encircled the camp, he knew. It began to occur to him now that there would be no battle. Geronimo's coffin was deposited gently on the ground, small portions of rocks and soil falling away. Hayden looked over at the base commander who shrugged.

"Your party, Agent Jaye. My orders are to give you everything you need."

Hayden moved forward as one of the diggers prized open the lid of the coffin. The team came forward. The lid lifted surprisingly easily. Drake peered over top of the frame and into the box's depths.

To see one of the greatest surprises of his life.

Hayden pulled away, frozen for an instant; the mission forgotten, her life forgotten, her friends suddenly gone as her brain petrified.

No way . . .

It was an impossibility. Surely it was. But she dared not tear her eyes away.

Within the coffin, mounted on a titanium bracket, hung a

state-of-the-art digital screen and, as they stared, it burst into life.

Canned laughter burst from the speakers. Hayden and the others jerked backward, dumbstruck. The laughter echoed artificially from the advanced screen as a plethora of colors filled it—starburst after starburst mushrooming outward. The team started to recover and Drake turned to her.

"Is this the right . . . I mean . . . what the—"

Dahl stepped closer for a better look. "Is poor old Geronimo still here?"

Hayden pulled him away. "Careful! Don't you understand all the connotations of this?"

Dahl blinked. "It means somebody left us a screen instead of a box. You think it's the weapon?"

"The Order didn't leave this," Hayden said. "Not the Nazi war criminal part of it anyway. This means that the Order is—"

But then the laughter stopped.

Hayden froze, unsure what to expect. She stared down, ready to duck and cover. She moved in front of Lauren. She wished that Kinimaka, Drake and Dahl weren't so damned close. She . . .

A logo flashed up on the screen, bright red on black, no more than a slash of blood to her mind.

"That's the Order's logo," Alicia said.

I don't understand," Mai admitted. "How could they have put this screen in place? And how could it still function?"

"They didn't," Yorgi said.

The logo faded and Hayden banished all else from her mind. The black screen reappeared and an artificially-lowered voice began to grate from the speakers.

"Welcome to your nightmare, boys and girls," it said and then paused for a burst of canned laughter. "Famine greets you, and you have to know that the last two Horsemen are the worst of all. If Famine doesn't get you, Death will! Ha, ha. Ha, ha, ha."

Hayden took a moment to wonder what kind of a twisted mind and warped imagination came up with this shit.

"Straight to the point then. The third Horseman will destroy you all, rather than let you destroy each other. Famine does that, am I right?" the guttural tones went on. "And now that you've advanced into the electronic age it's going to move much, much faster. You ever hear of Strask Labs?"

Hayden frowned, sent a quick glance around and included the base commander. He nodded and was about to speak when the voice went on.

"They're one of the big conglomerates, hellbent on taking over the world. Power. Influence. Immense wealth, they want it all, and are starting to move into the big leagues. The American government recently took Strask Labs into its confidence."

What does that mean? Hayden wondered. *And how recently?*

"In Dallas, Texas, not far from here, Strask own a bio testing facility. They manufacture drugs, diseases, cures and weapons. They run the whole gamut. If there's a deadly infection out there, a world-killing virus, a canister of nerve gas or a new bio-weapon, Strask in Dallas have it. Literally," he grunted, "it's a one-stop shop."

Hayden wanted to stop it right there. This was going in a very bad direction.

"The bio lab has been targeted. Famine will be unleashed. Your crops and those around the world will wither and die. It is a manufactured poison, deliberately targeting a specific strain of crop and it cannot be stopped. We are the Order of the Last Judgment. And like I said, this is *your* nightmare."

The recording stopped. Hayden blinked and stared, the

world and her problems entirely forgotten. If the Order were targeting a bio lab who'd made a precise crop infection and were planning to wipe out all reserves, then . . .

It was possible. And probable. No doubt the disease would be targeted toward the soil too, so that no edible crops would ever grow again.

Then, suddenly, the screen exploded into life once more.

"Oh, and now we're in the electronic age let me tell you this. By opening this coffin, by starting this recording, you put the whole thing into motion—electronically!"

CHAPTER TWENTY SIX

Fort Sill exploded into action. The base commander screamed for a techie to come over and take apart the recording, the screen and anything else they might find inside the coffin. Hayden saw bundles of old clothing and bones at the bottom and had to assume the Order had simply placed the screen inside and left it for somebody to find. Could a signal have gone out, piggybacking off the base's Wi-Fi the moment they opened the coffin?

I have to believe so. The unsealing started the recording. Most likely, sensors were involved. Whoever did all this was tech savvy. Which threw up another question.

"Have we just jumped forward from Nazi war criminals operating fifty years in the past to right now?"

"I don't get it," Smyth said.

The team had backed away from Geronimo's grave to allow others to get involved and now stood in a group underneath some trees.

"I thought it was pretty clear," Hayden said. "The guy said we *are* the Order of the Last Judgment. They still exist."

The base commander strode over. "Okay people, we've double and treble-checked our perimeter. No signs of your Special Forces enemies. Looks like they gave this one a clear miss, and I done blame them. Lots of firepower here." He indicated the soldiers stood around the fort.

"That doesn't mean the signal that came out of that grave wasn't broadcast elsewhere too," Lauren pointed out. "Any number of people might have seen it in one form or another."

"Whilst that is true," the commander nodded, "there ain't

a whole lot we can do about it. Now what we *can* do, is call Strask Labs and give those boys the proverbial heads up."

He indicated a man close by, already with a phone to his ear.

Hayden knew she should call Secretary Crowe but held off as the soldier's call went through on loudspeaker, the endless ringing tone making the SPEAR team glance worriedly around.

"This a twenty-four-hour manned laboratory," the base commander said. "On call to the military and the White House. I cannot impress how bad this is." He indicted the ringing phone.

"You don't need to." Hayden said. "Can you liaise with the local authorities? Get them to Strask and tell them we're on the way."

"Right away, Agent Jaye."

Hayden started sprinting for the chopper. "We have to get to Dallas! *Now!*"

CHAPTER TWENTY SEVEN

Karin took, what was for her, an immeasurable amount of time before even showing the flash drive to a computer terminal. She was well aware that somebody of Tyler Webb's wealth and reach could have installed all manner of tech on his computer—especially the one containing every dirty little secret he'd garnered through the years.

So here she was.

A girl. A computer. A flash drive.

How many names have they monickered me with in the past? Data Girl. Web Head. HacKaz. Long ago, far away, but still relevant.

Dino and Wu stood looking on, surveillance around the house already as good as it was ever going to get. They had sensors at every approach, and plans with backup strategies for both hard and soft evac situations. All three soldiers were currently at a low ebb—battered, bruised, healing slowly from the San Francisco jaunt. They were also hot, hungry and lacking funds. On Karin's guarantee, they had gambled everything on this. Right from the very beginning.

"Time to prove your worth," she said.

The early years never left her, the long duration she'd turned her back on the world. Self-destruction was one way to redemption.

"We believe in you," Dino said.

She smiled grimly as she inserted the flash drive and watched the large screen. She'd designed everything to work as fast as it was able and now there was absolutely no lag as a prompt flashed up onto the screen:

Continue?

Damn right.

She sat down and got to work. The keyboard rattled, her fingers flashed, the screen flickered. She didn't expect to find or even understand it all immediately—there were many gigabytes of information—and that was why she'd made everything as ultra-secure as she possibly could before booting the drive up. She'd also prepped several offshore accounts and a couple of Los Angeles based ones, where they may be able to deposit some quick cash. Of course, she remembered everything from her time at SPEAR; it was what had happened since Webb's death that may throw a wrench into the works.

Ignoring the bland but ominous title *Documents* for now and focusing on *Finance*, she made her fingers and the screen a whirlwind of information. Dino gasped as she fought to keep up.

"Sheeyit, and I thought I was a whiz at Sonic. I bet you get that prickly little fucker shooting all over the place, eh?"

"You know Sonic? From the Master System or the Mega Drive? Aren't we all a bit young for that?"

Dino looked blank. "PlayStation, dude. And retro is better."

Karin shook her head, forced to smile. "Oh yeah, that's totally retro, dude."

Delving into the finance file, she soon brought up account numbers, sort codes and key commands. She found source banks, most of them offshore. She found over seventy five different accounts.

"Unbelievable."

Dino pulled up a chair. "Yeah, I have trouble keeping track of two. And they're both empty!"

Karin knew she didn't have the time to investigate every account. She needed to whittle it down and cherry-pick the best. Cleverly, she'd already written a simple program that would trawl through a file and highlight the accounts with the highest numbers. She unleashed it now and waited five seconds.

The three flashing blue bars looked promising.

"Let's have a look at you."

The first account flashed up. It was based in the Caymans, unused, and showed a balance of thirty thousand dollars. Karin blinked. *You have to be joking!* She'd been aware that Webb had cut ties at the end in his reckless quest for the treasures of Saint Germain—he'd gone it alone and used massive funds to stay out of sight and enlist an army near the end, he'd paid off thousands to call in every last favor—but she hadn't expected his accounts to be this badly depleted.

In any case, she quickly sent the thirty thousand to a local LA bank account she'd already set up.

Risky, but if we're quick we can withdraw and take the cash. If anyone was monitoring the account, which seemed unlikely given its low balance, they should be able to make it happen before they caught on.

She moved on to the next account, saw a balance of eighty thousand dollars, and had to admit that was better. But nothing like the millions she'd been expecting. At her side, Dino remained silent. She took the cash and held her breath as she clicked on to the final account.

Bloody hell. Fifteen thousand?

She was forced to run through the remaining accounts, netting by the end a sum of around one hundred and thirty thousand dollars. It wasn't bad, but it wasn't lifelong security type money. This was taking time, and she was wary of staying plugged in any longer, but the scarcity of the pickings so far made the next step a necessity.

"Blackmail fodder," she said.

"I ain't comfortable with that," Dino said.

"Depends who it is," Karin pointed out. "And what they've done. We can expose the properly evil bastards—maybe through some kind of new, dedicated website—and discuss what we might do to those that could stand to lose a few quid."

Wu shook his head. "What?"

"A few *dollars*. Centarinos. Wonga. Shit, where do we start?"

The new file contained pages and pages of names, each highlighted in bold and accompanied by a photo and date. Karin scrolled down the list. "Right, well, they're in alphabetical order. That's something, at least. Any preferences?"

"I don't know any rich guys," Dino said. "Let alone any to blackmail."

"I recognize some of those names," Wu said as Karin scrolled steadily from A-C. "Celebs. Sports stars. TV personalities. Jeez, who was this Webb guy?"

"Who was he?" Karin felt the hatred rekindle. "One of the worst, creepiest and most altogether powerful creatures that ever lived. Evil incarnate, with the influence to touch any life on the planet."

"I could name a couple of those right now," Dino said.

"Yeah, so could anyone. But those are exactly the assholes whose radars we want to stay underneath."

Karin checked her system's firewalls, looked for any early warning signals that someone else was sniffing around. Nothing presented itself, but she wasn't conceited enough to believe somebody out there wasn't a whole lot smarter than she.

"Check the entire place," she said, removing the flash drive. "We need to monitor everything for a day or so from site B. Then, we'll see."

*

It was all part of her careful set up. If anything did go wrong and they were seen, captured or killed it wouldn't be through lack of preparation. Karin had used every trick in her considerable arsenal and every ounce of her immense intellect to safeguard them.

And my plan. My tiny retribution.

Dino, Wu and she removed themselves from their house in the desert and retired to a small shack they'd found in the middle of nowhere. It had taken weeks of methodical searching, but once found it proved the ideal place to act as a backup hideaway. Wu spent twenty four hours watching the house through CCTV. Karin and Dino drove to LA, withdrew a stash of money and deposited what remained elsewhere, whilst periodically testing her network's firewalls, its toughness, and the state it was in. Again and again she saw no sign that it had been tested in any way.

Methodical and careful, though; this was the only way they would stay free.

It was a whole thirty hours later when they returned to the house. More checks, and then Karin was ready to work on the flash drive once more.

"Checked the cameras?" she asked.

"Yeah, just do it."

It took just a few seconds and then, once more, she was scrolling through the list of names. After C of course, came D.

There was no Matt Drake listed.

But there was a separate section for SPEAR. Drake's name was on the list. So was Alicia Myles. Hayden Jaye and Mano Kinimaka she'd expected. She saw Bridget McKenzie—no surprise. Lancelot Smyth? Hmmm. Mai Kitano. Lauren Fox. Yorgi. Interestingly there was no link to Torsten Dahl.

But there was a link to Karin Blake.

She stared at it for a moment, then chose to ignore it for

now. Other links associated with the SPEAR team and added to the foot of the front page were those belonging to Kimberly Crowe, the Secretary of Defense; Nicholas Bell, the prisoner; and a whole sub menu entitled *Family/Friends*.

Holy shit, this guy really went to town on them.

Good.

The first click just had to be on the name: *Matt Drake*.

Her gaze flickered, flinched and then started to widen; her eyes widened to the size of saucers.

"Fuck me," she whispered fearfully. "Oh. Fuck. Me."

CHAPTER TWENTY EIGHT

Matt Drake saw the Strask Laboratories sign long before they reached the place. On the outskirts of Dallas, it was still a tall building and its blue and white stylized 'S' logo was mounted near the very top of the structure. Their vehicles were moving fast though, and soon he saw the whole area opening up ahead.

Strask Labs looked unimportant, bland, a stick in a field of sticks, and that no doubt was the idea. Its windows were impenetrable, but many were. Its car park was covered by a nest of CCTV cameras, but it was that kind of world. No one could tell just how advanced the cameras were, or how far they ranged. There was no gate other than a flimsy barrier. No security visible at all.

"Any answer yet?" Dahl asked.

Hayden pinched the bridge of her nose. "Dead silence," was all she said.

Drake studied the landscape. The parking area made an L-shape around the building, front and east. To the west was a steep grassy embankment. No fence. The whole area was open plan. A network of roads ran around it, and dozens of smaller office buildings, warehouses and a strip-mall made up the immediate prospect.

"Police," Dahl said.

The DPD were already on site, parked outside the area along the side of the road. Hayden told their drivers to park up alongside, and jumped out.

Drake was quick to follow.

"You guys seen anything? Anything at all?" Hayden asked.

A tall bewhiskered officer looked up. "What you see is what we got, ma'am. We were instructed to watch and not take action."

Hayden cursed. "So we have no idea what we're walking into. Just a madman's promise that it's about as bad as it gets."

Alicia shrugged. "Hey, what's new?"

"If they have a bio-weapon in there, or a bio-device specifically engineered to target our crops then we don't have a choice," Dahl said.

"And how do you suggest we get inside?"

"Head on and head first," Dahl said with a smile. "Is there any other way?"

"Not for us," Drake said. "You ready?"

"Shit," Alicia mumbled. "I really hope you two aren't about to hold hands."

Hayden asked for the items they'd requested and handed them out. Drake took his gas mask and slipped it on. No chances would be taken at the lab.

Drake then slipped down the grassy embankment, and hopped over a gully at the bottom and into the parking area. About forty cars were dotted about, everyday runners in varying stages of age and cleanliness. Nothing out of the ordinary. Dahl jogged at his side, Alicia and Mai to the right. They were fully prepared and guns were at the ready. Drake was expecting the worst, but so far all that had greeted them was an ominous silence.

"You think word did get out to the other teams?" Kinimaka was staring around the perimeter. "If some of those countries get wind that such a bio-weapon is here and vulnerable in this lab we could face an attack. And Strask is far less protected than Fort Sill."

"Other teams?" Lauren sighed through the comms. "I'm worried the Order's recording was broadcast without restriction. And that the shitstorm might well and truly be on its way."

Kinimaka's mouth turned into a large circle. "Ooooh."

Drake and Dahl pushed on, threading through cars and keeping a watch on all the windows. Nothing moved. No alarms were sounding inside. They reached the walkways that led to the front lobby, and saw even these smaller windows were obscured.

"If I delivered here," Dahl said. "I'd guess straight away that this was no normal lab."

"Aye, mate. A nice pretty little reception is always best."

Dahl jiggled the door handles, and looked surprised. "Unlocked."

Drake waited for the team and Hayden's order. "Go."

Gas mask restricting his vision, he watched as Dahl threw the doors wide open and then slipped inside. Drake's leveled his new HK, searching for enemies. The first thing they saw were bodies lying next to the reception desk and in the hallways behind.

"Quick." Dahl ran to the first, covered by Alicia. Mai ran to the second, covered by Drake. The Swede checked quickly for a pulse.

"Thank God," he said. "She's alive."

"This one too," Mai affirmed, and pulled the victim's eyelid open. "I think he's been drugged. Sleeping gas, or whatever fancy term they call it."

Hayden carried a gas, vapor and fume detector. "It's something along those lines. Not toxic. Not deadly. Something light to put them to sleep, perhaps?"

"Weaponized vodka," Alicia said, her voice distorted by the mask. "That'd do it."

Kenzie looked over at her, shaking her head slowly.

"What you looking at, Bridget?"

"Well at least with that mask on I *can* look at you without needing to throw up."

"The gas must have been fast-acting with full coverage," Hayden said. "How the hell did they do it?"

"Vents," Lauren said. "Heating system, air con, that kind of thing. There may be some scientists locked in their labs somewhere though. Considering the type of facility this is, not every lab or storage unit will be connected to the main hub."

"Okay," Hayden said. "Then *why*? What have they gained by putting all the staff to sleep?"

A new voice broke into their conversation, not through the comms system but over some kind of loudspeaker system that probably covered the entire building.

"You're here? And the others? Oh, good. We can begin in around twelve seconds then."

Drake spun swiftly, watching the door. Lauren's voice broke across the comms like a tidal wave.

"Incoming! Israelis, I think. Breaching right now. And the Swedes!"

"If ever there was a place *not* to have a gun battle . . ." Alicia pointed out.

The gunfire had already started; the Dallas cops no doubt drawing on the infiltrators. Despite that, the attack came incredibly fast. Drake was already walking along the corridor and keying his comms, asking for the emergency override code that would open most of the interior doors. At this point, beyond the first set of doors, a large bank of windows exploded, grenades making short work of the triple-glazing. Drake saw razor sharp splinters imploding in a deadly, unstoppable wave, spilling through rooms. Shards embedded into every surface. Interior partitions and office windows also smashed or wilted. Drake aimed his gun at the doors.

Lauren's voice: "Two, three, five, eight, seven."

Quickly, he input the override code, then ran through, followed by the rest of the team. There were bodies everywhere, knocked out by the sleeping gas.

"Are we safe to remove the masks?" he asked.

Hayden had been monitoring the air quality. "I don't recommend it. Yes, it's now clear but whoever introduced the gas could do it again."

"With worse," Dahl added.

"Dammit."

Drake opened fire as he saw masked figures entering. Five at once, so that was probably the Russians, making free with their bullets and indifferent to whom they hurt along the way. Drake hit one on the vest, the others scattered.

"I think we can safely say the Russian team isn't government sanctioned. No government in their right mind would go along with this."

Kinimaka grunted. "We're talking about the Russians here, bud. Hard to say."

"And if they thought they could get away with it," Kenzie said. "The Israelis too."

Drake took cover behind a desk. The partitioning all around inside this inner maze of offices was flimsy at best. They should keep moving.

He waved Alicia and Mai past. "Lauren," he said. "Do we know where the bio-weapon is?"

"Not yet. But the info is coming."

Drake made a face. Bloody bureaucrats were probably weighing the cost of lives versus revenue. Hayden pushed past. "Go deeper," she said. "It'll be this way."

The Russians strafed the inner offices. Bullets shredded fiberglass paneling, sending the panels crashing down and aluminum struts tumbling everywhere. Drake kept his head down. Hayden crawled onward.

Drake glanced between debris. "Can't get a bead on them."

Dahl sat at a different vantage point. "I can." He fired a shot; a man fell over, but Dahl shook his head grimly.

"Vest. Still five strong."

Lauren broke over the comms. "Just a snippet of info, people. The command that released the sleeping agent definitely came from *inside* the building."

"Understood," Hayden said. "Lauren, where are the Swedes?"

Silence, then, "Judging by the way they came in I'd say on the other side of the building coming right at you."

"Crap, then we need to reach the center point first. Assuming that's the way down to the sub levels, Lauren?"

"Yeah, but we don't know where the bio-weapon is yet."

"It's down there," Hayden said. "They'd have to be stupid to keep it anywhere else."

Drake nodded over at Dahl. "You okay?"

"Of course. But, like you said earlier, no government would sanction this attack."

"Now you're thinking the Swedes are operating independently?"

Dahl frowned, but said nothing. Anything was possible at this point, and the new revelation that the Order may still be operating, updated to a modern infrastructure, also threw question marks across the page. *Just how many steps ahead of us are they?*

And the fourth? If Famine doesn't get you, Death will!

Drake rolled. Kinimaka crept toward the back edge of the office and hugged the outer wall, followed by Smyth as they converged on the inner hub. Hayden, Mai and Yorgi went straight through the middle. Drake fired shot after shot to keep the Russians pinned down. Kenzie crab-walked among them, gripping her gun but looking glum nonetheless. Poor thing was missing her katana.

Drake reached the end of the open-plan office area. Hayden was already there, surveying the open space that led to an elevator bank and another large area of offices beyond. Somewhere in there, were the Swedes.

"I hate to keep giving you bad news," Lauren said in their ears. "But the Israelis just breached too. It's a war zone out here. You're goddamn lucky you're in *there*."

Now Kenzie came back. "I highly doubt the Israelis are government endorsed. But I do believe they're Special Forces. Don't you have backup?"

"On its way. A boatload of it. I have no idea how these teams expect to get away afterward."

"Don't you believe it," Kenzie said. "There's always a way. You need to start securing the victims in here. Getting them the help they need."

Hayden came back. "Sorry, I can't agree to that yet. We don't know what we're dealing with. We don't know if the Order can release anything more deadly."

"Isn't that a reason to get them out?"

"The Order may be wanting us to do exactly that. Open the doors."

"Umm, dude," Alicia drawled. "Some twat already opened the windows."

Hayden thought about it. "Shit, you're right, but that makes it all worse. What if the Order's ploy is to release something lethal across Dallas?"

Drake glared at the elevators. "We need to know where that fucking bio-weapon is."

Bullets exploded from the Russian contingent, making a papier-mâché of various panels. Office implements jumped into the air: a set of pencils, a telephone, a whole ream of paper.

The team hit the ground.

Lauren's voice was barely heard. "Sub Level Four, Lab 7. That's where it is. Hurry!"

CHAPTER TWENTY NINE

Using the bank of elevators as a shield from the Swedes, the SPEAR team fired a non-stop volley at the Russians as they sped toward the steel doors. Hayden and Yorgi were freed up whilst Kinimaka and Smyth kept an eye open for the Swedes and the rest of the team concentrated on the Russians.

Hayden punched the button marked SL4.

If the elevators dinged, the sound was lost under the heavy gunfire. Drake kept low, but the enemy still managed to return fire and creep forward, coming around desk after desk and using the sturdier objects to shelter behind. Even then one man fell, shot through the head. Another shouted in pain as he was winged, and yet another was wounded in the leg. Still, they came.

The lights flashed above the metal doors and then they whooshed open. Hayden jumped inside, the rest of the team following. It was a tight fit, but they managed it.

Drake was crushed up against Dahl, the HK between them.

Alicia was chin-first against his back. "Who the hell is that behind me? With the wandering fingers?"

"That's me." Kenzie puffed as the tight space constricted them, leaving no room for movement as it sped down to Sub Level Four. "But my hands are trapped near my neck. Surprisingly, my fingers are there too." She waggled them.

Alicia felt the movement. "Well, somebody has something pressed into my ass. And it ain't a banana."

"Oh, that's probably me," Yorgi said. "Well, it's my pistol."

Alicia raised an eyebrow. "Your pistol, huh?"

"My gun. My handgun, is what I mean."

"Is it fully loaded?"

"Alicia . . ." Drake warned.

"Umm, yes it should be."

"I'd best not move then. Don't want it going off in such a tight space now, do we?"

Mercifully, just as Kenzie looked like she was about to send out a pithy reply, the elevator stopped and made its arrival sound. The doors opened and the team practically fell out into the corridor. Drake searched the walls for a sign. Of course, there was none.

"Where's Lab 7?"

"Turn right, third door along," Lauren said.

"Excellent."

Dahl led the way, still careful, but looking confident. The threat was largely above, but Drake didn't forget for one second the reason they were here. The Order of the Last Judgment. What else did they have planned?

Yorgi removed his mask, grabbing some air. Kenzie joined him, flouting the rules, and then Smyth followed suit, giving Hayden a blank stare when she spread her arms helplessly.

"Rebels," Dahl said, still walking.

"I'd say rogues," Kenzie said. "Sounds better."

She moved up beside him.

"If I weren't so well disciplined I'd bloody join you."

"Don't worry. We can work on that."

Drake nudged her in the back. "You know he went to a private school, don't you, Kenz? You'll never break him."

"Mossad have their ways."

Dahl glanced back over his shoulder. "Will you two shut up? I'm trying to concentrate."

"See what I mean?" Drake said.

"Concentrate on what?" Alicia asked. "Numbers one to four?"

"Here we are," Dahl said. "Lab 7."

"You count up all that way yourself, Torsty? Wait, I think I have a sticker somewhere."

Hayden pushed her way to the front. "Formation, people. Watch the back. Watch the elevators, both banks. I need Lauren on the comms, talking me to the bio-weapon, and I need the lab secure. Think you can do that?"

Without pause, they parted and took up their positions. Drake and Hayden were left to enter the lab on their own. First, they entered an outer office, littered with paraphernalia, every available surface cluttered with all manner of instruments. Drake had no idea what they were but they looked vital, and expensive.

Beyond a glass wall lay an inner, secure room.

"Lauren," he said. "Lab 7 consists of two rooms. Outer and inner. The inner is probably a control room for chemicals, capable of being sealed off and vented."

Nothing. The comms were dead.

Drake stared at Hayden. "What the—"

"Sorry, Matt. Hayden. Labs are always frequency shielded so signals can't get in and out. Lab 7 is on a different level to the rest of the facility and it took us a moment to turn the extra shielding off."

"No worries," Hayden said. "Where next?"

"Inner room. There should be a glass cabinet. Do you see it?"

Drake went over to the large glass wall. "Yep. Right in the far corner."

"The bio-weapon obviously doesn't look like a weapon. It should be stored in a canister about the size of a coffee flask. It can be identified by the code PD777. Got that?"

"Got it." He went over to the door's key code panel and typed in the override code. "Nothing." He sighed. "Could this room have a different code?"

"Let me find out. Problem is, all the bosses, techs and lab people are in there with you, sleeping."

"Not to mention the Russians, Swedes and Israelis. Be quick."

Drake listened as Hayden checked with the team. All was quiet, eerily so. Then Smyth growled through his coms.

"Movement on the eastern staircase. Here they come!"

"I got movement on the western one," Mai reported. "Hurry."

"Hold those elevators," Hayden said. "We're gonna need them real soon."

Drake considered shooting the glass. No doubt it would be bulletproof and potentially dangerous. There were glass cabinets in the outer room too, stocked with tubes and canisters that might contain any number of poisons.

Lauren shouted out a new code. Drake punched it in. The door swung open. He ran for the back of the room, slipped open the cabinet and started searching for the canister. Hayden stayed behind. Watching their backs, each team member keeping line of sight with the next.

Drake sifted through canister after canister. Each one bore an imprint in black, bold letters and numbers, and they weren't organized. A minute passed. Smyth opened fire up his staircase and Mai did the same a few seconds later. They were under attack, praying nobody was idiotic enough to send a grenade into the fray.

"Got it!"

He lifted the canister, took half a second to remember it contained a bio-weapon that could destroy at the very least—America, and tucked it under one arm. "Time to go."

As one, coordinated, they began the retreat. Mai and Smyth covered the stairs until Drake and Hayden reached the corridor and then Yorgi and Dahl covered them. Mai and Smyth retreated fast as Alicia pressed the elevators' button.

Doors whooshed instantly open.

"Faster!" Mai shouted, appearing fast around a corner. "They're seconds behind me."

She fired back, pinning them down.

Smyth came the other way, shielded now by Dahl, both men backpedalling for the doors.

And then the alarms began to sound, a huge claxon-like booming that filled the ears and sent the senses into overdrive.

"What the fuck is that?" Drake shouted.

"No. Oh no!" Lauren screamed back. "Get out of there. Get out of there now! They just released something into the system." She paused. "Oh my God . . . it's sarin."

It was already flooding through the roof vents of the corridor and the side vents of the elevator.

CHAPTER THIRTY

Drake quelled the initial surge of fear at the mention of the name sarin. He knew it was deadly. Knew it was considered a weapon of mass destruction. He knew Smyth, Yorgi and Kenzie had taken their masks off.

And he saw how what was said to be a colorless, odorless liquid seeped through the vents.

"I never doubted they stored sarin here." Hayden jumped at Yorgi. "But this . . ." She grappled with his mask.

Drake knew almost anything could be manipulated, engineered or generally re-imagined. The only limit was the imagination. A liquid nerve agent was infinitely pliable. Now he went hard for Kenzie, but saw Alicia and Mai were already there. They had the Israeli's mask on, but her eyes were already closed, her body slumping.

Sarin could kill in one to ten minutes depending on the dose.

"No," Drake said. "No, no, no."

Smyth slid down the side of the lift, already unconscious before Dahl managed to jam his mask fully over his face.

The elevator shot up, back to the ground floor.

"What do we do?" Hayden shouted over the comms. "How long do they have?"

"Who?" Lauren reacted naturally. "Who's hurt?"

"Just get a goddamn lab rat or a doctor and tell us what to do!"

Kinimaka hefted Smyth over one shoulder as the doors swept open. Drake saw him about to rush out, then threw himself out first, knowing the Hawaiian had probably forgotten about the waiting Swedes, Russians and Israelis.

Immediately he could see what looked like a faint steam leaking through all the high-level vents. His heart dropped. "It's been released up here too."

"The whole facility," Lauren said. "I have a lab technician right here."

"Don't need him," Kinimaka breathed. "We need atropine. Where's the fucking atropine?"

A new voice came on the line. "How many people infected? And to what level?"

Drake swept the area, ran for cover, weapon aimed. Alicia backed him up. Movement ahead made them pause.

"Fuck that!" Hayden cried. "We have three of our own and dozens of people already unconscious in the lab. You have to get in here with an antidote, and you have to do it now!"

"Sarin *is* deadly," the man said. "But it can take an hour to kill. We're on our way, believe me. We were prepared for this. Tell me, are the victims having difficulty breathing?"

Drake looked back. Hayden took a moment to check. "Yeah," she said with a catch in her throat. "Yeah, they are."

Drake saw Dahl now move over to Kenzie, gently remove her from Alicia and cradle her in his arms. He stared straight at Kinimaka. Nobody else. Nowhere else. The world was gone and only one thing remained in the Swede's conscience.

"Mano. What do we do?"

The big Hawaiian sniffed. "Atropine, and an auto-injector."

The voice responded immediately. "Med bays are situated on every floor. Several antidotes are included in each bay and atropine is one of them. You'll find auto-injectors there too. Just stab it into a thigh muscle."

"I know what to do!"

Drake waited for the lab tech to tell Kinimaka where to go then led the way. No sneaking, no dodging behind tables;

this time they went heads up and balls out, holding their fallen friends, daring any rogue nation to be stupid enough to take them on. The floor was still littered with bodies, only now those sleeping forms were curled up, wracked with pain, some already shuddering.

The front doors were destroyed. Men wearing masks and suits rushed in.

Drake kicked a chair aside and then spied the med bay in one corner of the room. He sprinted. A Russian body lay to the right, clad in Kevlar, the one they'd shot. Two more lay next to it; convulsing and dying. The sarin hit them hard too. The release of the chemical had effectively stopped the battle, and SPEAR still held the bio-weapon.

Hayden forged ahead, not holding a weapon, and wrenched the med bay door open. Inside, a dozen ampoules faced them, all full of glistening liquids. They were clearly marked, and Kinimaka bellowed at the atropine; Mai pulled out an auto-injector and filled it. Kinimaka jammed the needle into Smyth's face just a few seconds before Dahl did the same to Kenzie. Alicia and Mai handled Yorgi and then the team sat back on their haunches, exhausted, numb, scared that the hope that filled their hearts now felt so desperate.

Minutes passed. Drake turned to Kinimaka. "What happens now?"

"Well, atropine blocks the effects of sarin. They should come around."

"Watch for side effects," the lab tech said. "Hallucinations, mostly. But dizziness, nausea, blurred vision . . ."

"Don't worry," Alicia said. "All of that's nothing worse than a pub lunch for Team SPEAR."

"Dry mouth. Fast heart rate . . ."

"Yup."

Still more minutes passed and Drake stared helplessly at

Yorgi's face, wishing a hundred times a second that some life would flood back into it. Hayden asked the tech if they could flood the sarin out of the system and allow everyone to remove their masks but the situation was barely under control. Whoever released the sarin still might have other plans.

"We're in the system too now," Lauren assured them. "The FBI brought some high-level computer geeks down who've been poking around for a while."

"Any news on the other Special Ops teams?" Hayden asked.

"We think so. Just getting confirmation. It's all a bit of a muddle in there."

Drake tapped Yorgi's cheek, to the right of his mask. "Tell me about it."

The Russian moved slightly, raising his arms. His eyes fluttered open and he stared unseeing, straight at Drake. He coughed, tried to remove his mask, but Drake kept it in place. Atropine or no atropine, it was best to leave nothing to chance. Smyth struggled too and then Kenzie; Dahl breathed a long, audible sigh of relief. The team took the chance to share a brief, weak smile.

"Let's get them out into the air," Hayden said. "We're done here today."

Lauren came back on the comms. "They're okay? All of them?" She still had no idea who had been infected.

"So far so good, love," Drake said. "Could do with a doc to check 'em over though."

"We have a dozen out here."

"Coming to you now," Hayden said.

The team reformed and helped each other out of the front doors. Hayden clutched the bio-weapon to her chest, unsure even now who she could trust. She posed the question to Lauren across the comms.

"It needs taking to a safe facility in Dallas," Lauren said. "I have the details here. They're waiting for you."

Hayden stared over at Drake, eyes weary behind the mask.

It never ends.

Drake knew exactly what she was thinking. By the time they reached the ambulance set-up, removed their masks and found Lauren though, they were already starting to feel a little refreshed. Drake found pleasure in being brought a hot coffee and Alicia bleated for a bottle of water. Mai took it away from her, drank, then offered her a sip from the used bottle.

Kenzie reached up, grabbed it away from Mai, and sighed. "Why do I see four of you?"

Alicia reclaimed the water. "Still alive then? Hey, does this count as a three-way?"

Drake had been watching. "Y'know something? I'll know when it's time to quit this job when you two stop trying to wind each other up. *That's* when I'll retire."

Lauren left Smyth's side for a moment as a barrage of information came across her central comms system. This would include messages from the obnoxious guy in DC, the local Dallas operation and, to a lesser extent, the Secretary of Defense.

She waved for the group to listen up before remembering she could use the comms. "Hey, ah, well, hi. I'm gonna give you the address in Dallas and you should get on your way. The longer that bio-weapon stays loose the greater the danger. Now, we have a little bit of clarification. It seems the initial sleeping agent which was introduced to affect almost everyone working in the lab was triggered by a redundant code as soon as you opened Geronimo's coffin. It seems they think the cult may now *not* still exist, but at least one person might still be working for them. The sarin was also triggered by the same code and no doubt by the same person. An insider? Maybe. But don't forget we had to take down the lab's shields so a signal could have gotten in."

"You need to check for people leaving before the sleeping agent did its work," Hayden said.

"On it. But there's more. Bodies have been counted." She took a breath. "Our lab people and innocent civilian have fared well. They all seem to be responding to the atropine. It's assumed, since they were asleep on the floor, that they received only weak doses, and help came quick. Now, the IDs are hard, but since we knew the positions of the Russians and Swedes we have to assume we're correct. Three Russians dead, two missing. Two Swedes dead, one missing. And three Israelis dead, two missing."

"They didn't get atropine?" Dahl asked worriedly.

"Sure they did, but after the civilians. And it did hit them more aggressively."

By now, Smyth, Yorgi and Kenzie were on their feet, looking refreshed and hungry for action. Drake wondered if it might be one of the aforementioned side effects.

"Yorgi," he said. "Look at Alicia. What do you see?"

The Russian smirked. "Ice cream and hot chilies?"

Drake grinned. "He's fine."

Alicia frowned hard. "What the hell does that mean. Yogi? Yogi? C'mon, mate. You know I love you, but if you don't spill I'm gonna have to kill you."

Drake pulled her away toward the waiting cars. "Well done, love, you just proved his point."

CHAPTER THIRTY ONE

Speed was their choice, their savior, their God, and their best way to stay alive right now.

They had no illusions about what might await them on the way into Dallas. It didn't matter how many cops assisted; how many FBI SUVs and SWAT vans lined the route, the people they were up against were among the best in the world and they *would* find a way.

Depending on who they were really working for.

Drake saw the vehicles they'd been provided with for the short run through Dallas—two government issue, four-wheel drives—and pulled up short.

"That really ain't gonna work."

Remembering the car park and its contents, he nodded to a pair of parking spots near the exit.

"They will."

Lauren voiced her agreement. "I'll get the FBI to sort it out."

"Quickly." Drake was already headed that way. "Everyone? Load the fuck up. We're about to need every bullet we've got."

With Hayden in their midst they dashed toward the cars—a stealth-black Dodge Challenger and a baby blue Mustang with two white stripes down the bonnet. Dahl honed in on the Mustang, which was fine because Drake wanted the Challenger. Police cars screamed away, preparing to clear a route through the center of Dallas. A chopper hovered nearby, warned away because of the likely probability that Special Forces teams could shoot it down. Both cars were new enough to be hacked—the FBI didn't need the keys.

Drake climbed in, along with Yorgi—who grabbed the passenger seat—Hayden, Alicia and Mai. He fired the engine up, grinning happily.

"Now that," he said, "is a sound I'd get out of bed before six a.m. on a morning for."

Alicia ignored it. She was used to his childishness, and had let everyone know it.

Drake revved the engine. Dahl fired up the Mustang alongside and the two men grinned through two sets of windows, together at last.

Hayden tapped the canister against the back of his seat. "Bio-weapon."

"Umm, yeah. Okay."

He floored it, spinning the wheel and the car around a tight space in the car park and racing for the exit. The vehicle bounced over uneven asphalt, front end lifting and rear end scraping. Sparks flew.

Behind Drake, Dahl saw the sparks flashing across his windshield, covering it in fire for over a second. Clearly, he wasn't happy.

"'Kinell, Drake. Were you *trying* to hit that?"

"Just drive," Hayden came back. "The secure building's only nine minutes away."

"Yeah, on a race track maybe," Smyth said. "But this is Dallas, and these two ain't race car drivers."

"You wanna shot, Lancelot?" Drake breathed. "Climb over that Swede and take it."

"Whatever."

"Are you angry?" Alicia joined in. "Surely not, Lancelot."

"Can we—" Hayden tried again.

Lauren's voice overrode hers. "Hostiles are inbound," she said, then: "Don't get shot, Lancelot."

Drake held a great deal of oversteer by finessing the wheel and using both lanes of the road. A cop car stood ahead, blocking other drivers from crossing their path. The Challengers shot past a junction, high-rises now surrounding them. The Mustang blurred past half a second later, almost nosing the Dodge's rear fender. Drake glanced up into the rearview and all he could see was Dahl's gritted teeth.

"Now I know what it's like to be chased by a shark."

Somewhere ahead lay the remaining contingent of Russians, Swedes and Israelis, all tasked with one duty—retrieve the bio-weapon that had been specifically engineered to wipe out America's food supply.

"Why don't we just destroy it?" Kinimaka said as he hung onto a grab handle.

"Fair question," Dahl pointed out.

"It is," Lauren said. "But I've just been told there are protocols. Procedures. Do it the wrong way and you could kill yourselves and a whole lot of others."

Drake eased off the gas as a sharp bend appeared up ahead. Again, the police had blocked all other routes and he drifted the vehicle gracefully around the corner, shedding rubber and blasting through a red light. Dahl was a few feet behind him. Pedestrians lined the streets, staring, gesturing, but held back by cops with a bullhorn. Drake was always acutely aware that some might not listen.

"Cops can't handle all this," Hayden said. "Slow it down, guys. We're five minutes out."

At that point a pickup truck blasted out from a side street, almost running down a police officer who wasn't paying attention. It swerved into their path and then pulled alongside. Yorgi already had his window pulled down, and Mai broke out the glass in the back.

The pickup—a silver F-150—kept pace, coming closer. The grinning face behind the wheel stared over at them, watching them twice as much as the road. Yorgi fell back into his seat.

"Oh no, no, no. That is not good. I know her. *I know her.*"

Drake took a quick peek. "Looks like a Russian weightlifter to me."

"She *was* in Olympics," Yorgi said. "That was before she became military black-ops assassin, one of best ever to come out of Russia. She is Olga."

Drake slowed as a knot of pedestrians walked out in front of the speeding cars, most with cellphones held inches before their eyes.

"Olga?"

"Yes, Olga. She is legend. You never hear of her?"

"Not in this context. No."

The silver F-150 swerved hard, striking the wide of their Challenger. Free of the wandering herd, Drake goosed the throttle again and surged ahead, the Challenger responding with a satisfying roar. Olga swept over once more, aiming for the rear three-quarter wing but missed by inches. Her F-150 crossed over to the other side, right between Drake and Dahl. The Swede maneuvered his Mustang behind her.

"Can't ram her," he said. "Too risky."

"Can't shoot her," Mai said. "Same problem."

"How does she expect to escape?" Kinimaka wondered.

"Olga is invincible," Yorgi assured them. "And she never fails."

"That's lovely for her," Alicia said. "Maybe you two could hide under the same mattress."

The three vehicles raced along, other vehicles largely blocked and pedestrians warned by the unbroken shriek of police sirens. Drake followed Hayden's direction and Hayden sat glued to the screen of a portable satnav.

Drake saw a long straight ahead.

"Stay with me, Dahl," he said. "Box the bitch in."

He accelerated, keeping to the center of the road. A stray vehicle did start to wander out of a side street, but jammed all on when the driver saw the oncoming chase. Drake kept the hammer down, watching Olga behind and Dahl behind her. The engines roared, the tires rumbled. Glass shopfronts and office buildings flashed by in a blur. Pedestrians jumped out into the road to take pictures. A police car joined the chase, coming alongside Olga so that now Drake had two cars in his immediate rearview.

"Three minutes," Hayden said.

"Get your guns out, people," Alicia said.

"Let's hope the Russian bitch doesn't go down quietly," Kenzie said.

Yorgi gulped hard next to Drake.

Then, ahead, the oddest and most terrifying thing happened. Figures ran out into the center of the road, dropped to one knee, and fired.

Bullets strafed the front of the Challenger, clanging against metal and shearing through bolts. Sparks exploded into the air. Drake kept the vehicle dead straight.

"Hit the fucking deck!" he cried.

More shots. Police ran hard from the sidewalk, trying to stop the shooters. Civilians dived for cover. A contingent of SWAT broke cover and ran with the police, weapons aimed but unused because of the likelihood of hitting people on the other side of the road.

Drake's windshield exploded, glass tumbling over his jacket, his shoulders and down into his lap. The offending bullet thunked into the headrest just a few inches to the right of his ear. The Yorkshireman waited two more seconds, allowed the shooters to settle once more, and then swerved the Challenger with great violence.

Leaving Olga's F-150 in the firing line.

She wrenched at her own wheel, striking the cop to her right side, but the bullets still struck. The man sat beside her slumped; red burst across the inside of the car. Another Russian dead and only one remaining.

Dahl found himself suddenly in the direct firing line.

But by then the shooters were concentrated on the approaching cops and SWAT, just two of them turning and spreading out covering fire as they turned to run. Drake saw bullets hammer in among the crowd, saw the disdain with which these people—Israelis, at a guess—treated the civilians.

"Fuck it," he said. "That ain't gonna stand."

"Drake!" Hayden warned. "Two minutes."

Mai grabbed her shoulder. "This has to be done."

Drake stomped on the gas pedal, and ate up the ground between the car and the fleeing gunmen. Yorgi leaned out of one window and Mai leaned out of the other. Guns leveled, they fired three shots each down the dead straight street, without chance of other casualties, and dropped the running men.

Drake swerved hard around their falling bodies.

"Bastards."

In the rearview, the cops picked them up. Then Olga and Dahl were back, coming hard, racing each other down the center of the road. Olga's vehicle was bloody, her windshield missing, the fenders, sides and lights all smashed, one of the tires shedding rubber. But still she came, as implacable as a hurricane.

"Ninety seconds," Hayden read aloud.

"Where?" Drake asked.

She shouted out an address. "Take a hard right ahead, then left and the building will be dead ahead, blocking the road."

"On another note," Lauren put in. "That's the Israelis out of the fight. And the race."

"Unsanctioned," Kenzie said. "As I thought. No way would that have happened if our government was involved."

Dahl didn't take his eyes off the road. "That coming from you surprises me."

"It shouldn't. I am not saying they wouldn't operate, kill and maim on foreign territory. Friendly territory. I am saying they wouldn't do it so openly."

"Ah, that make more sense."

Drake slowed, standing hard on the brakes, and flung the roaring Challenger around the sharp right. Almost clipping the far curb, he powered on and heard the tires scrabbling for grip. At the last moment they caught, spit gravel, and helped propel the car forward. The hope was Dahl might be able to nudge Olga's backend as she turned, but the Russian was too savvy, cutting the corner recklessly and powering ahead. A litter bin jumped high in her wake, slammed by the front end.

"Thirty seconds," Hayden said.

Then it all went to hell.

CHAPTER THIRTY TWO

Olga risked everything, roaring up fast toward the Challenger's trunk.

Drake saw the left turn coming fast, and prepared to fling the car around.

At the back of his mind, this whole way, had been the nagging worry that the last remaining Swede was out there—somewhere. But he hadn't shown.

Until now.

The soldier burst out of a shop front, wicked-looking machine-pistol leveled, face bloodied and set in a rictus of pain. He was hurting, but he remained on mission. Another non-sanctioned attack. Another third-party using Special Ops men.

Drake reacted instantly. What were the options? It seemed that swerving dangerously into the tight left, trying to fit the Challenger perfectly into the new narrow street, he might be able to flip the backend into the onrushing Swede. It was the only play, and didn't account for the man's deadly weapon.

Hayden and Yorgi were sitting on that side of the car. The Swede looked like he was going to spray the entire vehicle as it slid past sideways. His finger tightened. Drake fought the wheel, keeping it tight, his right foot feathering the throttle at just the right rate.

The Swede opened fire almost point blank—seconds before the car's tail would swipe at him.

And then the whole world went crazy, upside down, as Olga smashed full force into the drifting Challenger. She hadn't slowed down one bit. She plowed her vehicle into the side of the Dodge, sending it spinning, crushing the Swede and flinging his body halfway across the road. Drake held onto the wheel, unable to see straight as the car spun; two rotations, then it hit the high curb and flipped.

It came down on its roof, still skidding, grating against concrete, until it hit the shopfront. Glass shattered and rained down. Drake fought for equilibrium. Alicia was stunned, Yorgi dazed.

Olga jammed the brakes on, and managed somehow to bring the F-150 to a sudden standstill.

Drake saw her in the upside-down side mirror. Windows were smashed on all sides but the gaps were too small to fit through easily. He heard Mai fighting her seatbelt, shrugging it off. He knew she was agile, but didn't believe she'd fit through the rear window. They couldn't defend themselves.

Olga stomped toward them, huge arms and legs working, face set with so much anger it might set fire to the entire world. Blood coated her features and ran down from her neck to her fingers, dripping onto the floor. She carried a machine gun in one hand and a rocket launcher in the other. Drake saw a spare magazine gripped between her teeth and a military blade at her side.

Closing the gap, she was inexorable. Death oncoming. Her eyes never blinked. Steam and now fire broke out of the car behind her, licking around her shape. Drake then saw a flash of blue and knew the Mustang had arrived. He saw Olga sneer. He saw the team jump from the other car in an explosion of action.

Olga fell to one knee, leveled the rocket launcher across one enormous shoulder, and zeroed in on the upended Challenger.

Would she destroy the bio-weapon then?

She's lost it. There's no rational thought behind that demonic face.

They were helpless. In the back seat the women were now animated, freeing themselves and trying to find some wriggle room. They didn't see what was coming, and Drake didn't tell them. No way could they do anything about it.

Olga squeezed the trigger and the rocket ignited.

Friends, family, this is how we go . . .

Torsten Dahl smashed his way through like a terrible battering ram; running at full force, with all his might, he crashed into Olga from behind. The rocket launcher slipped, its payload shooting askew and firing off on another trajectory. Dahl himself, whilst saving the day, must have experienced the utter shock of his life, for Olga did not move.

The Swede had just run headlong into the world's toughest brick wall.

Dahl fell back, nose broken, out cold.

Olga shrugged the Mad Swede off, barely noticing the great attack. She rose like a new mountain, threw the rocket launcher to the ground, and lifted the machine gun in one hand, blood still dripping underneath, spattering the floor.

Drake saw it all, turned to push Yorgi out, then Hayden. His head still spun, but he managed to catch Alicia's eye.

"We good?" She knew something wasn't right.

"I just saw Dahl hit Olga at full pelt, bounce off unconscious, and she barely noticed."

Alicia could barely find the breath. "Fuck. Me."

"And now she has a machine gun."

Hayden crawled free. Mai jumped after her, squirming through the small gap. Drake turned back, watching the mirror even as he attempted to squeeze through his own small windows of space. Olga steadied the gun, sneered once more, raised her free hand, and pulled free a tooth from her mouth, flinging it to the ground. At this point the rest of Dahl's teammates arrived.

And one of them was Mano Kinimaka.

The Hawaiian, in true fashion, launched himself at full speed, feet leaving the ground, arms outstretched, a human missile, a wrecking ball of muscle and bone. He struck Olga around the shoulders, a better aim than Dahl, and gripped hard. Olga staggered forward six feet, and that in itself was a miracle.

Kinimaka swung around her front, facing the Russian.

The machine gun fell to the floor.

Drake read her lips.

"You should be kneeling, little man."

Kinimaka swung a haymaker, which Olga deftly dodged, faster than Drake would have realized. Her own fist then buried itself deep into Mano's kidneys, sending the Hawaiian instantly to his knees and gasping for breath.

Kenzie and Smyth reached the battle. Drake couldn't shake the feeling that it wouldn't be enough.

He squirmed until the flesh tore off his stomach, until his hip bone shrieked. He wrenched himself out of the car and ignored the fresh blood. Signaling all but Hayden, he started to limp toward the battle as the sirens sounded around them, flashing blue lights filled his sight, and the roaring of people and cops and soldiers filled the air.

He shambled up the street, coming close to Olga. The Russian ignored Smyth as he shot her through the stomach; she grabbed Kenzie by the hair and flung her aside. Tufts of brown stayed gripped in the Russian's hands and Kenzie, shocked, flipped and tumbled along the gutter, scraping her flesh. Olga then smashed a hand down onto Smyth's wrist, sending the gun to the ground and making the soldier scream.

"You shoot me? I will tear your arm off and choke you with bloody end."

Drake gathered his strength and hit her from behind, a

three strike blow to the kidneys and ribcage. He'd have used his gun, but had lost it in the crash. Olga didn't even notice the attack. It was like hitting a tree trunk. He looked around for a weapon, something to use.

He saw it.

Mai ran up, followed by Alicia and then Yorgi, white as a sheet. Drake hefted the rocket launcher, held it above his head, and brought it crashing down with all his might onto the Russian's back.

This time, she moved.

Kinimaka scrambled aside as the huge mountain crashed down to one knee. Her spare magazine fell from between her teeth. An RPG toppled from her belt. Drake dropped the weapon, panting hard.

Olga rose, turned, smiled. "I will trample you until you are but offal on concrete."

Drake staggered away. Olga's kick nicked his thigh and sent an explosion of pain from one end of his body to the other. Alicia waded in, only to be manhandled high into the air and flung on top of Kenzie. Kinimaka rose to a head-butt that sent him straight on his ass. Smyth dove in with countless body strikes, and then three to the throat and nose that made Olga break out into laughter.

"Oh, thank you, little one, that helped break down the phlegm. Please, one more."

She held her face out for Smyth to strike.

Alicia helped Kenzie up. Cops were rushing toward them. Drake couldn't help but wish they would stay away. This could be a bloodbath. He tried to rise, and managed it on one leg.

Olga gripped Smyth by the throat and flung him away. Kinimaka shook his great head, now at Olga's feet, and delivered half a dozen incredible blows to her thick thighs.

She punched Kinimaka in the head, laying him out. She

took Drake's next attack and flung him backward, though blood fell freely from her ears, her right eye and innumerable cuts and contusions over her forehead. A hole had opened up in her stomach where Smyth shot her and Drake wondered if that might be the way to stop her.

Mai caught Olga's attention. "Look at me," she said. "Look at me. I have never been beaten."

An expression of interest crossed the bloody mien. "But you are no bigger than one of my sweat glands. Are you Supergirl? Wonder Woman? Scarlett Johanssen?"

"I am Mai Kitano."

Olga lumbered forward, kicking Smyth and an approaching Alicia aside. Mai crouched. Olga lunged. Mai danced away, far away, and then pointed at Olga's right shoulder.

"And whilst I distracted you, my friend Yorgi will destroy you."

Olga turned shockingly fast. "Wha . . ."

Yorgi steadied the rocket launcher across his shoulders, made sure the last grenade was mounted correctly, and then fired directly at Olga's body mass.

Drake ducked.

CHAPTER THIRTY THREE

In the aftermath, the SPEAR team vanished. Whisked away from the scene after handing off the bio-weapon, they were driven through the heart of the unnaturally quiet city to one of the FBI's more rural safe houses. It was a ranch, necessarily small for security, but a ranch nonetheless, with its own house, stables and coral. Horses were kept to sell the illusion, and a ranch hand to train them, but he too worked for the Feds.

The team were so unbelievably happy to arrive at the safe house, and even happier to separate and shut the doors to separate rooms. To a person they were beat, weary, battered, bruised, bleeding.

Blood soaked them all, contusions and woolly-headedness too. Those that hadn't been knocked unconscious wished they had; and those that had, wished they'd been able to help. Drake and Alicia walked into their room, stripped, and headed straight for the shower. A red-hot burst of water helped wash more than blood away. Drake helped Alicia and Alicia helped Drake in the places where their arms were just too covered in bruises to help.

The team weren't broken, but they had been somewhat beaten.

"Always somebody out there—" Drake gasped as the water smashed into him full flow "—who can take you down."

"I know." Alicia piled handfuls of liquid soap into her palm. "Did you see the way Dahl bounced off her?"

Drake started to cough. "Oh, no, please. Don't make me laugh. Please."

It didn't feel off to Drake, that he might find humor so

soon after what he'd just witnessed. The man was a soldier, trained to deal with trauma and heartache, death and violence; he'd been doing it for most of his life, and soldiers coped differently. One of those ways was in camaraderie with their colleagues; another was to always look for the lighter side of things.

When possible. There were some situations that brought even a soldier to his knees.

Now Alicia, cut from the same cloth, recalled Kinimaka's tussle with the immense Olga. "Shit, it was like Godzilla's baby versus Godzilla. Bloody Mano was more shocked than hurt."

"He sure can take a head-butt." Drake grinned.

"Not!" Alicia laughed and they soaked for a while together, willing the pain away.

Drake later vacated the shower, donned a bath sheet, and walked back into the bedroom. A sense of unreality hit him. An hour ago they'd been at the very center of Hell, immersed in one of the hardest and bloodiest battles of their lives, now they were washing up on a Texas ranch, surrounded by guards.

What next?

Well, the bright side was they had won three of the four corners of the earth. And three of the Four Horsemen. The Order had concealed four weapons, so by Drake's admittedly slightly incoherent, fuzzy and wholly unsure calculation, that left just one. He laughed at himself.

Shit, I hope I got that right.

Footsteps sounded at his back and he turned.

There stood Alicia, fully naked and glistening with water from the shower, her hair plastered across one bruised shoulder. Drake stared, and forgot about the mission.

"Bloody 'ell," he said. "So there *are* times when seeing two of you is a good thing."

She padded over and removed his towel. "Do you think we have time?"

"Don't worry," he said with a smile in his voice. "This won't take long."

Later, and after they'd found and tried to avoid every bruised part of both their bodies, Drake and Alicia donned fresh clothes and wandered down to the vast kitchen. Drake wasn't sure why they chose the kitchen; it seemed the natural place to congregate. Failing sunlight slanted in through the picture windows, turning golden and burnishing the wooden floor and kitchen fittings. The place was warm and smelled of freshly baked bread. Drake sat on top of a bar stool and relaxed.

"I could spend a month here."

"One more Horseman," Alicia said. "And then we take a break?"

"Can we do that? I mean, it's not like the bell-ends of the word take a break, love."

"Well, we have to answer to Crowe anyway," she shrugged, "about Peru. And Smyth may have problems. We shouldn't be away on a mission when a member of our family is in trouble."

Drake nodded. "Aye, agreed. And then there's SEAL Team 7."

"Someday," Alicia sighed, sitting on a perch next to him, "our holiday will come."

"Ey up, look what the cat dragged in!" Drake cried, sighting Dahl.

The Swede eased his way through the door, stepping carefully. "Bollocks, I'm trying to walk but am seeing double of everything."

"You think walking's tough?" Drake said. "You wanna try shagging."

Dahl felt his way to a bar stool. "Someone fetch me a drink."

Alicia slid her bottle of water across. "I'll go get another."

Drake eyed his friend worriedly. "You gonna have to sit the rest of this out, mate?"

"In truth, it's getting better by the minute."

"Oh, 'cause I remember you sitting out the fight with Olga."

"Piss off, Drake. I don't ever want to remember that."

Drake chortled. "As if we're ever gonna let you forget it."

The rest of the team emerged in dribs and drabs and, twenty minutes later, they were all sat around the breakfast bar, nursing coffee and water, fruit and bacon strips, and more wounds than they could count. Kinimaka wouldn't meet anyone's eye and Smyth couldn't hold anything in his right hand. Yorgi was immensely subdued. Kenzie couldn't stop complaining. Only Mai, Lauren and Hayden seemed their normal selves.

"Y'know," Hayden said. "I'm just happy we're all through that together. It could have been much worse. The atropine did its job. Any after effects, guys?"

Yorgi, Smyth and Kenzie blinked. Kenzie spoke for them all. "I think Olga beat the after effects away."

Hayden smiled. "Good, because we ain't done yet. Those teams who didn't attend Fort Sill and Dallas were searching for the final clue. Luckily, the DC think tank and the NSA were able to keep tabs on the main players."

"SAS?" Drake guessed.

"Well, the Brits, yes. Followed by China and whatever remains of the French—"

"SEAL Team 7?" Dahl asked.

"Unknown, undeclared, and unsanctioned," Hayden said. "According to Crowe."

"There are higher entities than the Secretary of Defense," Kinimaka said.

"President Coburn wouldn't hang us out to dry," Drake protested. "I have to believe he knows nothing about the SEALs."

"Agreed," Hayden said. "And whilst I agree with Mano, that there are higher entities than Crowe, there are many more insidious ones. The kind that come sideways at you, out of the blue, and give you little choice. I have to believe there's more going on than we know."

"Doesn't help our problem." Smyth grunted, and lifted a glass of milk with difficulty.

"True." Hayden grabbed a handful of fruit and settled herself. "So, let's concentrate on ending this bad mother and get home. We're still the biggest team, and the best. Even now the Brits only got about a day's head start. The Chinese too. Now, it seems out of all the rest only the French are revitalized. They have sent another team, three strong, to hook up with the only remaining original."

"So in the battle of the Special Ops forces," Dahl said. "We're on top."

"Yeah, but it's hardly relevant. And false. It's not like we're hand to hand, or in the wilderness together."

"It's raw, unpredictable battle," Dahl said. "It's as real as it gets."

Hayden nodded and then quickly went on. "Let's recap the Order's text. 'At the Four Corners of the Earth we found the Four Horsemen and laid with them the blueprint of the Order of the Last Judgment. Those who survive the Judgment quest and its aftermath will rightly reign supreme. If you are reading this, we are lost, so read and follow with cautious eyes. Our last years were spent assembling the four final weapons, the world revolutions: War, Conquest, Famine and Death. Unleashed together, they will destroy all governments and unveil a new future. Be prepared. Find them. Go to the Four Corners of the

Earth. Find the resting places of the Father of Strategy and then the Khagan; the Worst Indian Who Ever Lived and then the Scourge of God. But all is not as it seems. We visited the Khagan in 1960, five years after completion, placing Conquest in his coffin. We found the Scourge who guards the true last judgment. And the only kill code is when the Horsemen arose. The Father's bones are unmarked. The Indian is surrounded by guns. The Order of the Last Judgment now live through you, and will forever reign supreme.'"

She finished and took a drink.

"All right? It makes more sense now, I guess. The Order are dead, long gone, but there's still some small element of them in on this. Maybe a mole. A loner. Maybe something else. But he's good enough to hack that Dallas lab, and good enough to take a whole lot of Special Forces down, so we can't underestimate that."

She paused as Drake waved. "Yeah?"

"You know the best place for him to be?" he said. "Inside the think tank in DC. Or working for the NSA."

Hayden's eyes widened. "Crap, that's a real good point. Let me think on it." She poured black coffee from a glass jug.

"Time flies, my friends," Mai said.

"Yeah, I'm with you." Hayden gulped down a mouthful. "Breaking the text down then: the last corner of the earth is Europe. We have to find the tomb of the Scourge of God, who is the Horseman of Death and guards the true last judgment. The worst of all. And the kill code being when the Horsemen arose? I don't understand that as yet, sorry."

"I guess the think tank has been on this a while?" Yorgi said.

Lauren now spoke up from her position leaning against the enormous fridge. "Sure have. An ancient leader was once labeled with the questionable title 'Flagellum dei', by the Romans that he fought and murdered. He was probably the most successful of the barbarian rulers, and attacked the east and west Roman empires when he lived circa 406–453. He was the most feared enemy of Rome and once quoted: 'There, where I have passed, the grass will never grow again.'"

"Another aggrandized, ancient mass murderer," Dahl said.

"Attila the Hun," Lauren said, "murdered his brother in 434 to become sole ruler of the Huns. Notorious for his fierce gaze, Attila was known to roll his eyes often 'as if to enjoy the terror he inspired' according to Edward Gibbon, a historian. He also reputedly claimed to own the actual sword of Mars, the Roman god of war. You can imagine the fear and horror this might inspire on the Roman battlefield."

"We get it," Drake said. "Attila was a bad, or good, boy depending on which side you were on. And who wrote the history books. How and where did he die?"

"Several conflicting accounts describe how he died. From a nosebleed to a knife, at the hand of his new wife. When they found his body the men, as was the custom of the Huns, plucked the hair from their heads and cut deep, hideous wounds in their faces. It was said that Attila, being so terrible an enemy, had his death announced by the gods as a fantastic windfall. A blessing. His body was put in place at the center of a vast plain, inside a silken tent, for all to see and admire. The best horsemen of the tribes rode around and around in circles and spoke over campfires of his great exploits. His was a great death. It goes on to say a celebration was enjoyed over his tomb." Lauren continued to repeat the pertinent points DC whispered into her ears. There was no point setting up a speaker.

"They sealed his coffins with gold, silver and iron, for he had three. And they believed these three materials befitted the greatest of all kings. Of course, arms, riches and rare gems were added. And, also as custom it seems, they slew everyone that labored on his grave to keep its site a secret."

Alicia glared around the table. "One of you dies," she said. "Don't be asking me to bury you. Not a friggin' chance."

"You'll be both unhappy and glad to hear Attila's tomb is one of the greatest lost burial sites in history. Of course, from some of the others—King Richard III's long-missing body turning up under a parking lot in Leicester a few years ago—we have faith that they can still be found. Cleopatra, maybe? Sir Francis Drake? Mozart? Anyway, as for Attila's it is believed that the Hun engineers diverted the Tisza River long enough to dry up the main river bed. Attila was buried there in his magnificent, priceless triple coffin. The Tisza was then freed, concealing Attila for all time."

At that moment they heard the sound of an approaching helicopter. Hayden swept her eyes around the room.

"I hope you're ready for another fight, boys and girls, because this ain't nowhere near finished yet."

Drake stretched aching muscles. Dahl steadied his head on his shoulders. Kenzie winced when she touched the scrape down her back.

"To be fair," Drake said. "I was getting bored here anyway."

Hayden smiled. Dahl nodded as best he could. Mai was already on her feet. Lauren headed for the door.

"C'mon," she said. "They're gonna brief us more on the way."

"Europe?" Yorgi asked.

"Yeah. And to the final Horseman of Death."

Alicia jumped off the barstool. "Great pep-talk," she said sarcastically. "You make it sound so thrilling, even my toes are starting to tingle."

CHAPTER THIRTY FOUR

Another flight, another struggle on the horizon. Drake settled into the comfortable seat and listened as Lauren voiced DC's judgments and findings on the case of Attila the Hun. The team sat around in varying poses, taking in what they could and trying to shrug off the hurt after the newly named 'Olga incident.'

"Attila's grave lost to history," Lauren recapped. "Never found, although there have been a few bogus discoveries. Now—" she paused, listening "—have you heard of a gravitational anomaly?"

Dahl looked over. "There is more than one meaning to that term."

"Well, this is our meaning. Quite recently, scientists discovered a huge and mysterious anomaly buried beneath the polar icecap. Did you know that? It has vast dimensions—151 miles across and a depth of almost a thousand meters. Spotted by NASA satellites it presented a gravitational anomaly because changes in its vicinity indicated the presence of an enormous object sitting in a crater. Now, discounting the wild theories, this object represents a gravitational anomaly. It doesn't sit right, doesn't move like all else around it, and can thus be detected by high-powered radar."

"You're talking GPR," Dahl said. "My old specialty."

Drake made his eyes widen. "Are you sure? I thought that was male stripping at hen parties. The Dancing Viking, they called you."

Dahl gave him weary. "Cut it out."

Alicia leaned over. "He seems grumpy," she stage-whispered.

"Rebounding off an unsuspecting old lady will do that to you."

Amazingly, Smyth had tears in his eyes. "I gotta say," he choked, "I've never seen anyone bounce off someone so hard without a trampoline involved." He hid his face, trying to compose himself.

Kinimaka patted his shoulder. "You okay, brah? I never seen you laugh before, man. It's weird."

Lauren cut in, saving the Swede from more ribbing. "GPR, but on an intense scale. I mean, Google Maps have the strange Antarctica object. You can see it from your laptop. But to find something as small as Attila's tomb? Well, that involves using machines and software that NASA haven't even admitted to owning yet."

"They use a satellite?" Yorgi asked.

"Oh yeah, all the cool nations have it."

"Including China, Britain and France." Drake pointed out their list of rivals.

"Of course. From space the Chinese could identify a man sitting in his car, check the Internet sites he's browsing through, and categorize the contents of the sandwich he's eating. Any man. Almost anywhere."

"Just men?" Kenzie asked. "Or women too?"

Lauren grinned and whispered, "I have a man in my ear, relaying this. Sounds a tad young, like he hasn't discovered women yet."

Drake listened as the chopper split the skies between America and Europe, the third and fourth corners of the earth.

"Right, well, anyway . . ." Lauren winked. "Piecing together the obscure geography of Piscarus, it is said in one text that Attila's famous palace was seated between the Danube and the Tisza, in the Carpathian Hills, on the plains of upper Hungary and neighboring Jazberin. In a far more obscure passage it states that Attila's grave was across from his palace."

"But buried beneath a river," Mai stated.

"Yes, the Tisza traverses Hungary from north to south, a huge tributary of the Danube itself. The path of the river will help our scientists. Hopefully, their investigations with geophysical technique will combine satellite, magnetics, MAG and GPR. Magnetic surveys are supplemented by GPR profiles across selected anomalies. They also say they can see if and when a river was ever diverted." She shrugged. "We're talking thousands and thousands of images for a computer to crunch, then make a determination."

"All right, all right, so we're heading for Hungary." Alicia faked a headache. "Just say *that*."

The team settled back, wondering how their aggressive counterparts were doing.

Hungary, the Danube and the Tisza looked just as black as the rest of Europe at night, but Drake knew right now it was far more volatile. The most powerful of the Four Horsemen lay down there—Death—and those that found it might well shape the future of the world.

The team landed, took off again, landed once more and then jumped in a huge, non-reflective van to complete the last leg of their journey. The number crunchers hadn't concluded anything yet, the areas were still large and the target small, not to mention old and potentially degraded. It would have been nice to find the Order's own workings out, but their sudden killings all those decades ago put paid to any backtracking.

They set up a camp on the plains, put a guard around the outside, and settled in. The winds were high, ruffling the tents; the surreal reality of all they had done during the last few days still trying to sink in.

Are we really here now, camping halfway up the side of a Hungarian hill? Drake wondered. *Or are we still being pummeled by Olga?*

The blooming tent canvas spoke the truth, and so did the wriggling shape at his side. Alicia, wrapped in her sleeping bag so that only her eyes peered out.

"Cold, love?"

"Yeah, get in here and warm me up."

"Please," Dahl said, from somewhere south of Drake's feet, "not tonight."

"Agreed," Kenzie stated from the east. "Tell the bitch you have a headache or something. Who knows where she's been? Number of diseases etcetera, etcetera."

"A foursome's out of the question then?"

"It is," Mai added from near the tent opening. "Especially since there are five us."

"Nuts, I forgot you were here, Sprite. I still can't believe they stuck us all in one bloody tent."

"I for one fancy sleeping out on the plains," Dahl said, rising. "Then, perhaps I'll sleep."

Drake watched the Swede head out, assuming he'd take the chance to call Johanna. Their relationship remained up in the air, but the day would come, and soon, when somebody made an unalterable decision.

The day dawned, and the DC boffins came up with half a dozen sites. The team separated and started to dig, putting the great scenery out of the minds and hearts: the flashing blue snake of the Tisza, wide and then oddly narrow in places, the grassy rolling Carpathian hills, the endless clear skies. The cool breeze, blowing across the wide spaces, was welcome, easing weariness and soothing bruises. Drake and the others constantly wondered where their enemies were. The British, the Chinese and the French. *Where? Over the closest hill?* Nobody ever saw the faintest hint of surveillance. It was as if the other teams had given up.

"Not your most conventional relic hunt," Drake said once. "I hardly know where I'm at next."

"Agreed," Dahl said. "One moment we're all at loggerheads and the next it's plain sailing. Still, it could be worse."

The first day passed quickly, then a second. They found nothing. The rain came and then the blinding sun. The team took turns resting and then let some hired hands take over for a while. Men and women that spoke no English were appointed from a nearby village. Once, Alicia found a void in the earth, an old tunnel perhaps, but the elation was quickly quashed when her scrabbling came to a dead end.

"Useless," she said. "We could be a meter away and still not find it."

"How do you think it's stayed undetected all these years?"

Dahl continued to scratch his head, sure there was something they were missing. "It's right on the tip of my tongue," he repeated more than once.

Drake couldn't help it. "You mean Olga, don't you? It was a very brief experience, mate."

Dahl growled, still perusing.

Another night and another few hours in the tent. The most intense of these nights was when Drake brought the conversation around to Webb's statement, his legacy and his secret stash of information.

"We have to concentrate on that next. The secrets he gathered could be destructive. Overwhelming."

"For who?" Dahl said. "The ones directed at us weren't so bad."

"Except for the one we don't know yet," Mai said.

"Shit, really? I forgot. Which one is that?"

The Japanese woman lowered her voice and spoke softly. "One of you is dying."

Silence reigned for a long, distressing moment.

Alicia broke it. "Gotta agree with Drake. It's not just us. Webb was a specialist stalker and mega-rich asshole. He must have had dirt on everybody."

A false alarm sent them scrambling out of the tent, into the soil and mud and down among the rubble and grit of an ancient burial site. To their deep annoyance, it turned out not to belong to Attila. At least, not as far as they could tell.

Later, in the tent, they returned to their thoughts.

"So much to confront," Hayden said. "Perhaps this search for Webb's stash, and what we subsequently discover, might protect us from what may be coming."

"Joshua's death in Peru? Our insubordination? Questionable judgment and indefinable leash? We have to answer to someone. One tarnishing you can get away with. But three? Four? Our accounts are in the red, people, and I don't mean overdrawn."

"Hence SEAL Team 7?" Dahl asked.

"Maybe," Hayden muttered. "Who knows? But if they come at us with prejudice, by God I will strike back with comparative force. And so will all of you. That's an order."

Another day dawned and the hunt continued. Rainfall hampered their efforts. The DC think tank came back with seven more sites, making a total of twenty three. Most had yielded nothing but voids or old foundations, buildings long gone, skeletons that were in tatters. The majority of another day passed, and the morale of the SPEAR team went into decline.

"Are we even in the right place?" Kenzie asked. "I mean Hungary. Across from Attila's palace. How long ago was the man born? Sixteen hundred years ago, right? That's, what? Fourteen hundred years before Geronimo. Maybe Attila's the wrong 'scourge'. I assume the Catholic Church have labelled many."

"We're detecting a great variety of anomalies," Kinimaka said. "Just so many, and none of them correct."

Dahl stared at him. "We need a way to narrow it down."

Lauren, always connected to the think tank, looked across. "Yeah, they say. Yeah."

The winds blew softly through the Swede's hair, but his face remained impassive. "I got nothing."

"Maybe another look at Attila?" Mai suggested. "Something in his history?"

Lauren told the DC gang to get on it. The team rested, slept, looked out for trouble and found none, and attended two more false alarms.

At last, Drake rounded the team up. "I think we're gonna have to call this one a failure, people. The Order say they found it, *maybe*, but if we can't then the other countries can't. Perhaps the fourth Horseman is best left where he was buried. If he's even still there."

"It is possible the grave was ransacked—" Hayden spread her arms "—soon after interment. But then surely the relics would have shown up. Clothing. The sword. Gems. Other bodies."

"Hard to leave a weapon so potent out there," Kenzie said with a faraway look on her face. "I know my government would not. They would never stop searching."

Drake nodded in agreement. "True, but we surely have other crises on the boil. We can't stay here forever."

"Same thing they said in Peru," Smyth said.

Drake nodded at Lauren. "Do they have anything for us?"

"Not yet, except for eight more potential sites. Readings all the same. Nothing firm."

"But couldn't that be just what we're looking for?" Dahl said ever so softly.

Hayden sighed. "I think I may have to call this one, and contact the Secretary. We're better—"

"Be careful," Alicia warned. "That may be the signal the SEALs are waiting for."

Hayden clammed up, eyes now unsure.

Dahl finally caught their attention. "Ground Penetrating Radar," he said. "Searches for anomalies, gravitational or magnetic or whatever. It finds an awful lot, naturally, since this is a very old planet. But we *can* narrow it down. We can. Oh hell, how could we be such fools?"

Drake shared a worried frown with Alicia. "You okay, pal? Not still feeling the after effects of that Olga you tried to take, are you?"

"I'm *fine*. I'm perfect, as always. Listen—remember those bozos that found the tombs of the gods?"

Now Drake's face grew serious. "That was us, Torsten. Well, most of us."

"I *know* that. We found the bones of Odin, and Thor, Zeus and Loki." He paused. "Aphrodite, Mars and more. Well, what were their weapons and armor made out of? Some of their gems?"

"An unknown substance that later helped us on another mission," Drake said.

"Yeah." Dahl couldn't stop grinning. "And whose sword was buried with Attila?"

Lauren jumped on it. "Mars!" she cried. "The Roman god of war gave Attila his sword through the Scythians. It was called the Holy War Sword. But if it did originate from Mars' own hand . . ."

"You can recalibrate the GPR to look for just that element," Dahl said. "And that incredibly rare element only."

"And boom!" Drake nodded at him. "Just like that. The Mad Swede returns."

Alicia still looked pained. "You couldn't have thought of that friggin' days ago?"

CHAPTER THIRTY FIVE

Eight more hours and they were ready. The DC team reset the GPR after contacting the Icelandic archaeological unit who were still investigating what was left of the first tomb of the gods. *It always comes back to Odin,* Drake thought as he waited. Understandably, the Icelanders had kept much of the details of the find and all the samples. It was a matter of a few moments to send the rare element's data to DC.

Or so they said, Drake later imagined. He'd be shocked if the Americans didn't already have it on file.

A test and then a hot signal was sent down. A ping on a site they'd already skirted and the ancient Sword of Mars was a clear pinpoint on a map.

"That's it," Mai said. "The tomb of Attila the Hun."

Excavations began in earnest. The villagers started widening the hole they'd already hollowed out. Before they reached a void that ran in perfect parallel with the sword, they paid off the villagers and pretended despondence as they watched them walk away.

"The other side of this," Mai said, "is the immense cultural find."

"We can't worry about that now," Hayden said. "This is the weapon of Death. It has to be neutralized before we declare anything."

Smyth, Yorgi and Kinimaka jumped in, attacking the earth. Dahl still looked and felt a little woozy, though Alicia and Kenzie took the opportunity to call him every name from 'idle arse' to the Mad Sloth.

It didn't take long to break into the void.

Drake watched as the trio widened the gap. Mai and Alicia were out checking the terrain, ensuring there were no surprises about to come creeping through the tall grass. Lauren was going to stay near the hole; a line of sight between the two women and those below.

"Since we don't know how far down we're going," Drake said, "the comms may be useless. But I guess we'll play it as we find it."

"All we need is the box," Hayden affirmed. "We don't spend time staring at anything, or anyone, else. Agreed?"

They nodded. Yorgi went first, being the most agile of the team. Kinimaka came next, still nursing a head wound, and then Smyth. Drake jumped into the hole, followed by Hayden and Dahl. The Swede was to stay near the entrance. Drake ducked under the jagged earth and found himself inside a dark tunnel. One minute of crawling and squeezing between walls, led to the wider void, where the team turned left. Yorgi had the sword on a handheld GPS and shouted out the distance between them and it every few minutes.

Drake kept his flashlight steady, joining beams with those ahead. The passage never deviated, but skirted around the sword's resting place until they were slowly headed away from it.

Yorgi stopped ahead. "We may have to break through."

Drake cursed. "It's solid rock. We'd need big machinery to break through there. Can you see how thick it is?"

Yorgi made an unhappy noise. "Twice the width of this passage."

"And the sword?"

"Just on the other side."

Drake felt the distinct impression that they were being toyed with. The old gods again, having fun. It sometimes felt as if they'd been dogging him this whole way, throwing him into this adventure and that, sometimes returning to make their presence felt.

Like now.

He made the decision. "Push on," he said. "We need to see where this passage goes."

"Well, one of the anomalies lies ahead," Yorgi sent back. "A large unknown shape."

Alicia's voice crackled over the comms. "Is it moving?"

Drake knew the wicked tone of humor. "Quit it."

"How many legs does it have?"

"Alicia!"

Everyone below ground took their handguns out. Drake tried to crane his neck to see ahead but Kinimaka blocked his view. The only thing he succeeded in doing was knocking the top of his head against the tunnel.

Dust sifted through the air. Drake was sweating, his fresh bruises throbbing. The team crawled on as fast as they could. Yorgi led them around a slow bend. It was only then that the young Russian stopped.

"Ah! I have something."

"What?" Several voices rang out.

"Wait. You can come up here with me."

Soon, Drake rounded the curve to see the side of the passage widen into an eight-foot-high, four-man-wide archway of rock. It was buff-colored, smooth and presided over a narrower hole that had been cut into the very rock—a small, door-like entrance.

Drake eyed the blackness of that opening. "So maybe they hollowed out the bedrock a little, ensuring Attila would remain here forever?"

"But there's no river above us," Yorgi stated. "That has been on my mind."

"River courses change through the years," Hayden said. "We can't tell at the moment if the Tisza once flowed this way. As it is, it's only a few meters to the south."

Drake walked toward the darkness. "I'm game. Shall we see?"

Yorgi jumped up, maintaining his position in front. At first, the new door was just a shape of utter blackness, but as they approached and shone their flashlights, they saw hints of a large room on the other side. A room no larger than a good-sized dining room, full of dust motes and utter silence, and with a knee-high pedestal at its center.

Atop the pedestal sat a stone coffin.

"Incredible," Yorgi breathed.

"You think Attila's in there?" Kenzie asked.

"The sword is, I think." Yorgi consulted his GPR. "So says this thing."

"We stay on mission." Hayden hadn't even looked at the coffin. She was busy scanning the floor. "And that right there? That's it."

Drake looked to where she pointed. The team had moved through the entrance arch now and were fully inside the room. The familiar wooden box with the Order's seal on top sat on the pedestal itself, at the foot of the coffin. Hayden strode toward it.

"Make ready," she told Lauren through the comms. "We're on our way. Tell DC we found the last box."

"Did you open it up?"

"Negative. I don't think that's a good idea down here. We'll wait till we're topside."

Drake stared at the coffin. Yogi moved closer. Kenzie climbed onto the pedestal and peered over the top.

"Anyone gonna give me a hand?"

"Not now," Hayden said. "We have to go."

"Why?" Kenzie remained bolshie. "It's not like the other teams are here. Makes a nice change to have a minute to ourselves, don't you think? A nice change not to have someone trying to restrain me."

Drake keyed the comms. "Dahl? You're a bastard."

"Whaa?"

Kenzie inhaled. "It's just a stone lid."

Drake saw the relic smuggler in her, the passion for treasure. Of course, it would never quieten. It was a part of her. He nodded at Hayden.

"We'll catch you up. Promise."

He ran over to the other side of the pedestal, took hold of the stone and heaved.

Hayden hurried out of the tomb, Yorgi and Kinimaka close behind. Smyth lingered in the doorway. Drake watched as the treasures of Attila the Hun's tomb were unearthed.

In the glow of the flashlight, his eyes were blinded; glittering green and red, sapphire blue and bright yellow; hues of the rainbow shimmering and free for the first time in almost a thousand years. The riches shifted, a sword unsettled by the movement. Other blades gleamed. Necklaces, anklets and bracelets lay in heaps.

Beneath it all, still wrapped in a few tatters of clothing, lay the body of Attila. Drake believed it so. This site had never been found by grave robbers; hence the presence of the riches. The Nazi's required it only for their wider schemes, and drawing attention to a monumental find would only draw attention to them. Breathless, he jumped on the comms.

"Lauren," he whispered. "You gotta get someone to guard all this. You just gotta make it happen. It's . . . incredible. The only thing is . . ." He paused, searching.

"What is it?"

"There are no swords. The Sword of Mars is missing."

Lauren breathed out. "Oh no, that's not good."

Drake's face became strained. "After all we've been through," he said. "I bloody well know that."

Kenzie grunted. Drake looked over. "The Sword of Mars is here."

"Bloody hell, you are good. Relic smuggler and thief extraordinaire. You nicked that from right under my nose." He stared. "It's fabulous."

"You can't take anything." He saw her lift out a bejeweled object. "But trust you to go for the most valuable item in there."

"More than Attila?"

"Yeah, of course. You can take him. But, whatever you do, keep the sword."

Kenzie laughed and withdrew her hand, leaving the bejeweled treasure behind but keeping the sword. "I've seen it all now," she said with a kind of reverence. "We can go."

Drake was happy that she'd shown an inner desire, and that he'd helped her fulfill it. "All right, then. Let's go see what the Horseman of Death is all about."

CHAPTER THIRTY SIX

Kneeling in the direct sunlight, the SPEAR team studied the final box of the Order of the Last Judgment.

Kinimaka waited for approval as Alicia and Mai drifted in from the boundaries now that friendly choppers could be seen on the horizon. Hayden gestured to Kinimaka.

"Get on with it, Mano. We have to see what's inside before company arrives; friend or foe."

The Hawaiian nodded and snapped the lock. Drake leaned forward as the lid came up, knocking heads with Dahl.

"Fuck!" he shouted, blinking.

"Was that your attempt at a kiss, Yorkie?"

"I'll give you a kiss if you stick that shaggy mop you call a head into my face again. A bloody Yorkshire kiss."

Of course, nobody heard him. They were all concentrating on the new revelation.

Hayden peered inside, craning over Kenzie. "Sheeyit," she said offhandedly. "I never imagined it would be that."

"Nor me." Mai was standing.

"The true last judgment," Lauren said, reciting the text again. "The worst one of all."

"Well, I don't know about you guys," Alicia muttered. "But all I see inside is a fucking scrap of paper. Looks like my shopping list."

Mai looked over. "Somehow, I can't imagine you inside a supermarket."

Alicia shuddered. "Just once. All those trolleys, aisle-blockers and choices totally freaked me out." She studied the approaching attack choppers wistfully. "This is much better."

Kinimaka reached inside the box, lifted the scrap of paper

out and held it so that everyone could see. "It's just a set of numbers."

"Random," Smyth said.

Drake felt anger. "So the Order of the Last Judgment sent us halfway around the world to find a scrap of paper in a tomb that has lain hidden for hundreds of years? A place we'd possibly never have found if we hadn't had experience with the tombs of the gods? I don't get it."

"The Nazis were relic and treasure hunters," Kenzie said. "You know that incredible mass they recently found under the polar ice? Some say it's a Nazi base. They looted everything from ornaments to scrolls and paintings. They tried to make zombies, sought eternal life and lost thousands of men in perilous quests. If they chose to leave *that* inside Attila the Hun's tomb rather than steal the wealth—there's a terrible reason."

Lauren pointed to her ears. "DC want to know what it is."

Hayden took it from Kinimaka. "Right guys, it's an old scrap of notepad paper, quite thick and torn around two sides. It's yellowing and feels quite brittle. Now, there is a line of writing across the middle that consists only of numbers." She read them out: "483794311656 . . ." She took a breath. "There's more . . ."

"A geek's wet dream." Alicia sighed. "But what the hell do we do?"

"Get out of here," Drake said, standing as the helicopters touched down. "Before the Huns find us."

A pilot jogged over. "You guys ready? We're gonna have to keep this under the radar."

The team walked with him back to the choppers. Hayden finished her recital and passed the scrap of paper around as they settled into their seats. "Any ideas?"

"You couldn't even do the lottery with those," Alicia said. "Useless."

"And what do they have to do with death?" Drake said. "And the Four Horsemen? Since numbers seem to be important, could this have anything to do with birth dates? Death dates?"

"We're on it," a voice said in his ear, and he was reminded again that they were universally connected unless they turned DC off for a mission, in which case they only connected to Lauren.

"Not only on it," another voice said. "We got it."

Drake listened as the choppers rose slowly into the air.

"Those numbers, broken down, are coordinates. Easy. The Nazis left you a big ass target, people."

Drake started to check and prep his weapons. "Target?"

"Yeah, the first set of numbers points to the Ukraine. The sequence is one long, unbroken number so that's why it took us a while to break it down."

Alicia checked her watch. "I don't call five minutes a while."

"You don't have an IQ of one-sixty."

"How the hell do you know, smartass? I never got it checked."

A moment of silence, and then: "Anyway. We input the entire sequence and plugged it into a satellite. What we're looking at now is a large industrial area, maybe eight square miles in total. It's full of warehouses mostly, we've counted over thirty, and appears to be empty. Something from the war era abandoned. It could be an old storage area for the Soviets, now disused."

"And the coordinates?" Hayden asked. "Do they point to anything in particular?"

"Still checking." The line went quiet.

Hayden didn't have to inform the pilots; they were already headed for the Ukraine. Drake felt himself relax a little; at least their rival teams couldn't beat them to this one. He looked over at Hayden and mouthed, *Can we turn these off?*

She made a face. *Would look suspicious.*

Mole? He mimed it slowly, leaning forward.

Hayden did too. *There is no one we can trust.*

Alicia laughed. "Fucksake, Drake, if you wanna kiss her just do it."

The Yorkshire man sat back as the helicopter scythed through the skies. It was almost impossible, working at full capacity when you weren't sure if even your own bosses had your back. A weight settled into his heart. If they were being plotted against by anyone—they were about to find out.

The comms squeaked.

"Whoa."

Hayden's head came up. "What?"

The super-geek in DC sounded terrified. "Are you sure, Geoff? I mean, I can't tell them this and later discover it's just guesswork."

Silence. Then their liaison took a deep breath. "Wow, I have to say. This is bad. This is real bad. The coordinates appear to lead directly to the Horseman of Death."

Dahl paused in the middle of loading a magazine into his handgun. "That makes sense," he said. "But what is it?"

"A nuclear warhead."

Hayden gritted her teeth. "Can you pinpoint it? Is it live? Are there—"

"Wait," the geek breathed, catching his breath. "Please, just wait. There's more. I didn't mean 'a nuclear warhead.'"

Hayden frowned. "Then what did you mean?"

"There are *six* nuclear warheads inside three warehouses. We can't see through the walls, since the buildings are lead lined, but we can see through the roof with our satellites. Images show the nukes are eighties era, probably worth a fortune to the right bidder, and heavily guarded. The security is mostly inside, with the occasional drive around the empty base."

"So the Order of the Last Judgment secreted six nuclear weapons inside three warehouses for later use?" Mai asked. "That does sound like the Nazi thing to do."

"Weapons are operational too," the geek said.

"How do you know that?"

"The computer system is operative. They can be armed, guided, released."

"Do you have an exact location?" Kenzie asked.

"Yeah, we do. All six are strapped to the back of flatbed trucks, sitting inside the warehouses. Strangely, the activity inside has recently doubled. Of course, they could also be moved."

Drake looked over at Hayden who stared back.

"Mole," Kenzie said aloud.

"And the rival teams?" Dahl asked.

"Chatter has increased according to the NSA. Doesn't look good."

"I'd love to know what they're hoping to find," Mai said. "Apart from six old nuclear warheads."

"The Sword of Mars."

Drake twisted his neck around fast. "What?"

"Everyone got the coordinates, assuming this mole works here. Everyone tasked a satellite. Our imaging software is equipped with all manner of sensors and, since the Odin thing and subsequent near misses, we can detect the rare element associated with the tombs and the gods. Our instruments display the approximate size and shape of the object, and it matches up with the missing sword. They all know we found the sword and are headed for the nukes. We *have* to."

"Leave the sword on the chopper." Smyth shrugged.

Drake, Dahl and Hayden exchanged glances. "Not a

chance in hell. The sword stays with us."

Drake hung his head. "The one bloody thing that's more valuable than Genghis, Attila, Geronimo and Hannibal combined," he said. "And we're forced to take it to the nukes."

"Foresight," Mai said. "And they need it for any number of reasons. Wealth."

"Reward," Smyth said.

"Greed," Kenzie said.

"A failsafe," Hayden said with conviction. "For all those reasons combined. Where are the six nukes?"

"Two inside Warehouse 17," the geek said. "The other nukes are in Eighteen and Nineteen, and I'm pinging you over their exact locations right now. It's a big base, and we're counting heat sigs from at least two dozen bodies, so be careful."

Drake sat back, looking at the roof. "One more time?"

Hayden knew what he was thinking. "You believe it'll all change after this?"

He smiled sadly. "I do."

"Then let's hit it hard," Dahl said. "As a team, as colleagues. Let's do this one final time."

CHAPTER THIRTY SEVEN

The SPEAR team came in hard. The old, abandoned base was simply a haphazard arrangement of large, elongated warehouses with a network of flat dirt roads running between them. The roads were extra wide to allow for larger trucks. Drake imagined it had been some kind of storage depot once, a place to shout at for a vast array of military equipment. The helicopters came down on the outskirts, outside a rusted, wilting fence-line, and powered down almost instantly.

"Team ready," Hayden said into her comms.

"Go," DC told her. "Ensure the warheads are disabled and the other item is safe."

Dahl grumbled at the ground. "Talk about locking the stable door after the horse has bolted."

The team had already fixed the position of all three warehouses in their minds, and had a good idea of the twisting road network. Basically, everything crossed with everything else. There were no dead ends, no cul-de-sacs, no exit routes except one. The perimeter warehouses all backed up against dense forest, but the interior ones—the vital three—sat in the midst of others in a random arrangement.

Together, they ran.

"We'll have to split up, neutralize the nukes, then find a way of getting them out of here and to a nicer place," Hayden said. "Romania's not far."

Lauren was with them now, fully plugged in to DC and, having proved that she could think under pressure, they might need her when it came to handling the nukes. A steady head capable of relaying information through channels couldn't be underestimated. They stayed low, fast, and on course for the warehouses.

A dirt road opened up before them, deserted. Beyond that the entire area was bare earth and shale with just a few tufts of straggly brown grass. Drake surveyed the scene and gave the order to move. They ran out into the open, guns at the ready. The smell of dirt and oil struck his senses and a cold breeze slapped his face. Their gear jangled, their boots struck the earth hard.

They came up against the first warehouse wall, and paused with their backs against it. Drake glanced down the line.

"Ready?"

"Go."

He examined the next leg of their route, knowing they didn't have any CCTV to worry about since instruments detected no signals coming out of the base except cellphones. The nukes themselves gave off a low frequency hum. Beyond that, the place was barren.

Another run and they came up against another warehouse. Each one had its designated number painted in black scrawl across the side. Each one appeared rundown, tawdry, with runnels of rust descending from the roof to the floor. Guttering swung free, jagged lengths pointing at the ground, dripping dirty water.

Ahead now, Drake made out the left corner of Warehouse 17. "We cross this road," he said. "Make our way up the flank of that warehouse until we reach the end. That way, we're only twenty feet from Seventeen."

He moved out, then paused. A security vehicle passed along the road ahead, traveling the path that intersected theirs. Nothing happened though. Drake heaved a sigh of relief.

"No friends here," Dahl reminded them. "Do not trust anyone outside the team." He didn't have to add, "Even Americans."

Now Drake moved, hugged the warehouse wall and made his way forward. Warehouse 17 had two small windows looking out front. Drake cursed silently, but saw there was no other way to go.

"Move," he said urgently. "Move it now."

CHAPTER THIRTY EIGHT

They ran for the warehouse doors, splitting up into three groups. Drake, Alicia and Mai took Seventeen; Dahl, Kenzie and Hayden took Eighteen, which left Smyth, Lauren, Kinimaka and Yorgi with Nineteen. They hit the main doors as one.

Drake kicked it in, smashing it off its hinges. A man was just exiting an office inside. Drake took him under his arm, wrenched hard and flung him against the opposite office wall. The narrow passage they were in opened up ahead into the warehouse proper so Alicia and Mai bypassed him.

Drake finished the man off, left him comatose, and checked the small offices before joining the women. A spectacular sight met his eyes. The warehouse was vast, long and high. At its center, facing a set of roller doors, sat a long, low flatbed truck—a big-engined cab at the front. Two nuclear warheads sat on the back of the truck, plain as day, their nosecones facing the front, black straps fastening them down at regular intervals. The straps would allow flexibility without great movement—a good idea for transit, Drake guessed, since nobody wanted a deadly missile smashing against an immovable object. A vast bundle of side-curtains lay at the side of the huge truck, which he guessed would be attached before departure.

"No guards," Mai said.

Alicia pointed out another office to the right of the truck. "My guess."

"You'd think they would be more concerned," Mai said.

Drake couldn't help but check for CCTV, finding it hard to rely totally on a band of geeks sat in an air-conditioned office. "Our old friend, complacency, is probably at work," he said. "They've been sitting on this secret a long time."

Through the comms they heard sounds of combat, the other teams were engaged.

Alicia sprinted for the truck. "On me!"

Dahl picked up the closest man and threw him toward the rafters, getting a decent amount of air time before seeing him smash awkwardly down to earth. Bones broke. Blood oozed. Kenzie slipped past, firing her machine pistol, striking running men who then introduced their faces to the ground hard. Hayden ranged to the other side, favoring her Glock. The enormous truck they'd found sat at the center of the warehouse, with a trio of offices alongside and several rows of crates. They had no idea what lay inside, but thought it might be prudent to find out.

Hayden headed for the truck, eyes scanning the pair of nukes seated above her head. Damn, they were enormous at this distance. Monsters with no purpose other than to lay waste. Assuredly then, they were Death, and clearly a part of the fourth Horseman. Attila was the second most ancient figure of the four, born seven hundred years after Hannibal and, coincidentally, seven hundred years before Genghis Kahn. Geronimo was born in 1829. All horsemen in their own right. All kings, killers, generals, unequalled strategists. All had defied their supposed betters.

Was this why the Order chose them?

The DC mole, she knew, was mocking them with knowledge.

No time to change anything now. She crossed behind the flatbed, angling for the crates. Some of the lids were askew, others leaned against the wooden sides. Straw and other packing materials leaked out of the top. Hayden shot one man, then traded bullets with another, and was forced to dive to the ground and take cover.

She ended up at the rear of the truck with the tail end of a nuclear warhead looming over her.

"What the hell happens if a bullet hits one of these things?"

"Don't worry, it would have to be a good shot to directly strike the core, or the explosive," a voice told her through the comms. "But I guess there's always the chance of a fluke."

Hayden ground her teeth. "Oh, thanks, buddy."

"No problem. Don't worry, it's unlikely to happen."

Hayden ignored the bland, unemotional commentary, rolling out into the open and firing an entire magazine at her adversary. The man fell, bleeding. Hayden rammed in another mag as she dashed over to the crates.

The vast warehouse surrounded her, resounding with gunshots, spacious enough to be unsettling, the rafters so high they could easily hide an unfriendly antagonist. She peered over the top of the crates.

"I think we're good," she said. "Seems that they have more than one operation going on here."

Kenzie ran up, brandishing the Sword of Mars. "What is it?"

Dahl crouched by the flatbed's huge wheel. "Keep an eye out. We have more than one enemy here."

Hayden sifted the straw. "Stolen goods," she said. "Must be a waypoint. Quite an assortment here."

Kenzie drew out a golden statue. "They have teams doing house raids. Burglaries. It's a huge business. Everything gets shipped off, sold on or melted down. The conscience behind these crimes rates is below zero."

Dahl whispered, "To your left."

Hayden ducked behind a crate, sighted her prey and opened fire.

*

Lauren Fox followed Mano Kinimaka into the lion's den. She saw Smyth take out an adversary and leave him for dead. She saw Yorgi pick the lock of an office door, enter and declare it obsolete in less than a minute. Every day, she tried desperately to keep up. Every day, she worried she might lose her place in the team. This was part of why she courted Nicholas Bell's favor, why she ran the comms and looked for other ways to help.

She loved the team, and wanted to stay a part of it.

Now, she stayed at the back, Glock in hand and hoping she wouldn't have to use it. The flatbeds took up most of her vision, outsized and terrible. The warheads were a dull greenish color, non-reflective, surely one of the most menacing shapes the modern human mind might summon up. Smyth engaged with a large guard, took several blows and then disabled the guy just as Lauren was sneaking up to help. To her right Kinimaka shot two more. Bullets began to crisscross the warehouse as the rest realized they were under attack.

At the back, she saw several guards break for the cab of the flatbed.

"Watch out," she keyed the comms, "I can see men headed around the front. My God, are they gonna try to *drive* them outta here?"

"Oh no," DC voiced the reply to everyone. "You *have* to neutralize those nukes. If these guys have the launch codes, even one being loosed would be catastrophic. Listen, all six must be neutralized. *Now!*"

"Fuckin' easy for you to say," Alicia muttered. "Wrapped in your dressing gown and sipping yer frothy cappuccino. Wait, I see them heading for the cab here too."

Drake switched directions, seeing that he could race down this side of the flatbed and meet no opposition. Waving to Alicia, he set off fast.

Mai's voice cut through his concentration. "Watch your feet!"

Wha...?

A man wearing a thick black leather jacket came sliding under the flatbed, legs outstretched. By luck or clever design they struck Drake at the shins and sent him tumbling. The machine pistol skidded on ahead. Drake ignored the new set of bruises and scrambled under the truck just as the guard opened fire. Bullets scored the concrete in his wake. The guard pursued him, gun out.

Drake scrambled right under the truck, conscious of the enormous weapon above his head. The guard ducked, then crouched. Drake fired his Glock, and took the man's forehead apart. A scramble of footsteps came from behind and then he was tackled hard, the weight of another man crashing down on top of him. Drake's chin struck the ground, sending stars and blackness swirling into his vision. His teeth smashed together, tiny chippings cracked off. Pain exploded everywhere. He rolled, smashed an elbow into a face. A gun came up, fired; the bullets missed Drake's skull by an inch and went straight up, into the base of the nuke.

Drake felt the adrenaline surge. "That's a—" he grabbed the man's head and struck it against the concrete as hard as he could "—fucking. Nuclear. Missile." Each word a slam. In the end the head lolled. Drake scrambled back out from under the truck, and met Alicia sprinting on.

"No time for a nap, Drakey. This is some serious shit."

The Yorkshireman snatched up his machine pistol and tried to shake the ringing sound from his ears. Alicia's voice helped.

"Mai? You okay?"

"No! Pinned down."

A roar came from the engine of the flatbed.

"Run faster," Drake said. "A few more seconds and these live nukes are outta here!"

CHAPTER THIRTY NINE

Drake poured on the speed. These days it was uncommon that he see straight, so today was business as usual. The door to the cab came up ahead, over head-height. Drake reached up, grabbed the handle and pulled. Alicia aimed her Glock.

A hand grenade bounced out.

Drake stared in utter disbelief. "Are you fucking kiddi—"

Alicia struck him around the chest, propelling him backward and around the front of the truck. The grenade exploded violently, shrapnel spitting in all directions. Drake rolled with Alicia, the two held together. The truck's door went spinning and tumbling ahead of the vehicle. When Drake looked up there was only one man sat in the cab, high up, grinning evilly down at him. He goosed the gas pedal.

Drake knew there was no chance in hell that the vehicle could set off fast enough to run them down. He glanced to the side and saw three more guards rushing them. The truck bellowed, its wheels started to grip and propel it forward an inch at a time. The roller doors hadn't moved, but that wouldn't stop it.

The comms burst to life.

"They're driving the trucks out of here! Cabs are bulletproof. And damn hard to reach." It was Hayden's voice. "

"No way inside?" Kinimaka asked.

"No. It's sealed. And I don't want to use too much force, if you know what I mean."

And though Drake knew their own truck was now missing

a side door, there were still two more to worry about.

"Jump up onto the flatbed," he said. "Start unfastening those nukes. They'll be forced to stop."

"Risky. Friggin' risky, Drake. What if one of the warheads comes loose?"

Drake ran around the side of the cab, firing at their attackers. "One bloody problem at a time. What are we—whiz kids?"

Alicia shot a pursuer. "More like 'iffy bastards' these days I'm afraid."

Together, they leapt up to the flatbed and came face to face with the nuke.

"This works on two fronts," Drake now said through the comms. "We can neutralize and detach at the same time."

Hayden grunted. "Try not to sound so smug about it."

"Yorkshiremen don't do smug, love. We do simply awesome with just a dash of humility."

"Plus a few thousand crap things." Dahl sounded like he was running. "Yorkshire puddings. Terriers. Beer. Sporting teams. And that accent?"

Drake felt the truck starting to move beneath him. "Where's the control panel, people?"

A tech answered immediately. "See the warhead is made up of approximately thirty curved panels? It's the eighth one from the pointy end."

"My kinda language."

More shots rang out. Alicia was already concentrating on the pursuit. Mai had just leapt up onto the back of the flatbed. Now, she looked over the backend of the nuke.

"Bad news. The British are here."

"I think we have the Chinese," Dahl spoke.

"French," Kinimaka said. "A new team."

Drake leapt at the control panel. Do we know where the Sword of Mars is?"

"Yes, Matt. But I can't exactly say it out loud now, can I?" a voice answered.

"Duh," Dahl said.

Drake grimaced and pulled out a small electric screwdriver with a universal bit. Quickly, he undid eight bolts and let them drop out. He was faced with two small control panels the size of car satnav screens, a keyboard panel, and an array of flashing white symbols.

"Cyrillic," he said. "Of course it is."

"Can this day get any worse?" Alicia shouted across.

The Yorkshireman hung his head. "It bloody will now."

The truck picked up speed, heading for the roller door. The British came in tight formation from the rear of the warehouse. The guards spread out all around them.

The nuke flashed, fully live, awaiting the launch code or the kill code.

Drake knew they had to move. He knew they couldn't move. The only thing he didn't know—who would die first?

The guards rushed first, firing. Drake was a large target, and unmoving, bullets flashed past Alicia, striking the warhead. For a second Drake's life passed before his eyes, then Alicia felled one guard and Mai another. He saw more coming though and knew more came from their blind side. The white symbols flashed, a cursor blinked and waited.

"Do you think the guards might detonate?" Smyth said suddenly, quietly. "Could that be their orders?"

"Why would they die?" Kenzie asked.

"We've seen it before," Kinimaka said. "Families receiving huge payouts, needed medical attention or desperate relocation when their family head dies. If they belong to a mafia or a triad for instance. It's possible."

Drake knew they couldn't stay lucky much longer. Alicia managed to loosen a strap as the truck rolled along.

Hopefully, the driver would see. But then would he care? Drake saw no other option.

He raced down the flatbed, toward the back, waving his arms madly.

"Wait! Stop, stop. Don't shoot. I'm English!"

Dahl's grunt said it all, no words needed.

Drake dropped to his knees at the back of the truck, the tail fin of the nuke to his left, hands in the air and facing the oncoming five-man SAS unit completely unarmed.

"We need your help," he said. "There's too much at stake for us to wage war."

He saw a younger man switch to comms, saw two older men fix onto his face. Perhaps they would recognize him. Maybe they knew of Michael Crouch. He spoke again.

"I'm Matt Drake. Ex-SAS. Ex-soldier. Working for an international team of Special Forces called SPEAR. I trained at Hereford. I was trained by Crouch."

The name registered, all of it. Two of the five weapons were lowered. Drake heard Alicia's voice over the comms.

"You could mention my name too."

He winced slightly. "Probably not the best idea, love."

Mai and Alicia kept the guards at bay. Seconds passed. The British SAS soldiers fired on more approaching guards, ducking behind oil drums used to fill up the flat bed. Drake waited. The man with the radio finally finished.

"Matt Drake? I'm Cambridge. We met earlier. What do you need?"

Happy day, he thought. *The SAS are on board.*

"Help us secure this warehouse, stop this truck and neutralize that nuke," he said. "In that order."

The British jumped to it.

Splitting and running down both sides of the flatbed they picked off the oncoming guards, working beautifully as a team. Drake saw it and reveled, remembering the older days. There was a fluid grace to the movement of the team, a regal bearing and an implacable confidence. He'd thought SPEAR was the best team in the world, but now . . .

"Drake! Mai cried. "The nuke!"

Oh yeah. He raced back to the control panel, stared at the screens, the keyboard and the digits.

"Geeks?" he asked. "Do we know the code?"

"It could literally be anything," someone answered.

"That's not exactly fucking helpful, ya bloody bell-end."

"Sorry. If we knew the identities of the Order we could try their birthdays?"

Drake knew he was talking to a man that didn't care. It was a man they'd conversed with earlier, the obnoxious asshole.

Lauren shouted up, "You mentioned the Order. If they were here, they probably programmed the nukes. I can't believe they wouldn't leave a note of the codes."

"Maybe there is no code, babe," the asshole said. "Remember the signal you loosed by opening Geronimo's grave? Maybe that happened here too, and armed the nukes."

Drake stood back. "Shit, are they armed?"

"Fully. The flashing white symbols you see are numbers on countdown."

Sharp ice water flooded his body and he could barely breathe. "How . . . how long?"

A cough. "Sixty-four seconds. Then you and your bastard brethren are history. The Order will forever reign supreme! They live through me! I am the Order!"

A scuffle and a large amount of shouting followed. Drake watched the seconds passing on his wristwatch.

"Hello? You there?" a young voice asked.

"Hi, mate," Drake murmured. "We have thirty one seconds."

"I've been thinking about that. Your friend Lauren mentioned the Order. Well, they must have a kill code. And, since everything else is a part of the text, I just had a check through. Remember? It reads 'the only kill code is when the Horsemen arose.' Does that mean anything to you?"

Drake wracked his brain, but could think of nothing but the descending second count. "Arose?" he repeated. "Woke up? Resurrected? Think how the Order thinks? How the Nazis meant it. If a Horseman arises he—"

"Is born," the young voice said. "It's their dates of birth, maybe? But it can't be. Those eighties-era nukes usually have a three-digit kill code." He sounded desperate.

Nineteen seconds until destruction.

Kenzie spoke up. "Three digit, you say? Usually?"

"Yes."

Sixteen.

Drake looked around at Alicia, saw her crouched beside a strap, trying to unfasten it and shoot a guard at the same time. Saw her hair, her body, her amazing, astonishing spirit. *Alicia . . .*

Ten seconds.

Kenzie then shouted up, an affirmation of Dahl's belief in her. "I have it. Try seven hundred."

"Seven—oh—oh. Why?"

"Don't ask. Just do it!"

The young techie gave Drake the Cyrillic number symbols and the Yorkshireman hit the buttons.

Four—three—two—

"It didn't work," he said.

CHAPTER FORTY

"Yeah," Kenzie came back. "It did."

Of course, she'd disarmed their own and Lauren had disarmed theirs. Drake looked down the body of the nuke to Mai, where she stood in front of another keypad. All six nukes had been disarmed.

He stared at his watch. "We were at less than a second," he said.

All around the SAS made short work of the guards. Alicia undid a second strap and the warhead shifted slightly. Drake felt it picking up speed as it approached the roller doors.

"Anyone stopped their truck yet?"

"I'm on it!" Kenzie cried. "Literally!"

"Not a chance," Kinimaka said. "The French are everywhere the guards aren't. It's a riot in here."

Drake watched the SAS dealing with the guards; Alicia tugging at another strap and Mai flinging a guard against the truck's rear tire.

"Yeah, I know what you mean." The SPEAR team were unbelievably stretched.

"I can see something else going on," the young tech began. "I—"

Their link to Washington went dead.

"Say again?" Drake tried.

Ominous silence was his only reply.

"Shit, this can't be good." Drake swept the entire warehouse.

SEAL Team 7 hit them like all hell exploding.

*

Dahl ran behind the truck as it approached the roller doors of Warehouse 18. The Chinese raced across the front of the rumbling truck, heading for the far side door. They fired crosswise as they ran. Guards tried to stop them. Chinese Special Forces decimated them with bullets and hand-to-hand. Hayden was unlucky enough to be at the front of the flatbed when the action began.

She broke a guard's neck, then used his body to shield her as the Chinese opened fire indiscriminately. Bullets thudding into the body sent her backward. Her shield flopped. Dropping him, she leapt behind one of the forward, rumbling tires, walking behind it as it rolled forward. The Chinese crossed the front of the truck.

Dahl laid down fire, sending them scattering like bowling pins. Incredible to watch, it served to demonstrate their almost inhuman reaction. Even leaping away they returned fire.

Dahl took cover hastily, ducking behind the truck, then peeked out and fired more rounds. The Chinese were momentarily pinned down as guards came at them from behind. Dahl glanced over at Kenzie.

Not where she was supposed to be.

"Kenz? You okay?"

"Oh yeah, just picking up an old friend."

Dahl turned instinctively, saw her rummaging inside the crates, her head well inside, stomach perched on the edge of the lid, ass high in the air.

"That's a little off-putting."

"What? Oh, missing the wife? She might be cooler than you are, Torst, but remember—that only makes you hotter than she is."

He looked away, feeling torn. He lived in that state between marriage and divorce, and yet with the chance to do something about it all. What on earth was he doing here?

My job.

The Chinese burst into action again, shredding the approaching guards with machine-gun fire and pinning Dahl and Hayden down. The Swede turned to see Kenzie slithering out of a wooden crate.

"Oh, balls. Really?"

She held a new gleaming katana before her eyes, blade up. "I just knew I would find one if I dug deep enough. Robbers can't resist a sword."

"Where's the bloody Sword of Mars?"

"Oh, I dropped it in the crate."

"Damn!"

She ran, sword in one hand, machine pistol in the other, then vaulted right back onto the bed of the truck, a blur before Dahl's eyes. Dropping the katana she opened fire at the running Chinese.

"Where are they going?"

"Warehouse 17," Dahl said. "And we have to go with them."

Lauren saw the French contingent attack from the right side of Warehouse 19. Kinimaka and Smyth were already over in that direction and engaged immediately. Yorgi was crouched behind barrels, taking potshots at the guards. Lauren felt her heart lurch when the truck carrying the two nukes moved forward.

Remembering all that had been said, she jumped atop the truck, using the wheels for purchase. Then she set about loosening the first strap. If they could make the load highly unstable the trucks would be forced to stop. She poked her head up, peering over the nuke by stepping onto one of the large chocks, and saw Smyth fist fighting with one of the French guys.

DC came in over the comms. "Just confirmed by an agent

in Paris. Remember Armand Argento? He's helped you guys a few times over the years. Well, he says the French contingent are unsanctioned. Totally. There could be some savage warfare inside there."

Lauren gulped and watched Smyth fall backward, going down on one knee. The Frenchman above him took hold of his hair, tore a strip from the roots and threw it aside. Smyth cried out. A knee to the nose sent him reeling. The French guy jumped on top. Smyth struggled. Lauren looked from him to Kinimaka to Yorgi, the nuclear warhead and the approaching shutter doors.

What do I do?

Make some goddamn noise.

She emptied the magazine of her Glock high above the enemies' heads, making them flinch and duck. It gave Smyth and Kinimaka precious seconds. Smyth saw space and fired up into it, felling his attacker. Kinimaka broke a man's neck, another's face, and shot point blank into a third, sending him reeling, out of the battle.

One Frenchman remained.

Lauren dropped as a bullet clanged off the shell of the nuke. How scary was it that it didn't even bother her? How inured had she become? But she was part of this team and determined to stay with it as long as they would have her. She'd found this family, and would support it.

The enormous truck picked up rapid speed as it accelerated hard, straight at the roller shutter door, impacting it, making the front cab rebound slightly, and then smashing straight through.

Lauren threw herself down onto the bed of the truck.

Drake winced as the SEALs engaged the SAS and SPEAR alongside a moving nuclear warhead, wondering if any battle could get more fucked up, or become more deadly than this. A few words from the comms told him it most certainly could.

All three trucks, carrying six nukes, burst through the roller shutter doors at the same time. Metal shrapnel flew everywhere as the ripped-open doors sagged. The trucks bounced through. Men leapt at the trucks, jumping aboard, sensing they would only pick up speed. Drake now saw two Chinese soldiers sprinting alongside. He steadied himself on the flatbed, and saw Alicia and Mai further back, sheltering behind one of the wooden chocks. The nuke shifted as they hit one of the world's biggest potholes.

Drake cringed. If the enormous, heavy weapon freed from its chocks and broke its straps they were all in trouble.

Out into the daylight they raced. Twenty miles per hour and then thirty, the three flatbeds roared as their drivers hit the gas pedal. A wide open road opened out ahead, almost straight toward the base exit about two miles away. Now alongside each other, Drake could look across from his own truck to Dahl's and then to Kinimaka's. The sight of massive, shifting nuclear missiles, battling men alongside, guns being fired, knives and fists being used, people being thrown off, no quarter given, the road bending and all three trucks downshifting into the turn, stunned him to the core. It was a bedlam of greed and violence, a glimpse into Hell.

But now the SEALs took his full attention.

Four strong, they had first attacked the SAS, taking one down without concern. The British rallied and came back hard, forcing the SEALs to take cover. Four men now ran behind the trucks, hoping to jump aboard. The SAS commander, Cambridge, fought hand to hand with a SEAL, both taking blows. Mai and Alicia were busy kicking off guards and trying to find a hole in the melee.

Drake came face to face with the SEAL team leader. "Why?" he said.

"Don't ask questions," the man growled and came at Drake. The blows were precise and incredibly harsh, much like his own. He blocked, felt the pain from those blocks, and punched back. He kicked solidly. A knife appeared in the other man's hand. Drake parried it with his own, sending both weapons flickering away and off the truck.

"Why?" he said again.

"You fucked up. You and your crew."

"How?" Drake backpedalled to gain some space.

"And why would the bastards want to kill us?" Alicia asked, popping up behind the man.

He struck instantly, catching her across the temple. Drake shoved a boot into his kidneys, and watched him fall. Alicia planted her own foot into his face. Together, they threw him spinning over the side.

Ahead, the road widened.

Mai dispatched two guards. Another SAS man went down and now the British and the Americans were evenly matched. Three versus three. Drake saw the two Chinese he'd seen earlier creep like spiders over the top of the nuke.

"Watch it!"

Too late. They fell upon him.

Dahl knew, in essence, that they were headed to Romania. That was good. It was the half-hour-long drive that might kill them before they got there.

He fought the Chinese and the guards, kicked them back and found they jumped up, wanting more. The Chinese slipped around his guard, hitting with force, and twice almost skewering him with their wicked blades. More guards surrounded him. Hayden resorted to flinging them off the truck until their numbers wilted.

At the rear, Kenzie dispatched the last of her enemies. The machine gun was empty, the katana dripping red. She stalked back up the flatbed, now narrowing her eyes as two Chinese came at her together, stabbing with knives. She parried, stepping around. They pulled guns. She leapt into their faces, surprising them. A shot went under her arm, glancing off the nuke. She found herself next to one of the chocks with a handgun pointed at her face.

"Crap."

The only way was up. She kicked the arm that held the gun, flinging it away, and then scrambled up the chock and onto the body of the nuke. She reached the top, found it was simply a gentle curve up there, but hazardous to balance. Instead, she sat astride the nuke, katana in hand.

"Come and fucking get me!" she screamed. "If you dare."

They went up fast, perfectly balanced. Kenzie stood on top of the warhead, twirling her sword and they came at her with knives. A thrust and a swipe. She parried, but they drew blood. It spattered onto the missile. The truck jounced at thirty miles per hour. The Chinese adjusted supremely. Kenzie lost her balance, slipped, and once again fell astride the missile.

"Ow."

The wind gusted through her hair, cold as a freezer. A knife came down at her. She switched the katana to the other hand, caught the wrist between her fingers and then jerked harshly to the side. The wrist broke, the knife fell. She wrenched the body that way too, and saw it fly headfirst from the truck. The second man was already attacking. Kenzie threw the katana back to her right hand and let him run right into the point. He hung for a moment until Kenzie cast him aside.

Then she looked down from her perch atop the nuke, katana blade dripping blood onto those that battled below.

"Two Chinese down. Three to go."

Alicia was looking over at her from her won truck, having

watched the battle atop the warhead. "That looked so friggin' awesome," she said. "I do believe I have an erection."

Dahl stared up at her from his own truck. "Me too."

But then the warhead began to shift.

CHAPTER FORTY ONE

Dahl noticed the shift immediately, saw the two straps they'd managed to unfasten flapping in the wind and then a third—twanging apart like the world's craziest rubber band, slapping viciously against the nuke and the bottom of the flatbed. On its first powerful snap-back it struck a guard in the pit of the stomach, sending him flying, arms and legs akimbo, straight off the side of the truck and point blank into the rear wheels of the one traveling alongside. Dahl winced at the result.

The nuke shifted again. Dahl felt a red mist fall over him as Kenzie struggled on top, and Hayden fought right underneath its shadow with no idea what was coming. He shouted, bellowed, to no avail. The tire roar, the screaming, the focus required to do combat; it all hampered their hearing. He jumped on the comms.

"Move. The nuke's about to go!"

Kenzie stared down. "Go where? You mean take off?"

"Nooo!"

At the end of his tether, the Swede ran like a madman, close to Hayden, and put his shoulder against the incredible missile's bulk. "The nuke's coming down!"

Hayden rolled fast, the guard too. The warhead slithered another inch. Dahl hefted it with every ounce of strength he'd ever mustered, every muscle shrieking.

A heavy thud sounded next to him.

Crap.

But it was Kenzie, still holding the katana and with a sarcastic smile across her face. "Damn, you are one crazy motherfucking hero. You really think you can hold that even for a second?"

"Ummm, no. Not really."
"Then *move*."
The Mad Swede dived clear.

Drake and Alicia managed to snatch a second to share the spectacle.
"What the hell is Dahl doing?" Alicia asked. "Is he hugging the goddam nuke?"
"Don't be a fool," Drake snapped with a shake of the head. "Clearly he's snogging it."
Drake then leapt aside to help the SAS boys, pulling a SEAL away from a younger man and hurling him against the nuke. The man's entire frame shuddered. Punches were exchanged and then the SEAL was lying unconscious, prone but alive. Drake intended to keep him so.
Another SEAL died and then an SAS soldier, both stabbed at close range. Cambridge and the young man were all that remained. They teamed up with Drake to face the last SEAL. At the same time, Alicia and Mai joined them. The truck thundered along the dirt road, touching the one beside it once and careening off. The collision managed to stabilize Dahl's nuke, jamming it down onto its outsize chocks. As one, the three vehicles smashed through the exit gate and continued on, heading for Romania. Steel and concrete were utterly destroyed, bursting to and fro. By now the choppers had lifted off and were flying alongside the trucks, men with heavy artillery leaning out of the doors and focused on the drivers.
Drake stayed the attack on the SEAL. "Wait. You're Special Ops. American. Why would you try to kill us?"
In truth, he'd never expected an answer, but in response, the man attacked. He felled Cambridge and then winded Drake. The young SAS man fell to the side. The SEAL was tough and without mercy, delivering blow after crushing blow. But then Mai faced up to him.

Eight seconds later and the fight was over. Again, they let him live, groaning in a heap, disarmed.

Drake turned to Cambridge. "I can't say how much we appreciate your help, Major. I'm so sorry for the loss of your men. But please, if you would, let these men live, they were only following orders."

The two surviving SEALs looked up, surprised and perhaps wondering.

Cambridge nodded. "I understand and agree with you, Drake. In the end, we're all pawns."

Drake made a face. "Well, not anymore. The American government just tried to kill us. I don't see a way back from that."

Cambridge shrugged. "Strike back."

Drake smiled grimly. "A man after my own heart. It was good to meet you, Major Cambridge."

"And you, Matt Drake."

He nodded at Mai and Alicia then headed precariously toward the back of the truck. Drake stared after him, checking the stability of the warhead at the same time. All looked well.

"You know they're gonna jog back and nick the sword?" Alicia prompted him.

"Yeah, but you know what? I don't give a fuck. The Sword of Mars is the least of our problems." He keyed the comms. "Hayden? Dahl? How you doing over there?"

"Good," Hayden came back. "The last of the Chinese just jumped off. Going for the sword."

Kenzie cackled. "No, they saw me in action."

"Didn't we all." Drake smiled. "I ain't gonna forget that sight in a while."

Alicia slammed him right on the shoulder. "Cool off, soldier boy. Next you'll be wanting me to stick a nuke between *my* legs."

"Nah, don't worry," Drake said as he turned away. "I'll do that for you later."

The choppers bullied and threatened and cajoled the drivers to slow their vehicles. Of course, at first it didn't work, but after somebody put a large caliber round through one of the windshields, the men that thought themselves untouchable suddenly began to doubt. Three minutes later, the trucks slowed, hands came out of the windows, and all motion stopped.

Drake caught his balance, used to the constant jarring and forward momentum. He jumped down to the ground, aware that the comms had suddenly fired back into life and now keeping a very close eye on their pilots.

No sound came from the comms. DC, for once, was silent.

The team gathered after destroying their earpieces. They sat on a grassy knoll overlooking the three missile carriers, wondering what the world and its more malevolent characters might throw at them next.

Drake eyed a pilot. "Could you fly us to Romania?"

The man's eyes never flickered. "Sure," he said. "Can't see why not. The nukes are headed there anyway, to be stored inside a base. We'll get a head start."

Together, they departed another battlefield.

Together, they remained strong.

Hours later, the team vacated a Romanian safe house and took a bus to Transylvania, alighting near Bran Castle, the supposed site of the home of Count Dracula. Here, among high trees and tall mountains, they found a dark, quiet guesthouse and settled in. The lights were low. The team now wore civilian clothes, taken from the safe house, and possessed only what weapons and ammo they'd been able to carry, as well as a good stash of money from the safe that

Yorgi had picked. They had no passport, no papers, no identities.

They congregated in one room. Ten people, no comms. Ten people on the run from the American government with no idea whom they might trust. No clear place to turn to. No more SPEAR and no secret base. No Pentagon office or DC home. What families they had were out of bounds. What contacts they might use could be compromised.

The whole world had changed on some unknown, obscure executive order.

"What next?" Smyth broached the issue first, his voice pitched low in the poorly lit room.

"First, we finish the mission," Hayden said. "The Order of the Last Judgment sought to take the world down by secreting four terrible weapons. War, through Hannibal, which was the great gun. Conquest, through Genghis Kahn which was the linchpin code we destroyed. Famine, through Geronimo which was the bio-weapon. And finally Death, through Attila, which were six nuclear weapons. Together, these weapons would have reduced our society as we know it to rubble and chaos. I think we can safely say we neutralized the threat."

"With the only loose end being the Sword of Mars," Lauren said. "Now in the hands of either the Chinese or the British."

"I do hope it's us," Drake said. "The SAS saved us back there and lost some good men. I hope Cambridge doesn't get a reprimand."

"Moving forward . . ." Dahl said. "Even we can't do this alone. First, what the hell are we going to do now? And second, who can we trust to help us do it?"

"Well, first we find out what made the Americans turn on us," Hayden said. "My guess is the Peru operation, and . . . other stuff . . . that happened. Is it just a few powerful men against us? A splinter group influencing others? I can't believe for one second that Coburn would sanction this."

"You're saying we should sneak in for a chat with the President?" Drake asked.

Hayden shrugged. "Why not?"

"And if it is a splinter group," Dahl said. "We take them down."

"Alive," Mai said. "The only way we survive all this is to catch our enemies alive."

The team sat around the large room in various poses, the curtains drawn tight against an impenetrable night. Deep in Romania, they talked. Planned. It soon became clear that they did have resources, but those resources were sparse. Drake could count them on the fingers of one hand.

"Where next?" Kenzie asked, still hanging onto her katana, letting the blade bask in the dim light.

"Forward," Drake said. "We always go forward."

"If we ever stop," Dahl said. "We die."

Alicia held on to Drake's arm. "And I thought my days of running away were over."

"This is different," he said, then sighed. "Of course, you know that. Sorry."

"It's okay. Dumb, but pretty. Finally, I realized—that's my type."

"Does this mean we're on the run?" Kenzie asked. "Because I really wanted to get away from all that."

"We will get this sorted." Dahl leaned closer to her. "I promise you. I have my children too, don't forget. I will overcome anything and everything for them."

"You didn't mention your wife."

Dahl stared and then sat back, thinking. Drake saw Kenzie shift a little closer to the big Swede. He shed it from his thoughts and studied the room.

"Tomorrow is another day," he said. "Where do you want to go first?"

THE END

For more information on the future of the Matt Drake world and other David Leadbeater novels please read on:

Matt Drake will return around the middle of 2017. I'm looking forward to see where we can take the team from here, and how they will cope with the new situation. For now though, we'll leave them in peace.

Next up will be the start of a brand new archaeological action/adventure series—same style as the Drake books, same genre, plenty of camaraderie, action and some great archaeological quests, but with brand new characters. Look out for the first release in May.

If you have enjoyed this or any other of my books, please leave a review. Even a short line or two helps to ensure future releases.

Other Books by David Leadbeater:

The Matt Drake Series
The Bones of Odin (Matt Drake #1)
The Blood King Conspiracy (Matt Drake #2)
The Gates of Hell (Matt Drake 3)
The Tomb of the Gods (Matt Drake #4)
Brothers in Arms (Matt Drake #5)
The Swords of Babylon (Matt Drake #6)
Blood Vengeance (Matt Drake #7)
Last Man Standing (Matt Drake #8)
The Plagues of Pandora (Matt Drake #9)
The Lost Kingdom (Matt Drake #10)
The Ghost Ships of Arizona (Matt Drake #11)
The Last Bazaar (Matt Drake #12)
The Edge of Armageddon (Matt Drake #13)
The Treasures of Saint Germain (Matt Drake #14)
Inca Kings (Matt Drake #15)

The Alicia Myles Series
Aztec Gold (Alicia Myles #1)
Crusader's Gold (Alicia Myles #2)
Caribbean Gold (Alicia Myles #3)

The Torsten Dahl Thriller Series
Stand Your Ground (Dahl Thriller #1)

The Disavowed Series:
The Razor's Edge (Disavowed #1)
In Harm's Way (Disavowed #2)
Threat Level: Red (Disavowed #3)

David Leadbeater

The Chosen Few Series
Chosen (The Chosen Trilogy #1)
Guardians (The Chosen Tribology #2)

Short Stories
Walking with Ghosts (A short story)
A Whispering of Ghosts (A short story)

Connect with the author on Twitter: @dleadbeater2011
Visit the author's website: www.davidleadbeater.com

All helpful, genuine comments are welcome. I would love to hear from you.
davidleadbeater2011@hotmail.co.uk

Printed in Poland
by Amazon Fulfillment
Poland Sp. z o.o., Wrocław